STAY WITH ME

DIAMOND IN THE ROUGH 3

REBEL HART

AMORE PUBLISHING

1

CLINTON

My knees curled against my chest. I felt the blood caking on my face. My head spun from the aftermath of the fight with my father. How aggressive things had gotten. How proud I was of Cecilia standing up to him.

How much my heart hurt that Rae witnessed any of it.

I closed my eyes and listened to the sound of Michael's SUV pull out of the driveway. No, not pull out. Peel out. Tires squealed along the concrete and the smell of burned rubber filled the air. I placed my head against my knees as the rain came down harder than ever. Thunder boomed in the distance. Lightning flashed above my head. When had it started raining?

Could it wash away my sins?

I felt sick to my stomach. I wanted to vomit on the porch. The silence was deafening. And yet, it brought me peace. My father wasn't yelling. Cecilia wasn't crying. Things were simply… silent. The sound of the rain soothed my soul, but the booming of thunder reminded me of reality.

Reminded me of the presence of my unconscious father.

My back rested heavily against the railing as I slowly looked up. I stared at the house as water dripped from the tendrils of my hair. I wanted to go after Rae. I wanted to wrap her up in my arms and tell her I didn't mean it. But I couldn't. I knew I couldn't. Because I was bad news, and I always would be.

She had her life ahead of her.

And I had nothing in my future.

My eyes slowly gravitated to my father, lying unconscious on the porch. I didn't even know what to do with him. Did I need to call 9-1-1? Was he even still breathing? I saw his back softly moving, and I almost regretted it.

Almost regretted not having killed my father when I had the chance.

What kind of person does that make me?

I grimaced and turned my eyes away from him. Maybe if I ignored him long enough, he'd go away. Maybe if I blinked my eyes rapidly, it would somehow rewind time. Back to the last time I'd been pressed against Rae's body. Back to the last time I'd been in her arms and gazing into those gorgeous eyes.

So I blinked as quickly as I could. Faster, and faster, while I prayed it took me back in time. That, somehow, blinking in quick succession was the key to time travel.

It wasn't, though.

It only served to hold back my tears.

Rae deserves someone better.

Those four words kept rushing around in my mind. The storm grew and the wind howled. My leather jacket shrunk against me as the rain continued to batter it. Rae did deserve someone better. Someone more worthy of her time. And far less dangerous. The life I lead wasn't a life to pull someone into. The family I had wasn't a family I needed to add to.

And it killed me inside.

She went after him, though. She cares about you.

It was true. I'd seen her lunge at him. I'd seen Michael holding her back as she tried to get to me. Which only fueled my need to let her go. If she ever got hurt because of me, I'd never forgive myself. If my father ever hurt her, for any reason, I knew I'd kill him. I'd sit in prison with a smile on my face about it, too. Rae deserved much better than that. She deserved a family that would take her in. Make her feel loved. Make her feel safe. Make her feel wanted.

None of which my father could ever provide for anyone.

I still couldn't remember bits and pieces of the night, though. I couldn't remember how we ended up on the porch. Or the exact moment where I knocked my father out cold. I remember Cecilia screaming. I remember her chest heaving with tears. And the next thing I knew, we were on the porch. Before Michael and Rae pulled up. Then Rae had tried to come to my defense.

And the next thing I know, Dad was on the ground. Unconscious, in a pool of his own blood.

Or possibly mine.

Slowly, pain filled my body. An excruciating pain I didn't know what to do with. My face throbbed. My neck stiffened. My eyes fluttered closed as more tears pushed themselves to the surface. The night came back in bits and pieces. Rae, screaming from Michael's arms. Trying to pull away and get to me. Cecilia, crying on the porch as she yelled for both of us to stop. My father, chuckling in his maniacal way as his eyes briefly fell on to Rae.

My knee, connecting with his groin.

I slowly looked back over at my father. Sounds other than the rain slowly dawned on me. Cecilia's voice, rambling aimlessly as she stood in the doorway of the house.

"Yes, unconscious. Yes, he's breathing. Uh huh. From the nose. Um, it just—it all happened so fast—I know his nose is broken again. I can just tell by looking at it."

My eyes gravitated to my stepmother. To the way she looked upon me with worry and hurt. She slipped out, tiptoeing around my father's body as she came for me. She dipped down, propping a cell phone against her shoulder. She reached out and touched something on my neck. My eye twitched. Her hand cupped my cheek. And when she brushed her finger across my temple, I felt myself get sick to my stomach.

I leaned over, away from her, and began to heave. My stomach turned itself inside out as burning bile worked its way up my throat. Concussion. I had a concussion, right?

I felt my stepmother's hand softly rubbing my back as I continued to puke on the porch.

It felt like my entire body was revolting against itself. Rising up and refusing to operate anymore until I got into better circumstances. It was like my physical form had finally given up. Had finally waved the white flag of surrender. I worked my way onto my hands and knees. I shook violently as the world spun around me. Tears dripped down my face. Snot fell from my nose. And with every heave, I felt my nose rush pain around the back of my head.

"Cecilia," I whimpered.

She patted my back. "I'm right here. The paramedics are on their way. Just hold on, okay?"

I couldn't gain control of my body. I felt helpless. Pathetic. Weak, like my father had always called me. My leather coat had tightened so badly around my arms that I couldn't feel my hands any longer. And that made me cry even harder. My mother's leather coat. The one she gave me when I was a young teenager. Sent to me, for my birthday. As a present and some sort of pathetic excuse for never being in my life. For leaving me behind with a man she knew to be an abusive piece of shit.

I suddenly didn't want to wear it anymore.

I leaned up and struggled to get it off. I stumbled around as spit dripped down my chin. I felt someone tugging at my coat, trying to help pull it off me as I slowly peeled it away from my body. I coughed and sputtered. Sobs fell from my lips because I didn't have the strength to hold back my tears any longer. I felt an arm wrap around my stomach, holding me as grunts and growls came from behind me.

It wasn't until the coat finally ripped away from my arms, however, that I figured out Cecilia was holding me. Cecilia was grunting with me. Cecilia was cradling me close.

"Come here. I've got you. They'll be here soon, Clint."

I leaned heavily against her. Despite the fact that my massive body was easily twice her size, I curled into her like a newborn child, afraid of being too far away from her. I coughed as my sobs came in hiccups. The taste of puke in my mouth was fucking awful. My nose hurt unlike anything I'd ever felt and Dad still lay there. Unconscious on the fucking porch.

The thunderstorm was moving away, though.

Slowly, but surely.

The sound of sirens fell against my ears and I sighed. Cecilia positioned herself against the house and I leaned even harder against her. I didn't know what this meant for us. What this meant for our family. Would she tell the paramedics how this all happened? Would I be arrested?

Would it even matter?

I might have a better quality of life in prison.

"It's okay. Breathe for me, Clint. I need you to settle down a bit."

My chest hiccupped. "I'm sor—so—sorry, Cec—cec—"

"Sh-sh-sh-sh. They're almost here. I see the ambulance now."

The siren's sound grew to a deafening roar. And only then did my father start to stir. Footsteps landed against pavement as people made their way onto the porch. Helping my father to wake up. I heard him groaning. Grumbling. Growling out my name. I slowly opened my eyes and watched him bat people away. He even ripped a small flashlight out of one of their hands and tossed it over the railing of the porch.

"Where the fuck is my son?"

I cowered against Cecilia's body as her hand smoothed over the side of my face.

"Where the hell are you, Clinton?"

The paramedic sighed. "Sir, I need you to stay still. You could have a concussion."

My father bolted upright. "Where the fuck are you, you piece of shit?"

"Sir, can you please—"

"I'm going to rip you a new one. You don't get to knock me out on my own porch and get away with it. Cecilia!"

She snickered. "Shut up, Howard."

He snarled. "What did you say, you stupid bitch?"

"Shut up, Dad. Seriously."

He whipped his head around. "Come here, you little dipshit."

"You two. Inside, now. The paramedic will tend to you in there."

We listened to the command of the woman trying to help my father. But he was combative the entire time. His curses and slurs followed me inside, where my stepmother and I switched roles. Once I got myself on my feet, I took her in my arms and held her closely as the paramedics examined me. They flashed lights in my eyes and checked my temples. The man fiddled with my nose and it nauseated me. I felt myself heave again and Cecilia quickly stepped away, watching with wide eyes while people fussed over me.

"No concussion. But he's in mild shock."

"Pupil dilation's good."

"We need a brace for his nose!"

"He'll need surgery to fix it eventually."

I reached out for Cecilia's hand and she took it. Then, with a squeeze, she stepped back out onto the porch. She closed the door, muting my father's yelling and cursing. And as I stood there, alone, I let the tears silently fall.

In front of a paramedic that kept tossing me pitiful glances.

"This is gonna hurt. Just bear with me."

"One, two—"

I closed my eyes and let myself fall into a happy place. I saw Rae's face, smiling at me as she called out my name. I was used to traveling to happy places. That's how I'd gotten through the hurt and the pain of my childhood. I didn't even feel them snap my nose into place. I didn't feel them inject me with pain medication. I didn't feel them poking around at my bruises or putting a brace over my nose.

Because I'd lost myself in my own little world.

A world where Rae was still there. Safe from harm,

and able to fall into my arms without a care in the world. I lost myself in a field of flowers as our backs fell to the petals, casting them upward as we made love underneath the summer sun. I lost myself in her laughter. In her scent. In her smile and her touch and her kiss.

And when I opened my eyes, one last tear slipped down my cheek.

No more, after this.

"Thank you, I really appreciate it. Yes, I'll make sure to file a police report. Yes, self-defense. I can promise you that. Handcuffs might be necessary to transport him. Uh huh. I'll be along in a little while. He'll be fine. Yes, thank you so much."

Cecilia's voice filled my ears and my eyes panned over to her. I saw her ushering the paramedics out. I heard the exhaustion in her voice. She closed the door and locked it, then turned to face me.

"I told them to take your father to the hospital."

I nodded slowly. "Okay."

"You really should go yourself. But they insisted you were fine."

"If something happens tonight, I'll check myself in somewhere."

She snickered. "You'll do no such thing alone."

Then she came over and took my hands within hers. "You really should call her, you know."

I nodded mindlessly. "Okay."

"I'm serious, Clint. She could really help you right now."

"I'll take that into account."

"Clint. Look at me, sweetheart."

My eyes fell to hers and I tried my best to focus.

"Call. Rae. Promise me."

I nodded slowly. "I promise to consider it."

Then I pulled away from her and walked my ass upstairs. Because I sure as hell didn't want to be part of this world anymore. I wanted to be part of my dreams.

Part of the only place where my father didn't exist.

2

RAELYNN

I sat in the passenger seat of Michael's car as we drove back to my place. I kept my eyes on the outside mirror, looking back, just in case Clint started running after us. But he didn't. He receded into the horizon as another storm unleashed, pouring forth more rain than I'd ever seen. Booming the loudest thunder imaginable. Flashing etches of lightning throughout the sky and blinding the whole of Riverbend for seconds at a time.

My heart had never hurt this badly before.

My soul shattered. It felt as if my heart were dripping blood as it slowly sank to my stomach. The butterflies in my body died, giving way to maggots that felt as if they were eating me from the inside out. It was the only way I had to explain the pain no one could see. It was the only way I knew how to explain how much Clint had just hurt me.

Maybe he didn't mean it?

It was my only hope. Maybe it was just a show he put on for his father. But that didn't make sense. His father had already been knocked unconscious. Was it possible the show was for Cecilia? Maybe she secretly didn't like me, or something like that. Or maybe, he meant it now but wouldn't mean it tomorrow.

Yeah, he'll call. Once tensions settle and he gets some rest.

"He's just got a lot on his plate right now. Give him some time."

Michael's voice pierced my thoughts, but I had nothing to say.

"You know he cares about you. I certainly know he cares about you. Just give him some space. A lot has happened in a short span of time to him."

I nodded aimlessly. "Yeah."

"He's probably just overwhelmed, and he'll call you tomorrow once he feels better."

"Maybe so."

"And besides, if we really want to be real for a second?"

I sighed. "Don't."

"We all know Clint can be sort of an ass sometimes. That's just kind of how he is."

I closed my eyes. "This was different, and you know it."

Michael didn't respond, which furthered the dread in my gut. He'd always been the voice of reason. The person that worked gracefully under pressure. Part of me was hoping he'd go against what I said. Tell me that this wasn't any different. That Clint was simply, well, being Clint. But when he didn't argue, I wanted the world to open up below me.

Taking me, and Clint's father, along for the ride.

We weaved slowly through the neighborhood as the sounds of sirens wailed in the distance. I whipped my head around, trying to figure out where they were headed. Had someone called 9-1-1? Was Clint all right? Who called? Did Michael call?

I looked over at him and he held up his hands.

"Don't look at me. My guess is his stepmother called."

Cecilia. "That makes sense."

I settled heavily into the seat as we turned down my street. I closed my eyes, feeling Michael's SUV park itself in my driveway. I didn't want to get out. I wanted to go back to Clint's place and force myself into his orbit. Force him to tolerate me until he came to his senses.

Michael's voice broke through my thoughts. And I wanted him to shut the hell up.

"Look, I know this time is different. But I want you to know I'm here for you. Me and Allison. You're not alone, even if you might feel like it right now."

I sighed. "I appreciate it."

"And if you need anything at all, we're only a phone call away. Anything. I mean that."

"Can you get Clint back for me?"

He paused. "Well, anything but that."

I snickered and opened my eyes before a groan fell from my lips. Fucking D.J.'s bullshit, rundown car was sitting in the middle of the damn driveway. Just my luck. Just what I fucking needed after this hellish night. I shook my head as I unbuckled my seatbelt. I couldn't unlock the door, though. I couldn't bring myself to open it and get out.

Michael cleared his throat. "You can always come back to my place, you know. Crash on our sofa. My parents wouldn't mind."

I nodded. "You lucked out with them, you know."

"I know. A lot of kids who are adopted end up in terrible situations. I came out lucky."

"Don't ever take that for granted."

He shook his head. "I don't. And I won't. I promise."

"Thanks for driving me home."

"The offer still stands if you don't want to be here."

"I know. I just want to be alone right now, though. I'm sure I can avoid them when I walk inside."

"Well, if you can't, I'll stay parked out here for a little bit. If you get to your window and wave me off, I'll leave. If you don't, I'll assume you're coming back out with your things."

I smiled softly. "Sounds like a plan."

I finally got my hand to move to the door handle. I shoved it open, then reached for my purse. I let myself out of his car, clutching my purse close to me. Trying to root myself in anything akin to reality. It felt like the world was spinning. Like I was floating up to the darkened heavens. None of this felt real. And yet, I knew it was real.

This torture was real.

The sirens grew, coating the neighborhood with their sounds as dogs began barking. Cats began meowing. The whole of the dirt of our side of the fence slowly woke up. People flicked on their lights. Others cursed at the animals to shut the hell up. I closed Michael's car door and made my way to the porch, fishing my keys out of my purse.

Please don't be downstairs. Please don't be downstairs. Please don't be downstairs.

I took one last peek back at Michael before shoving my key into the door. I unlocked it as silently as I could, then eased the door open. I didn't hear the television going. I didn't see any lights on. And as I slipped inside, I breathed a sigh of relief.

No one was downstairs.

I closed the door behind me and leaned against it. Heavily. I wanted to sit down and cry. But, I couldn't. Our foyer was like a fucking acoustical stereo. If there was any part of the house that required my silence, it was here. I locked the door softly, wincing as the sound of the latch echoed off the damn corners of the walls. I paused, holding my breath. Waiting for the hallway light to click on before D.J. yelled down the damn stairs at me.

But no sounds came.

I tiptoed into the kitchen. I opened the fridge and pulled out a bottle of water. It took a couple minutes of rummaging around to find a decent-enough snack. But, after finding an unopened bag of chips, I headed up stairs. I skipped the ones I knew creaked. The ones I knew might wake my mother up. And as I made my way down the hallway, I heard soft panting. Soft groaning. Soft, murmured curses coming from my mother's bedroom.

For fuck's sake.

I rushed the rest of the way to my room. I closed my door silently and locked it. I reached for my headphones and slipped them over my head, plugging the port into my phone. I turned on some music to block out the sounds. I walked over to my bedroom window and waved down at Michael. He flashed his lights before backing out of the driveway, and I stood there. Watching him leave.

With tears brewing behind my eyes again.

I had to take my headphones off in order to shed my wet clothes. I piled them onto the floor, racing the steady sounds of my fucking mother in the room next to me. I stripped myself bare, shivering as I walked over to my dresser. And as I pulled out a long shirt, the sounds grew. Morphing and growing, as if I weren't here.

Then again, they didn't know I was here.

It made me sick to my stomach to listen to. Then again, I should've been used to it. I ripped the shirt down against my body before quickly putting my headphones on again. I fell onto my bed and reached for the chips. I eased them open, careful not to disturb the disgusting party going on next door to my room. I snuggled underneath the covers and cracked open my water, chugging it back as I grabbed my remote.

I turned on my box television before immediately muting it.

I listened to music and watched the silent images of Golden Girls flash by. Mom and I didn't have cable. We each had cheap antennas on our televisions. But that was it. The nice one that D.J. purchased her was downstairs for movie nights. And the box television we'd had down there made it into my room as a 'gift.' I mean, don't get me wrong. I was grateful for it. But, knowing this television had made its way into my room because of D.J. never did sit right with me. Almost made me feel dirty every time I used the damn thing.

But I needed the distraction tonight.

I munched on chips and sipped my water. I watched the images on the television aimlessly as one song poured into another. Rock anthems. Rap songs. A few random musical numbers I'd come to enjoy. I mindlessly ate until the entire bag was gone, even though I knew damn good and well I'd hear about it tomorrow. I rolled my eyes and licked at my fingers. I tossed the empty chip bag into the small trash can beside my bed. I finished my water and threw that away, too. Then, I took a chance and eased my head-phones off my head.

Only to be met with louder, more fervent sounds.

I rolled my eyes and slipped them quickly back over my ears. I wiggled down into bed, turning off the tele-vision in the process. I lay there, staring up at the ceiling and trying to figure out what the fuck to do next. I kept checking my phone. Every few minutes, I checked to see if Clint had called. Or texted. Hell, fucking emailed me or some shit like that. There was nothing, though. A text from Michael, telling me he'd gotten home safely. A text from Allison, asking me if I needed anything. Another text from Michael, asking me to respond so he knew I was still alive.

So, I shot him a quick message back.

Me: Alive and well. Uh, kind of. Avoided D.J. and Mom. About to pass out.

Then my phone fell back to my chest.

The songs fell into the background. The entire world kind of faded away, really. The ceiling darkened and the room spun around me. Almost as if the chips had made me drunk. I felt my eyes closing and my body sinking into the mattress. My head fell off to the side as my breathing evened out, but I didn't quite feel asleep.

Oh, no.

Suddenly, I saw it. The bridge. The skid marks. I heard my own voice yelling for Michael to stop the car before I leapt out, rushed to the edge and peered over it. And as I gazed into the darkness below me, I called out his name.

"Clint!"

I tried jerking myself awake, moving, opening my eyes. But it was no use. I kept calling out his name while Michael pulled me away from the edge. And the more I fought against him, the angrier he got with me. I felt licks of fire kissing the back of my neck. I tore away from his grasp. And when I whipped around, I didn't see Michael behind me.

Just a fiery being that looked like Michael.

"You're pathetic."

I shook my head. "No, I'm not."

"You want to go for him?"

"You need to help me. He's down there. His bike's right over there!"

"What bike, Raelynn? What bike do you see?"

I whipped my head over to see the bike, but it wasn't there. And neither were the skidmarks. The fire in front of me grew, engulfing Michael and swallowing the rest of him whole. I felt my body lock up. Fear coursed through my veins. And as a fiery tongue made its way for me, I leaned back.

All the way over the railing.

"It should've been you, Raelynn."

The tongue wrapped itself around my throat and hoisted me over the edge. I cried out for help. I cried out for Michael. Then I cried out for Clint. Tears slid down my cheeks. I tried wrapping my hands around the fiery tongue, trying to get a grip on it so it would let me go. So it would stop searing my skin. So it would stop torturing me.

Then the tongue dropped me.

And as the darkness swallowed me whole again, I finally jerked myself awake. Just as the sun started streaming through my window.

Signaling the beginning of a new day.

3

CLINTON

I barely slept that night. Between the pain in my face and the hurt in my heart, sleep stayed away. I hated it. Every fucking second of it. The worrying. The turning in bed, over and over. I'd written more in my journal that night than ever before. Page after page of angry musings, random poems with Rae at the center, and a list.

A half-done list of all my possibilities after I graduated.

The list had more numbers than suggestions. It was depressing, really. Making a list, then putting two things on it. 'Get a job' and 'move out.' Those were the two things on my list.

And I still had no idea how to actually accomplish those two things.

The sun slowly rose and I eased myself out of bed. My entire body hurt. I shuffled into the bathroom and turned on the light, shielding my eyes. My head hurt.

Still. My hips hurt. Still. My knee hurt and my knuckles were bruised and even I knew my ribcage was black and blue again.

Nothing could have prepared me for the sight of myself in the mirror, though.

"Holy fuck."

The bags underneath my eyes were fierce. The soft red marks around my throat reminded me of more things that happened last night. Things I hadn't remembered until I looked at the marks on my body. The scratch marks. The bruises. The way that fucking thing on my face held my nose upright.

"I can't wear this shit to school."

I tried taking it off, but it felt like it was plastered to my nose. The bruises on my cheekbones made me angry. The light black and blue marks that peppered my ribcage made my blood boil. I turned my back to the image of myself and decided to suffer through a shower. I knew it would hurt, water battering against my abused body. But I stunk. I smelled of rain water, sweat, and hopelessness.

And if the plan was to do research today, I needed my wits about me.

I got into the shower and groaned all the way through it. Every droplet hurt. It felt like my body had gone into overdrive, like my nerve endings were exposed. I probably should've gone to the hospital. But I didn't want to be in the same facility as my father.

When the hell was he coming home anyway?

I slipped out of the shower and dried myself off, pressing the towel softly against my skin as I walked into my bedroom. Everything felt muted. It almost felt like I wasn't piloting my own body. Not really, anyway. I felt out of place. Out of time. Alert, but not really there.

Until a knock came at my door.

"Clint?"

Cecilia's voice caused me to pause. I quickly wrapped the towel around my waist before I reached for the door. I closed my eyes, drawing in a deep breath. Because I knew seeing me like this would throw her for a loop.

Then I opened the door.

She gasped. "Clint, you need a doctor."

I opened my eyes. "I'm fine."

"Your ribs. You—come with me. Come on. I'll get you somewhere."

"Cecilia."

"Your nose doesn't look much better, either. We need to schedule surgery."

"Cecilia."

"Come with me. You can skip school and—"

I snipped at her, "Cecilia."

She paused. "Yes?"

I sighed. "You shouldn't be here when my father gets home from the hospital. Whenever that is. It won't be safe for you. Not after you calling the paramedics and having him hauled off last night."

"I'm not concerned about that right now. I'm concerned about you. We need to go get you checked out. For all we know, your father's knocked something loose or busted stitches somewhere we don't know about."

"I'm fine. It's all topical."

"And how do you know that?"

I snickered. "If I were bleeding internally, I'd technically already be dead."

She stared at me and I took her in. Really, truly took her in. The color of her eyes that had slowly faded. The disheveled nature of her hair as she piled it at the crown of her head. The bags under her eyes were heavier than I'd ever seen them. And, without makeup, she looked ten years older. She had crows' feet at the corners of her eyes. Her lips were downturned, causing her entire face to sag. Her shoulders were hunched. She favored her left side.

I nodded slowly. "Didn't get much sleep, either?"

She brushed off my question. "I won't take you to the hospital your father's at, but you have to see someone."

"I'll make an appointment with the doctor I saw."

"That's the hospital Howard's at right now."

"I'll figure it out, then."

She sighed. "Why won't you let me take you?"

"Because it's not your responsibility."

I saw the hurt in her eyes. And had I not already been dead inside, it would've killed me. The truth of the matter was that all this was my mother's responsibility. But she'd abandoned me. None of this should've happened. Dad shouldn't have been an abusive fucking asshole. Nobody should have had to bear the responsibility of it.

I wouldn't let Cecilia dig her hole any deeper.

Just like I wouldn't let Rae do it, either.

"You really should take advantage of this time. Withdraw some funds. Pack up your things. Get the hell out of here and find a better life for yourself."

She stepped forward, placing a hand against my arm. "While that's sweet, it's not your job to look after me, Clinton. I appreciate it, but right now I'm worried about you. You can't go to school looking like this."

"Then I won't."

"There's nothing I can do to convince you to let me get you to a doctor?"

I shook my head. "No."

"Are you staying here for the day?"

"No."

"Where are you going, then?"

I shrugged. "Anywhere but school and here. I need to clear my head for a bit."

"Do you want me to come with you?"

"No."

"Is there anything I can do for you right now?"

You're much too good to me. "No, there isn't."

She sighed. "Well, at least keep in touch, okay?"

I nodded. "I can do that."

Reluctantly, she left my room. She walked down the hallway toward her and Dad's bedroom, but stopped in the doorway. I watched her back expand with her breath. I saw her shoulders roll back. And as she suddenly held her head high, she let out the longest sigh I'd ever heard in my life.

Before slipping through the large double doors and disappearing behind them.

You're too good for any of us, Cecelia.

I finished getting myself ready for the day and covered up the best I could. I slipped on a pair of sunglasses and went rummaging around for a coat. Anything to slide up my arms in case there were bruises I'd missed somehow. I found a light jacket shoved in the back of my closet, neatly hanging from a hanger. A bomber jacket, made out of some light-weight material, that Cecilia had gotten me for Christmas a year or two ago.

I ripped it off the hanger and slipped it on. I grabbed my notebook and pen from my bedside table and slipped my wallet into the back pocket of my jeans, cursing myself for... well, everything.

Then I made my way downstairs.

With my eyes covered and that bomber jacket covering the rest of my body, I made my way out the front door. Nothing in tow except my wallet and that fucking notebook. I had one goal in mind for the day. And that shit had nothing to do with school. By the time I was done today, I'd have that entire list filled with ideas on how to get the fuck out of here. How to start a life for myself with mediocre grades and no life skills to speak of.

There had to be a way for me to get out without using resource shelters in the area.

I walked toward school, then kept on walking. I walked past Valley High, down the mile and a half stretch until the main part of our little side of town came into view. I crossed the road, eyeing the railroad tracks off to my right. Fear seized me as images of that night bombarded my mind's eye. Including the moment where I was sure that damn river would sweep me away.

Rae saved you. And look at what you're doing to her.

"I'm saving her from me," I murmured to myself.

I trotted across the road and found my way into a coffee shop. The one next to the grocery store, actually. I walked inside and felt all eyes on me. Some random high school kid with sunglasses on, a navy blue jacket that almost didn't fit, and a nose brace on his face. But, thankfully, it was still early. Which meant the morning rush was all drive-thru. No one really came inside.

Giving me the privacy I needed.

I ordered my coffee and stood there to wait for it. I was thankful to be there. The last place I wanted to be was at school. I couldn't face Rae. I knew she'd corner me and ask me about last night. About us. About what the fuck happened. I couldn't face her right now. Because I knew if I looked her in the eyes, I wouldn't be able to lie to her.

So my only option was to avoid her at all costs.

"One large black coffee with rosewater and caramel?"

I reached out for it. "Thanks."

"Can we get you anything else?"

I paused, reliving the memory of Rae in my bed that morning. "Actually, yes. Do you have computers here for the general public to use?"

The barista nodded. "Through the doorway in the corner and immediately to the right."

"I appreciate it."

I took large gulps of the coffee as I walked through the small coffee shop. I did as I was told, and found myself in a small room with seven or eight different computers. All of them were as nice as the ones my father had at the house. It was shocking, really. This dinky little coffeehouse with such up-to-date technology.

I wasn't complaining though.

I sat down in the far corner, thankful that I was tucked away from the world. I opened my notebook and logged in using the log-in information taped across the top of the monitor. After navigating to the web browser, I picked up my pen. I scratched out the two things I'd written last night in my sleepy stupor, then typed in my first search.

What to do after high school with terrible grades.

Much to my surprise, a lot popped up. I filtered through the articles and clicked on a couple of them. I scanned through and jotted down some valuable information. The articles I really wanted to read, I emailed to myself. Good reading material if I couldn't sleep again tonight. I jotted down a few things to research. Community colleges in California with the best rates. Scholarships and shit I could get without proving good grades. Jobs I'd be eligible for as an eighteen-year old with a high school diploma.

Literally, anything that might get me out of this fucking place.

I didn't want to stay in Riverbend. And eventually, I'd want out of the state altogether. I needed to get the hell away from this shit. The hell away from my father. The hell away from my life. I needed a fresh start. With people that didn't know me and police departments that didn't profile me. My search poured me into an overall state search. States that had the best services for runaway children and had the best social programs to help people get back on their feet.

And after emailing myself over thirty links to articles to read later, I sat back and stared at the screen as I finished the coffee that reminded me of Rae. Then a thought hit me. A thought that lingered a little too long. A thought I wanted answers to, even if I didn't follow through with it. So, I typed my question into the internet search bar just to see what would pop up.

Is it legal for an eighteen-year old to steal from their parents?

A last ditch effort, just in case nothing else panned out whatsoever.

4

RAELYNN

I stood at the entrance to my neighborhood, staring up at the sidewalk. As Michael and Allison walked down to me, I held out hope that Clint might show up. That he might come meet me like we'd done those few times before the accident. Michael kept looking at me with that pity-filled stare and Allison rubbed my back. I shrugged her touch off, tired of their antics and their pity and their bullshit.

I was tired of everyone's fucking bullshit.

Michael sighed. "You know he's not coming."

Allison shushed him. "Come on, let's get to school before we're late."

"Maybe he'll show up after lunch. Once he gets some rest."

"Or maybe he went to the hospital when he got up this morning. You never know."

"Not helping, Allison."

"Sorry."

I walked aimlessly with them into the school. I peeked over my shoulder just before we walked inside, and there was no trace of him. We took up our usual spot outside of my locker, my head on a swivel for him. And while my heart refused to give up hope, my mind already had. Rationally, my mind knew he wasn't coming. Maybe not for the rest of the week. Maybe not ever again. I wouldn't blame him for that, either. Running away and never coming back.

I wanted to run away and never come back.

Allison linked her arm through mine. "Come on, it's homeroom time."

I wandered through the day aimlessly. Listlessly. I didn't pay attention in my morning classes or even take notes. I sat at the back of the classroom and worked on homework, trying to knock it out. Because I knew once I got home, I wouldn't be able to focus. I felt hollow. Empty inside. Like someone had shoveled out my soul and replaced it with helium. I was late to classes because I kept pausing in the hallway, letting my mind take over and memories rip me back into the past.

I missed Clint more than I could stand.

My heart continued to remain optimistic, though. Because apparently, torturing me wasn't enough. I stared out the window of class and counted down the minutes to lunch. That was my only remaining hope. That Clint would simply show up for school late because of a doctor or a need for sleep or another brawl with his father, and I'd see him at lunch. My eyes followed the hands of the clock. My teacher's voice stayed muted the entire time. After quickly finishing my homework for the night, I abandoned all thought processes and relegated myself to the spinning hell of my mind.

Of my heart.

Of the war raging between the two.

The bell rang and it ripped me from my trance. I gathered up my things and made a beeline for the door and raced toward the cafeteria. My legs carried me as quickly as I could run. I didn't even bother stopping by my locker to discard my morning books. I wanted to get to Clint as soon as possible. If he was here, I wanted to be the first to greet him.

But when I turned the corner, I saw the cafeteria completely empty.

"Huh?"

A voice cleared itself behind me. "Can I help you?"

I whipped around, gazing into the eyes of our football coach. He quirked an eyebrow at me. "Skipping class?"

I paused. "Uh, no. I—it's lunch time, isn't it?"

He furrowed his brow. "No. It's not. It's only ten-fifteen."

"What?"

"Are you okay? You look a little pale, Miss…?"

"Sorry. Uh, sorry. I have to get to class."

I rushed past the football coach, feeling his eyes follow me down the hallway. I'd only gotten through first period? I felt disoriented. Confused. I could've sworn I'd gone to both of my morning periods before lunch.

"Rae?"

I heard our school guidance counselor call out my name. I slowly turned around as tears rushed my eyes. She came over to me, ushering me toward the main office. And before I knew it, we were in her office. With her door closing behind me. As my books fell from my arms.

While tears streaked my cheeks.

She handed me tissues and urged me to take a seat in front of her desk. I didn't want to talk. The last thing I wanted to do was tell anyone else about what was happening. But, she didn't ask me questions. She simply typed away on her computer, her eyes glued to the screen. Giving me as much privacy as she could while I sobbed my eyes out in her fucking office.

Like a damn child.

You are a child.

I didn't feel like a child, though. I hadn't felt like one in years. The shit I'd dealt with. The bullshit my mother put us through. All this insanity with Clint and his father. Children didn't deal with this. Adults did. Adults tackled these kinds of issues.

Guess the grass isn't always greener on the other side.

I cried until I had no more tears. The guidance counselor—I couldn't recall her name—continued working until my crying subsided. I cried so hard my eyes swelled shut. I slumped into the chair until the back of my neck sat against the top crook of its cushion. I gazed up at the ceiling, wondering what Clint was doing. Wondering where he was.

Wondering if he was all right.

"Do you want to talk about it?"

I sighed, closing my eyes. "No."

"Are you sure?"

"Yeah."

"Is it something to do with Clint?"

I paused. "Why do you ask?"

"I noticed he's absent today."

"How do you know that?"

"I have more jobs than tending to the mental and emotional well-being of the student population here."

I sighed. "Gotcha."

"Would you like some advice?"

I snickered. "I haven't told you anything."

"Doesn't mean I don't have advice."

"Sure. Go ahead, then."

"Whatever's going on, address it head-on. Talk to whoever you need to in order to get things cleared up. This is your most important year. This is when you determine plans for college. Nail down your grades for scholarships. Create rapport with teachers who will give you shining recommendations for school. Whatever's happening that has you so distracted, talk to whoever you need to in order to fix it. Because when it comes to your future, you're allowed to be selfish."

It sounded like some shit out of a self-help book. And yet, it made all the sense in the world. The only problem with her advice was that I couldn't talk to them. Clint wasn't here, and if even I thought about talking to his father, I was certain he'd beat me into the ground, too. And even if I could get my mother to sit down and have a serious conversation with me about

D.J., she'd brush off anything I had to say to her because 'You're a teenager and don't get it.'

But it was sound advice.

"Thanks," I murmured.

"Anytime. You're free to go to class whenever you want. But you're more than welcome to stay here. You know, until another student comes knocking on the door or something."

I slowly sat up. "How many students do you see in a day, anyway?"

She sighed. "More than I like to admit with issues I still can't believe most days."

"In a good way, or…?"

"'Or.' Yes."

Guess the grass really isn't greener on the other side.

"What time is it?"

The counselor peeked over at me. "Almost time for the lunch bell."

"I've been in here that long?"

"You have, yes."

I sighed. "Great."

"Do you lose time like this often?"

"No. Just today."

"Another reason why you should unload the stressors off your chest."

I nodded. "Yeah. I got it."

She grinned. "Just making sure."

"Actually, I'd like to ask you something."

She turned toward me. "Ask away."

"Is it possible for an eighteen-year-old to survive in

this world with a high school diploma and nothing else?"

"Generally speaking? Or is this for something specific?"

"Just general. I'm curious."

She paused. "Uh huh."

"Really. I am."

"Okay. I'll bite. Yes, generally speaking, it's possible to make a good life for oneself without a college degree. But it's still hard. Most jobs will start people at the very bottom, and make them prove themselves twice over against their college-educated counterparts. And in bigger cities and states like California, that percentage drops significantly."

"So what you're saying is someone who only has a high school degree would have to get out of California before attempting to build a life for themselves."

She nodded. "For the greatest overall chance of success, yes."

"How can they do that without money?"

"There's the catch-22. I'll let you know once I know."

I snickered. "Well, thanks for the advice."

"My office is open to you anytime. But can you relay a message to Clint for me?"

I paused. "Sure."

"Tell him college is nothing like high school. Especially a community college. Let him know that even a two-year technical degree would set him up much better than only having a high school diploma."

I blinked. "I didn't ask that question for Clint."

"I'm sure you didn't."

She turned to face her computer just as the lunch bell rang. And while part of me was frustrated with her for assuming my position, I couldn't hate her for it. Because she'd been right. Maybe I was frustrated because she was right. Because I'd become so easy for people to read. I gathered my things and made my way for my locker, my mind in knots as I put my books away.

And pulled out my afternoon books.

As I made my way for the cafeteria—again—I wondered how long it might take for Clint to come back to school. Or if he'd come back at all. I hoped he did. His grades were slowly doing better. I mean, not by much. He was still a hearty C average student. But the one D he had in history had come up due to his last test score. If he worked really hard at it, he might be able to get some of his classes into the 'B' range before the end of the school year. Which would greatly affect his GPA.

And any chance he had at getting into a two-year technical college out of state somewhere.

"Hey there, beautiful."

"What's for lunch?"

"You want me to go through the line for you?"

"They've got discounted sodas today."

I rolled my eyes. "You guys can stop hanging off me now."

Michael chuckled. "Not our fault you haven't spoken to us all day."

Allison nodded. "Yeah, Rae. We're worried about you."

I rolled my eyes. "You should be worried about Clint."

Allison furrowed her brow. "What makes you think we're not?"

The three of us hopped into the lunch line and I kept my eyes peeled for him. I'd never seen Clint actually eat lunch here. So I kept darting my eyes through the glass-less window cutouts of the cement wall that separated the lunch line from the cafeteria dining area. I mindlessly paid for my food, grabbed a Dr. Pepper and headed for our seats in the corner. My backpack lay at my feet and my food stayed untouched as my eyes scanned the room, searching frantically for any sign of Clint.

But he was nowhere to be found.

Michael sat in front of me. "Just give him some time."

Allison patted my back. "He needs to rest. Recuperate. Process, and all that."

I shook my head. "I can't shake this feeling that something's just—"

I didn't know how to explain it.

I drew in deep, quick breaths as I cracked open my soda, chugging it back and relishing the burn of the carbonation. I tried to push my tears away, the hurt, the anguish. I didn't want people to see me break down and cry. I had cried in front of the school counselor, and that was enough. I didn't want the entire school talking about how I'd been bawling my eyes out at lunch over Clinton Fucking Clarke. Since he was nowhere in sight.

That didn't bode well for either of us. And told much more of a story than I wanted the school to know.

Especially since I had no idea what came next.

5

CLINTON

After sitting at that damn computer until almost eleven in the morning, I was out the door. I walked up and down the road, trying to figure out where to go or what to do next. No bike. No car. Forty bucks in my pocket. I didn't want to go home because I didn't want Cecilia questioning where I'd been or worrying even more about me. And I sure as hell didn't want to run into my father, just in case he came home from the hospital today.

I meandered until I came across a familiar sight. The park. That damned park I'd found Rae sitting in that night. I chuckled bitterly to myself. It was as if the world were conspiring against me today. Using everything it could to remind me of the girl I'd left behind. For a good reason.

Guess the world didn't care about my reasons.

I walked over to a bench in the corner, shielded by a few of the trees that still stood in the abandoned place. And as I sat down, I stared at that bench. The bench where Rae and I had our first kiss. Where I first felt her skin against mine. Where I found her, holding back tears and trying to put on a brave face while her entire world caved around her.

Like mine.

"What a fucking mess," I murmured to myself as I sat down. And the second my ass touched the bench, I felt something stiffen. I felt something preventing me from sitting down and I shot back up. I looked behind me. Had I sat on something? But I didn't see anything on the bench.

Holy shit, I have my phone with me.

I ripped my phone out of my pocket and sat back down. I opened up my email, clicking link after link as I read through the articles. Some of them were bullshit, and some of them were full of help. I pulled my notebook and pen back out, jotting down things on random pages that I wanted to remember. Names of community colleges in the state that would take high school kids with shitty grades. States in the country that would actually provide a free community college education to those who declared residency. I didn't even know that was a fucking thing, free education.

By the time I'd read through all those articles, I actually felt hope surge through my veins.

Maybe I can do this after all.

My stomach growling pulled me from my trance, so I slipped my phone back into my pocket. I gathered my things and walked back the same way I came, then slipped into the grocery store. Rae's grocery store. The one where all this bullshit started in the first place. I made my way to the deli and picked up a couple of sandwiches. Some fries. Even grabbed an energy drink from the machine. I felt people staring at me as I went through the line. The line Rae usually worked.

Only it wasn't Rae behind the register.

And I found that I didn't really like that.

You miss her.

I shook the thought away and walked my ass outside. I sat down on a bench near the front doors and tore into the food I'd bought. I wondered what Cecilia was doing. If she was worried about me. I wondered what she was thinking. If she was worried about the status of her marriage with my father. In my eyes? She needed to be more hellbent on taking care of herself. Finding a safe haven to run toward. Finding a way out of this hellhole. Because I knew my father would bring down hell on us all once he got out of that hospital.

She needed to take care of her own safety.

She's staying behind for you.

I growled to myself. The last thing I needed was yet another innocent woman going to bat for me. Rae tried it, and it almost got her hurt. And I didn't have the energy to push another good woman away. Cecilia had been a godsend. An adult who showed me what it really meant for a parent to care about a fucking child. I didn't want to push her away. The easy route would be for her to pack her shit and leave me behind. I knew how to deal with that. I knew how to write people off the moment they abandoned me. Mostly. Kind of.

Except your own mother.

Holy shit, I was a fucked-up human being.

I finished my food and tried not to give my thoughts any more energy to grow. Now I needed to concentrate on getting home. Even though cooler temperatures were falling over the city, that didn't stop the sun from beating down against our backs. Sweating me to my fucking core as I sat on the bench beside the sliding doors of the grocery store. I pulled my phone out of my pocket and checked the time. Fucking hell, it was almost three o'clock.

You'll need a ride to get home on time.

I searched for the taxi companies in the area before calling one up. I didn't want to make an Uber account and have to use it or anything. Because if I did, Dad would know I hadn't been in school. He'd see that charge to the credit card and flip his fucking nozzle. As if he didn't already do that, anyway. The last thing I needed was any more of a reason for my father to want me dead. Because I'd done enough to warrant him killing me.

I found myself dreading the moment that he got home from that hospital.

I ordered the taxi, and thirty minutes later it showed up. I rattled off my address and the man drove me home. And I just gave him the thirty bucks I still had left over from lunch. I didn't care how much the trip cost. I didn't care how much I was overpaying him by. The only thing I cared about was whether or not Dad was home. Whether or not I'd open this door and feel his wrath beating against my body.

Literally.

Until I bled to death.

I drew in a deep breath. As the taxi pulled away, I started for the front door. I opened it up and walked inside, bracing for my father's voice. But when I heard Cecilia yelp, I whipped my head up.

"What? What's wrong?"

Her hand pressed against her chest. "You scared the living daylights out of me, Clint."

I closed the door. "I didn't mean to startle you. It's just me."

I saw her book on the floor. She scrambled for it, trying to right herself on the couch again. Her cheeks were flushed, her eyes wide from the shock. My heart ached for her. How scared she was for my father to come home. But, when she lifted her eyes to meet mine again, the fear melted away. And replacing it was this cool sort of strength I'd come to learn she possessed.

A trait I envied quite a bit.

"How was your day?"

Her voice ripped me from my thoughts. "Uh, good."

"Did you make it to school?"

I nodded slowly. "Yep. I did."

"Are you sure about that?"

"Why wouldn't I be?"

"You want to try one more time?"

And when she grinned, I shook my head.

"No, I didn't make it to school."

She nodded. "I was home when the school called

and told me you were absent from roll call in homeroom."

"I don't think I've ever known you to linger in this house."

"I've never had a reason to, until now."

I chuckled. "Waiting for Dad and his wrath to come wafting through the door?"

Her face stayed serious. "No. Waiting for you."

Her words clenched my heart. It became hard to breathe. I'd never had someone do that for me. Hang around all day, waiting for me. I didn't know how to process that. How to feel about it.

I drew in a deep breath. "I'm worried about you."

Cecilia nodded. "I'm worried about you, too."

"I didn't mean to scare you or anything."

"You didn't. I know you can handle yourself. I figured you went on a walk into town, or something."

"I did."

"So… how's town?"

I snickered. "It's town. How was your day at the house?"

"It was… a day at the house."

I nodded. "It's not like you to hang around here like this. Just… sitting here and biding your time."

"I suppose we're all changing, in a way."

"How so?"

"Well, for one, you stood up for yourself. In a way I've never seen you do. I mean, I expected it eventually. But I didn't expect it to be for anyone other than yourself. Not only did you stand up to your father, but you did it for my sake. You've grown a lot, Clinton."

I didn't wince when she called me by my first name. "I guess that happens as life goes on."

"You shouldn't have to worry about your father, though. About whether or not he's home. You leave him to me. I'll figure this out."

"You know I'm not going to do that."

She got up from the couch. "I know you're not. But that isn't going to stop me from reminding you that it isn't your duty as the child of this house to meddle in adult affairs like this."

"I've been meddling in adult affairs ever since my father started using his hands to parent."

I watched as Cecilia approached me. She stood in front of me, clad in a pristine royal blue dress with dainty white gold jewelry peppering her body. Her makeup looked like perfection. Her hair was completely straight and pulled back, with wisps falling into her face. She reached her hand up and cupped my cheeks, flooding my body with warmth.

A warmth I only had memories of when it came to my mother.

"You've been through a lot in your life, Clint. And while I'm not your mother, that doesn't mean I don't worry about you."

I closed my eyes. "I know."

"My only regret is that I didn't step in sooner. That I never stopped your father from—"

"It's not your fault."

"No, it's not. But, I have a responsibility in all this. I knew what was taking place, and I never did anything to stop it. Or report it. That's on me, Clint.

Part of where you're standing right now is on
—is—uh—"

The second she drew in a shuddering breath, I
wrapped my arms around her. I pulled my stepmother closely into me and felt her arms drape
around me. Her warmth brought tears to my eyes.
Memories of my mother came flooding back to the
forefront of my mind. Memories of my mother
caring for me. Rocking with me. Loving me and
cherishing me and singing to me as she held me
close.

I buried my face in Cecilia's hair, trying to cling to
this feeling. To the idea that someone even remotely
akin to a parent could actually give a shit about me.

I sighed. "Please don't cry."

She nodded quickly and sniffled.

"Well, um, dinner's in the oven. And you smell like
you need a shower."

She pulled away from me as I chuckled softly.

"I suppose I don't smell the greatest."

She wrinkled her nose. "You really don't. Go get
cleaned up, and when you're done, dinner will be
ready."

I reached out and wiped a stray tear off her cheek.
I saw the pain and the guilt flooding Cecilia's eyes. I'd
never seen her like this. So downtrodden and… and
sad. Just plain sadness. It hurt me, truly. Because
through all this, I'd come to see how incredible of a
woman she really was. Strong, steadfast, dedicated, and
actually intelligent. Broken, like me. In a lot of ways
due to her family. Like me.

I stroked her cheek. "I'm proud to call you my stepmother."

She snickered. "And I hope, one day, I earn the honor of calling you my stepson."

She quickly turned on her bare feet and padded back into the kitchen, leaving me there to hurt even more. The fact that she didn't feel she could call me her stepson hurt. Especially after everything that had happened. Everything she'd helped me through. But I knew she said that because she felt guilty. Not because I'd done anything wrong.

So I dragged myself upstairs and got myself cleaned up for dinner.

I stepped into the shower with aches and pains in places on my body I didn't know existed. When I came out of the shower, wonderful smells filled my nostrils. I smelled basil and honey. Starches and gravy. I smelled butter and blueberries and sugar in the air. It pulled me downstairs. I went down for dinner in nothing but a pair of sweatpants and an old, ragged black shirt.

And I found dinner sprawled out on the kitchen table. With two place settings.

"We're eating at the table?"

Cecilia set our drinks down. "Why not?"

I paused. "I don't know. I'm just not—used to having family dinner. I guess."

She snickered. "Well, I'm not your father. I like eating with family. So get used to it is all I can tell you."

And when she winked at me, it made me smile. Truly smile, for the first time since yesterday evening.

"I can do that," I said.

6

RAELYNN

I didn't want to go, but I gave my word. During my last period, Michael and Allison both pressured me to join them for dinner tonight. Sushi, apparently. I didn't feel like going out, though. I didn't feel like joining them for anything. I wanted to run myself a bath, get into the pathetic tub and cry my eyes out while indulging in a bag full of cookies. But they were my friends and I knew they were trying their best to cheer me up.

So I promised them I'd be there.

Michael wanted to pick me up, but I refused. I'd get there somehow. Some way. I pulled on an old pair of jeans and a T-shirt, then threw my hair up into a bumpy ponytail. I looked like a hazard zone. The bags underneath my eyes were more prominent than ever and my skin looked pale. Well, paler than it usually was. I sighed as I walked away from the mirror, making my way downstairs.

"Where you headed?"

I paused at the sound of D.J.'s voice.

"Sweetheart?" Mom asked.

I sighed. "Heading out to dinner with Michael and Allison."

D.J. snickered. "You aren't going to eat dinner with me and your mother? She's been cooking."

I slowly turned around. "No, I'm not. I'll be back around eight or so."

"Where are you headed for dinner? So we know where you are."

"Not your responsibility to know where I am."

Mom sighed. "Please, just answer his question."

I glared at her. "Just because you put up with his antics so our bills get paid doesn't mean I have to."

Mom gasped. "Excuse me?"

D.J. stood up from the couch. "You apologize to your mother."

I scoffed. "Yeah, no thanks. No apologies needed for the truth, no matter how hard it is to hear."

"You get over here right now so we can have a talk. Your attitude has been atrocious lately."

"Pretty big word for a drug dealer."

Mom shot up from her seat. "You take that back right now, young lady."

"Do as your mother says."

I shrugged. "Sorry that I brought up a rumor on the street."

D.J. lunged at me and I dropped my purse. I was ready for a fucking fight. I was ready to take this asshole down with nothing but my hands. Mom held him back, talking softly in his ear as my nostrils flared in anger. I silently dared him with his eyes. Dared him to come at me. To lay his hands on me.

I'd get his ass thrown in jail and we'd all be rid of this fucker.

When the two of them sat back down on the couch, D.J. snuggled my mother. Ran his hands over her thighs. I watched her kiss his neck and it made me sick to look at. I picked up my purse and stormed out of the house, making my way for my bike. And as I threw my leg over the rusted piece of shit, I made my way into town.

Straight for the sushi place.

I parked my bike, but didn't have anything to tie it off. So I simply tossed the hunk of rust down onto the sidewalk and made my way inside. The breeze of the air conditioning felt good. I stood there for a second, letting it dry off the beads of sweat working their way down my face. And when I felt partially human again, I started meandering around the restaurant.

I found Michael and Allison in a booth.

"Shit, she's here."

"Hey, Rae!"

I quirked an eyebrow as the two of them leapt away from one another. I mean, Michael practically shoved Allison off his body. Their lips were red. Allison's neck was flushed. It didn't take a genius to figure out what they'd been doing in this back booth all by themselves.

It made me feel like the third wheel, though.

Which wasn't how I wanted to spend my dinner.

I ordered my drink as Allison made room for me on the other side of her. But I saw how they had their hands intertwined in the darkness. It made me miss Clint. It made me want him here. I wanted someone to kiss. Someone to snuggle against. Someone's hand to hold.

Specifically, his.

Michael whistled. "So what do you two want for dinner? It's on me, by the way."

I shook my head. "You don't have to do that."

Allison giggled. "That's so kind of you. Thank you."

Michael chuckled. "Hey, it's the least I can do."

Allison smiled. "You do so much more than that, you know. You're just... very kind. In general. I like that."

"Well, do you know what I like about you?"

I piped up. "What's that?"

The two of them looked at me before Allison's cheeks flushed.

"Oh, sorry. Thought you were talking to me."

I tossed them each a look before I buried myself back into the menu. I hated being that person. But I also wouldn't spend my entire dinner hour with them listening to their sickeningly, disgusting flirting back and forth. Yes, I was happy for them. But they had to respect what I was going through. Because if the tables were turned, I would've done the same damn thing.

Respected their circumstances.

The waiter came by and took our orders. Michael ordered for Allison and she giggled like the schoolgirl she was. I murmured my order before tossing the menu back to the waiter and thanking him for the extra water. I felt empty. Dead. Dark, deep within the pit of my soul. I didn't understand this kind of hurt. I'd never experienced it before. I mean, with my father, it wasn't my fault. He left well before I had any memories of him. But Clint?

Maybe I'd done something to push him away.

Maybe I'm the reason he's gone.

Michael cleared his throat. "So how's that bike holding up?"

I whipped my head up. "Huh?"

Allison smiled softly. "Your bike. That's how you got here, right?"

"Unless you took a taxi."

"You know she hates taxis, Michael."

"I mean, it's an option. You never know."

"You're so silly."

He smiled. "And you're so cute."

I rolled my eyes. "Yeah, I rode my bike. It's a hunk of rusted junk, but it gets the job done."

Allison giggled profusely. "That's what she said."

Michael snorted with laughter as I slowly panned my eyes over to her.

"What did you say?"

Allison smiled brightly. "Michael taught me those jokes. You know, using 'that's what she said' behind a phrase that could technically be construed as… dirty."

I snickered at the way she whispered 'dirty.' As if she'd be shot into the bowels of hell for saying it out loud.

"That was a good one, beautiful. Way to go."

She smiled. "Thanks, Michael."

Clint used to call me beautiful. "Well, it was a good one. Yes."

"Thanks, Rae."

Our food came and I entertained myself with eating. While Allison and Michael entertained themselves with, well, one another. They kept charging headfirst into conversations meant only for them. Which threw gasoline on the fire of my pain. When would this let up? When would it stop hurting so much? I mean, it'd only been one day. How the fuck was I supposed to keep putting one foot in front of the other and acting like things were okay if this was day one?

How did my two best friends expect me to sit here and watch them practically fondle one another when this was day one without Clint?

Every time they thought I wasn't looking, they snuck a kiss or shared bites of their food. At least, I thought so. I thought maybe they thought I couldn't see them. Because if that wasn't the case, then that meant they were blatantly making the conversation about them instead of including me.

And I didn't want to believe my two best friends were that cold-hearted.

I knew they were trying to get my mind off Clint. But, they had to know that what they were doing wasn't helping. Right? I mean, come on! They were pressing themselves against one another! I don't know when the hell their pseudo-relationship took a shift into the physical realm. But they needed to keep it behind closed doors.

Just be happy for them, Rae. They were happy for you.

Sushi was for dinner, but guilt was dessert. And instead of saying something to the two of them, I just let them roam. I didn't interject into their conversations and I turned my head every time they kissed one another. Because I knew I felt this way out of anger. And jealousy. Out of not having Clint in my life anymore.

Maybe they'll leave you, too. Now that they have one another.

Dinner wrapped up and I didn't fight Michael when he paid. I peeled away from the two of them to head outside. Because I wanted to get on my bike and go for a ride. I wanted to work off my anger. Work off my frustration. Ride around until D.J. was thrown off a bridge.

But I didn't see my bike on the sidewalk.

"Where's your bike?"

Michael's voice made me want to strangle him, for some reason.

"Uh oh. Should we call the police?"

Allison's voice grated on my ears as I stood there.

"You need a ride home?"

"Tell us what to do and we can get it done."

"Seriously, Rae. What do you need right now? Because we're here for you."

Yeah, when you aren't making out over dinner. "I just need a ride home."

Michael nodded. "I can do that."

I leaned my head against the glass of his backseat window. Allison took Michael's hand from across the console, their fingers laced together. Silent tears brewed behind my eyes. With every blink, they threatened to pour out. As if I hadn't already cried until my voice was hoarse over some asshole who didn't give a shit about me. They pulled into my driveway and I didn't bother looking to see if D.J.'s car was there. I just hopped out, happy to be out of their orbit so they could go fuck and get it over with already.

Allison rolled her window down. "If you need anything, call me. Okay?"

I nodded. "Will do."

"Promise?"

I sighed. "Yep. I promise."

"Same goes for me."

"Thanks, Michael."

Then Allison rolled up her window and the two of them took off.

I stood in the driveway, watching them fade away. Watching them ride off into their own little world. I used to do that on Clint's bike. I used to wrap my arms around him and cling to him as we rode around town. Or back to his house. Or back to my house. The horizon had been for our taking. Life had been ours to grasp. And now, I stood alone in my driveway. Watching my two best friends who were absolutely in love pave their own path into the sunset.

While I stood there.

Alone.

Like I'd always been in my life.

7

CLINTON

M idnight.
As I checked my cell phone for the time, midnight stared back at me. Midnight, on a school night, and I still wasn't asleep. I'd taken pain medication. I'd taken a sleep aid. And here I lay, staring at my fucking ceiling.

Wondering about Rae.

No matter how hard I tried, I couldn't stop thinking about her. Everything reminded me of her, and I hated it. I wanted it to be over. Every single part of this painful journey reminded me why I didn't do the fucking relationship thing. The pain in my broken heart reminded me of why I fucked and kept moving. Why I took what I wanted and gave very little back in return.

Because this was what heartbreak felt like.

I did it for her own good, though.

I rolled over onto my side. Despite the pain in my

face plate, I buried myself into the pillow. I stared at the wall, giving myself yet another muted surface to look at as my mind spiraled. I wanted to call Rae and tell her about all of the things I'd researched. All the possibilities that were apparently out there for me. And if she wanted to, she could be part of that. I wanted those words to come out of my mouth. I wanted to tell her how much I missed her. How much I wanted her. How much I needed her.

How much I love her.

I sighed as I rolled onto my back again. I was a stomach sleeper. So I knew I wouldn't sleep well. Or hard. But I wanted to sleep a little bit, at least. While my father wasn't at the house still. I didn't know his condition at the hospital. Frankly, I didn't care. Hell, I didn't give a shit if the hospital kept him for weeks on end because of complications stemming from the night before. So long as it kept him out of this house.

And away from us.

Rae could be over more.

I growled at the thoughts racing through my mind. I turned over onto my other side and grabbed my phone again. 12:06. I'd killed six entire minutes doing nothing but burying myself in my own thoughts.

Why can't it be six entire hours?

I tossed my phone back onto the bedside table. I snuggled down underneath the covers and closed my eyes. Maybe if I faked being asleep, my body would eventually slip into it. I mean, everyone said *Fake it until you make it*. Maybe that shit actually worked.

So I screwed my eyes shut.

Rae's face bombarded my memories. Her laughter echoed in the caverns of my ears. And I swore I felt her lips against mine. That soft plumpness pushing against me. My eyes ripped open. I panted softly for air. I rolled over and reached for my cell phone, trying to figure out what time it was.

One-fifteen in the morning.

I tossed my cell phone onto the pillow next to my head. Then I closed my eyes. At least it worked; pretending to sleep led to sleep. Not a restful sleep, though. I didn't want to see Rae in my dreams. I didn't want to relive the beauty of her body before waking up and finding myself in an empty bed. I couldn't take it. My heart couldn't tolerate it.

Should've thought about that before leaving her.

I growled as I turned to the side. I picked up another pillow and pressed it against my ear. I blocked myself away from the world, hoping it would all fade away with time. But the further I sank into my mattress, the more my mind swirled with thoughts of her. How was school? Did she have a lot of homework? What did we talk about in history? What did she do after school today? Did she have to work? Did she get home safely?

Does she miss me?

I peeked my eye open and saw my phone sitting there. Taunting me. Mocking me. Whispering things in my ear. *Call her. Just once. It'll be okay. Once you hear her voice, you can sleep easily.*

I almost caved, too.

Instead, I turned over onto my other side. I sandwiched my aching face between two pillows and forced my eyes to close. I drew in deep breaths, helping to push away memories of her. My mind fell blank. As my medication finally took hold, I felt myself actually drifting off to sleep. I welcomed it with open arms. I welcomed the pain medication as it continued to dull the ache in my bones. And as I hovered between sleepiness and being awake, I felt myself sigh.

I need to get out of this fucking town.

My mind gave way to thoughts of my future. Darkness swallowed me whole and dragged me under. I saw the list I'd made rushing behind my eyes. Reminding me of all the choices I had at my disposal, despite my insistence that I didn't. Community colleges and jobs that paid for schooling and only required a high school diploma. Entire lives I'd plotted out that were attainable for me the second I could get away from my father.

So many pieces soared around in my head.

For instance, would my father still be legally obligated to hand over my trust fund? I knew he had one set up for me. But could he take that away? It was technically mine. The second I turned eighteen, I gained control of it. I mean, he still lorded over it. Watched my every move with it. But I still technically had access to it. Could I shift that money into another account without his consent? Could I withdraw it and stash it somewhere so he couldn't take it back if he wanted?

The last thing before I got swept under by sleep was making a mental note. I needed to look into banking laws and call a few people so they could answer some questions.

Then, she appeared again.

"Clint?"

I turned around. "Rae?"

"Hey, Clint!"

I furrowed my brow. "What are you doing here?"

She paused. "What do you mean, what am I doing here? You called me."

"No, I didn't."

"Are you sure? Because I'm pretty sure you butt-dialed me while you were moaning my name."

A grin spread across her face and I looked down. And as the world tilted over on itself, I found my legs naked. Spread. With my cock resting in my hand. Rae's face darkened and she licked her lips, causing electricity to shoot through my body.

"I uh, I don't know where—"

Rae giggled. "Looks like you could use some help."

I panted. "Are you—willing to help?"

She quirked an eyebrow. "I can't believe you even have to ask that question."

In a flash, she was on top of me. Dressed in an outfit completely different from before. Her beautiful skin, softly sunkissed with summer's grace, was draped in red lingerie. A bra with her tits spilling out. A thong that emphasized her curves. A lacy robe slipped down her arms as she straddled me, gazing into my eyes. My cock pulsed in my hand. I felt it leaking as it begged to be within her. And as her hands fell against my chest, I licked my lips.

"How's this for help?"

Her lips fell to mine and I wrapped my arms around her.

Both of them. Leaving my cock to do as it wished. Her warmth drew me in. Her taste reminded me of the drug she'd become. I rolled her over, grunting as I pinned her beneath me.

Then I ripped that thong clear off her body.

"Clint!"

"You're mine, Rae."

She gasped as my lips fell to her neck.

I raked my teeth along her skin, pinning her wrists above her head as I kissed down her chest, feeling her excess fill the divots of my body. I brought her hands to my hair and had her fist the locks I'd grown out just so she could cling to me. And as I kissed my way down her body, I sucked against her skin, leaving marks that made me grin as she jumped and darted around.

"Clint. Oh, that tickl—! Oh, you—Clint, fuck."

I tossed her legs over my shoulders and settled in for a meal. Her scent filled my nostrils, letting loose the animal within its cage. I dove between her thighs. I felt her arousal coating my cheeks. I lapped until she shivered. Until she bucked ravenously against my face. I slipped my hands underneath her ass cheeks. I squeezed them, lifting her hips to my face. Feasting on the buffet of her body as her legs locked out against my back.

"Clint!"

I lapped heavily against her slit as she shook for me. I looked up, watching as her tits bounced for my viewing pleasure. Her skin flushed. Her back arched. Her sounds became choked as my tongue continued its assault. I didn't let up. I flicked her, faster. Harder. Visibly shaking her as I slowly lowered her back to the bed.

"No. No. Clint. I can't. No. I can't. Clint. Please. No."

I paused. "No?"

But she fisted my hair and pulled me back, causing me to chuckle against her pussy lips.

"More, please."

Her soft whimpers filled me with longing. The juice she offered me filled my stomach with need. My cock pulsed against the bedsheets and I started rutting, fucking their softness as I slid one finger into Rae's beautiful body. I crooked my digit and watched her jaw fall open. Her heels pressed into my back as she arched her hips closer to my mouth. Wanting everything I had for her.

So I gave it to her.

"Holy fucking hell."

Her growls encompassed me. I rocked harder against the mattress. I slid another finger inside her beautiful body, slowly working against her walls. I tickled the inside of her pussy. I felt her losing control of her body. Her toes curled and her body flushed against as broken syllables fell from her lips.

But I understood one of them. The only syllable I really wanted to hear.

"Come. Come. Come. Come."

She sprayed me and I chuckled with delight. I stuffed her full of my fingers before letting my pinky wander. Her thighs were drenched. My neck glistened with her mark. I lapped her swollen nub deeply, giving her a chance to recover as she heaved for air. Her hands fell away from my hair. She lay there, sprawled out. Ready for me to devour in any way I wished.

My pinky pressed against her puckered hole.

"Clint?"

My eyes found hers. "Yes?"

"I've never—I don't—"

I slowly rimmed her asshole with my fingertips, watching her gasp. *Listening to her sigh. I felt her ass release, ushering me in as I breached her virginal hole. Goosebumps traveled along my body. Heat rose at the base of my ballsack. She quivered around my fingers, moaning for more as I sank my fingers all the way into her body.*

"That's it. That's my beautiful girl."

"Oh, Clint."

"Take it, Rae. Take what you want."

"I don't know if I can come again."

"I know you can. I know you've got one more for me."

"Please, I can't. It feels too good."

"I'm not stopping until you come for me again."

She whimpered as I fucked her with my fingers. In, and out. Over and over as I watched her tremble. Her body was mine to do with what I wished. Her curves were flushed with the pleasure only I brought her. I wrapped my hand around my cock and stroked with delight. Her hips bucked against my hands as my thumb fell against her clit. I circled it softly, watching her eyes roll back. I stroked my cock to the rhythm of her hips, feeling that heady sensation finally taking over.

"Rae. I love you. I love you so fucking much."

8

RAELYNN

Brm! Brm! Brm! Brm! Brm! Brm!

My hand slammed against my cell phone, and I didn't know if I'd snoozed the alarm or turned it off. Either way, I rolled over, burying myself underneath the covers as I drifted back to sleep. I didn't struggle with sleep, either. All my body wanted to do was sleep. Sleep, cry, and sleep some more. I didn't want to do homework. I didn't give a shit about classes. Day two of absolute misery, and it threatened to swallow the whole of my future.

Because I didn't even give a shit about graphic design anymore.

I hadn't drawn in days. Which was unheard of. There were no doodles in the margins of my notes and textbooks. Mostly because I wasn't cracking open my textbooks or taking notes in class. There were no faint pen outlines on my arms of doodles I'd done before and after school. Because it took too much energy to pick up that pen. To trace those lines. To come up with an image I wanted to draw.

I was scared I'd end up drawing Clint's face everywhere.

Brm! Brm! Brm! Brm! Brm! Brm!

"Fucking alarm."

I slammed my hand against my phone again before a knock came at my door. I threw the covers off my head, my hair falling into my face. I blew at the tendrils, slowly working them out of my vision. And as I heaved a heavy sigh, I heard my mother's voice through the door.

"It's time to get up, honey. You have to leave in twenty minutes."

I sighed. "Great."

I threw the covers off my body and slowly eased myself out of bed. Every step I took, I groaned. Every time I lifted my arms, I grunted. I hadn't even bothered to change into pajamas last night. I still wore the clothes I'd worn to that dumbass sushi dinner. And they stank. I wrinkled my nose as I tossed them into the hamper, knowing damn good and well I'd have to do laundry after school today.

Then I shuffled to the bathroom in nothing but my underwear.

I cleaned myself up and splashed water in my face. I washed myself down with a soapy washcloth at the sink before drying myself off. I'd be late to school, but I didn't care. First time for everything, I guess. I slathered on the deodorant and threw my hair into a messy bun. I didn't have time to do anything else with it. Like wash it.

"Rae?"

I rolled my eyes. "I'm coming, Mom."

"Just making sure you're up."

I threw on some clothes and made my way down-stairs, hoping beyond all hope I didn't stink. I'd have to change my bedsheets, too. But that could be left for another time. The smell of breakfast wafted up my nose. Bacon and pancakes, which only meant one thing.

"Morning, tiger."

Fucking D.J. "Morning."

Mom smiled. "You sleep well?"

I snickered. "Sure."

D.J. slid me a glass of orange juice. "Your mother asked you a question. You don't have to cock such an attitude."

I pushed the glass away. "When are you going to get it through your head that I'm not your daughter?"

"Rae."

"I'm just trying to be a help to her. And I know she needs help with you sometimes."

"D.J.!"

I scoffed. "Yeah, whatever."

D.J. stabbed at his pancakes. "I care for your mother. I'll be around for a while. We might as well both get used to it."

"Oh, really? So, do you frequently beat on and bruise up things you care about?"

Mom pulled my chair out from the table. "That's enough. Come over here."

I rolled my eyes and followed her into the living room. What the fuck she was upset about, I'd never know. Even if D.J. married my mother, he still legally wasn't my father. So he didn't have a place to tell me what to do or give me some sort of morning pep talk.

"Can you make it quick? I'm going to be late for school."

Mom narrowed her eyes. "You're already late. So suck it up and listen."

I shook my head. "No, you suck it up and listen. I don't know what happened in your life to make you think you have to stick around with a man like him. A man that beats on you and makes you feel like shit. I don't know if you really do feel like you can't provide for this family or find a job that pays the bills, but it's not my issue anymore. And neither is he. If you want to ruin your life with a man like him, go ahead. But that doesn't mean I have to accept it or bring him into some fold. For years, Mom, it's been this way. For years, you've turned to men like D.J. for comfort and solace when all they do is stab you in the back and make you cry. And instead of bettering yourself and trying to pull yourself out of whatever bullshit mindset this is, you keep ending up with these guys. You keep pursuing them. You keep going out and getting drunk, and you drag me along with it."

Her eyes widened. "You take that back."

I shook my head. "No, I won't. Because you need to hear it. You're sick, Mom. Your head isn't right.

And until you get your head right, your life is always going to be like this. But just because you're willing to accept this doesn't mean I have to. I'm not listening to D.J. I'm not accepting him into my life. And I'm sure as hell not holding my tongue any longer in this house."

"I think you're done speaking to your mother that way."

D.J. came around the corner as Mom's eyes welled with tears.

"Yeah, well. Make sure not to beat on her too hard this time. Okay?"

Mom gasped. "Rae!"

I leveled my eyes at D.J. "But remember my promise. Always remember my promise."

I backtracked toward the front door and scooped up my things. My backpack, my purse, and my sanity. I tossed it all over my shoulders and ripped the front door open. Then I heard Mom's desperate voice behind me.

"Are you even coming home after school today?"

The question gave me pause. "I don't know, Mom. I'll see you when I see you."

I stepped out onto the porch and closed the door behind me. Hearing my mother cry on the other side of that door would've broken my heart had it not already been broken. I closed my eyes and drew in a deep breath. I'd already be late for school. I walked up my driveway and started for the opening of our neighborhood, wanting nothing more than to pack my shit and never come back.

Even if it meant not getting my high school diploma.

Maybe I should ask the guidance counselor about GED programs.

I walked away from my house as quickly as I could. I burst into a run before I started panting in the morning sun. I mean, come on. It was sixty-eight degrees outside. How the hell did the sun still feel hot? Just another thing to annoy me today before I got to homeroom.

"Rae!"

A horn honking caught my attention and I saw Allison hanging out of Michael's SUV. I snickered as they came screeching around a corner, blazing a trail straight for me. Michael came to a stop on the side of the curb. Allison reached back and threw open my door. I leapt in with my things and Michael whipped a U-turn, speeding off down the road toward our high school.

"Where in the world were you this morning?"

Michael cocked his head. "Thank fuck I decided to drive."

Allison gasped. "Michael. Don't use that kind of language."

He chuckled. "Sorry, beautiful."

I swallowed my groan as they leaned over and kissed one another.

"Thanks for picking me up."

Michael nodded. "Anytime."

Allison craned her head back. "What happened this morning? Why didn't you show up?"

"Yeah. We had to run back to my car before coming to find your ass."

"Michael."

I paused. "I thought you said you drove this morning."

And when they both fell silent, I decided I didn't want to know.

Allison giggled. "Anyway, how was your morning?"

Michael snickered. "I take it D.J. was around?"

I rolled my eyes. "He's always around. Only this time, I told my mother exactly what I thought of him. And her, for being with him."

"You did what?"

"What did you say to her?"

I shrugged. "What needed to be said a long time ago. That there was something wrong with her if she always gravitated to these types of men. That just because she needed him to pay the bills doesn't mean I had to accept him."

Allison's jaw hit the floor. "You said that to your mother?"

Michael's face fell. "Wow. That's pretty harsh."

I shrugged. "Had to be said either way. Not my fault she doesn't want to leave an abusive dickweed because he pays some of our bills."

Allison paused. "Does he really?"

I nodded. "Yep. Our dirty little secret."

Michael sighed. "I mean, at least you got it off your chest, right?"

Even though I made her cry, sure. "Yeah. At least there's that."

Allison sat down in her seat. "Did D.J. do anything this morning to bring that on?"

"I mean, other than trying to be my dad, not really. He was his usual asshole self. Told me he's trying to step in because, apparently, my mother needs help with me."

Michael balked. "What?"

"Yeah. That's what he told me."

Allison scoffed. "That can't be true. You've never given your mother any reason to worry. You've never really rebelled."

Michael chuckled. "Other than that one time me and her snuck out to go to a diner and got sick on milkshakes at two in the morning."

Allison paused. "You guys did what?"

I grinned. "No need to get jealous. It was three years ago."

"I'm not jealous."

Michael grinned. "That pouty bottom lip says otherwise."

I averted my gaze as he leaned in to kiss her. And the kissing evolved to giggling. Which evolved to him tickling her as we pulled into the back parking lot of the school. I gazed out the window, searching for Clint's bike. Well, not really bike. But any sort of vehicle that looked like it might have Clint in it. Part of me wanted to tell Michael to drive by his house. Maybe he just needed a ride to school.

Or maybe you know that's absolute bullshit.

I sighed and pushed my way out of Michael's SUV. He gave me a one-armed hug before Allison trotted around and wrapped her arms around my neck. I knew they were trying to cheer me up. Trying to offer me the bright side of life, or whatever. But I was slowly coming to the understanding that this was one of those things I had to ride out. There wasn't a way to make it pass any sooner. I just had to wait it out.

I glared at Michael. "If you hurt her like this, I will end you. Understood?"

Then I squeezed Allison one last time before relinquishing her to Michael.

Her new boyfriend, apparently.

I made my way to homeroom by myself. Because Michael and Allison wanted to walk hand in hand. It was the first time in my entire high school career I'd walked to homeroom alone. And it sucked. Hard. I crossed the threshold of the classroom just as the bell rang. And Allison came running in behind me just before the bell stopped ringing. She smelled like a mixture of her conditioner and Michael's aftershave as she sat down next to me.

A combination that brought tears to my eyes.

Allison took my hand. "You okay?"

I nodded, but didn't say anything.

"You're going to get through this, okay? And you're not going to do it alone."

Except, I was already alone. Mom had D.J. and didn't give a shit about my issues. Allison had Michael, and the two of them didn't give a shit as to how much PDA they graced the general public with. I was alone. Completely alone.

And I wondered if Clint felt this alone.

9

CLINTON

"Holy fuck."

I groaned as I rolled over. Something sticky and crusted slid against my skin. It made me grimace, causing me to reach for my sheets. And when I threw them off my body, memories came barreling back.

Memories of my dream.

"Are you shitting me?"

My boxers had a massive wet spot on them. My sheets were caked in cum. I snickered as I tossed my comforter off the bed, groaning at the smell. I hadn't had to deal with this shit since I was thirteen years old. And yet, some dream with Rae made me come like I'd just learned how to touch my dick for the first time.

"What a fucking mess," I whispered.

I threw my arm over my face. I didn't know what else to do. Every part of me hurt, my face included. And dream after dream last night haunted me. Every single one of them about her. Rae. That beautiful body and those soft curves and that excessive softness and those luxurious thighs. There wasn't a dream that ran through my head that hadn't been tainted by her presence. My balls felt empty. There was so much wetness on my bed.

How many times did I orgasm last night?

I sighed as I sat up. I ripped my sheets off the bed and tossed them to the side. I turned my fan on, needing to dry out the rest of my damn mattress before I inched my way out of my boxers. Feeling that crusted sensation sliding down my skin made me shiver. And not in a good way. I rushed into the bathroom and readied myself for a long, hot shower.

Hoping to wash the dreams away.

The one time I wanted to wake myself up, I couldn't. The one time I wanted to awaken myself from all those bullshit dreams, and I couldn't make it happen. I'd been practically sleepless for the past two nights. Then I pass out and my brain fucking tortures me. Just my luck, at this point. I turned on the hot water and let the steam fill the room. I stepped in, feeling the waterfall showerhead cascade hot streams down my back, carrying with it the stench of my sweat and the crusted evidence of my debauched dreams.

Tortuous dreams of a girl I couldn't have.

I scrubbed myself down. I washed my hair and winced as water beat against my face. I knew things would feel worse with my body before they got better. But I was tempted to go to a doctor. My nose fucking hurt. And it made me angry. Just what I needed to start my day. A large dose of fucking anger.

I hate my life.

I stood under the water until I felt it grow luke-warm. Then I turned it off and reached for a towel. Getting ready for the day took almost twice the amount of time. Especially since it felt like the marrow of my bones were filled with lead. I pulled on a pair of jeans and stretched out the collar of my shirt. I slid it over my face, trying not to hit my nose as I finished getting dressed. I gathered up my things and walked downstairs. I guess I didn't have a choice but to go to school today.

I didn't feel like it, though.

I picked up my bomber jacket lying on the floor. But instead of putting it on, I simply carried it into the kitchen. I figured the smell of coffee would greet me. Or breakfast. Or the sound of my stepmother's voice.

But nothing greeted me when I got into the kitchen.

"Cecilia?"

I furrowed my brow as the emptiness of my father's sprawling mansion-esque home greeted me. I didn't hear Cecilia call out for me, so I called her name again. And again. I repeated it as I walked around the house. I darted into guest bedrooms and checked the laundry room. I went back upstairs as fear gripped my heart. Hell, I even risked opening my father's bedroom doors to see if she was in there.

No one was around, though.

"Cecilia!"

My voice roared through the house. I dashed around in a frenzy, trying to locate her. It wasn't until I found the front door ajar, though, that I looked outside. And I found her. Standing there. At the end of the driveway.

With her back to me.

I narrowed my eyes and watched her unwavering body. She almost looked like a statue. One I didn't recognize. Her state of dress shocked me. Her hair was disheveled. She had her fucking robe on. Slippers on her feet with her nightgown peeking out from beyond the fluffiness of her robe. I'd never seen her step out of the house without a full face of makeup on. Designer heels. Thousands of dollars' worth of clothing and jewelry. And there she stood. Like any other stay-at-home mother.

Staring down at the ground.

"Cecilia?"

I walked toward her, leaving the front door hanging wide open. I tossed my bomber jacket onto the railing of the porch as the morning sun greeted me. The wind was brisk. Colors splashed against the sky. I kept an ear out for my father, just in case he was around. Something told me he wasn't, though.

Then, I got to Cecilia's side.

"What the—?"

She wasn't looking down. She was looking at our mailbox. Specifically, at the sign swinging below it. I blinked a few times, trying to bring the words into focus. Trying to convince myself I wasn't seeing what I knew was so plainly there.

"I don't even know when he came by."

Her voice sounded so defeated. Breathless.

Exhausted. Cecilia sniffled as she raked her hand through her knotted hair. I looked over at her and saw tears dripping down her cheeks. Tears of defeat. Tears of fear. Tears of wariness. My eyes gravitated back to the sign. I reached out and touched it, trying to convince myself it was real.

Then I snickered. "Can he do this? I mean, your name's on the house too, right?"

She shook her head slowly, not saying a word. And my stomach fell to my toes. In that moment, I realized that Cecilia was more like me than I could've ever understood. A prisoner in her own home. Where nothing was hers and everything was held over her head in spite. I raked my eyes over her, watching her unwavering body. The way she stood eerily still despite the tears that flowed down her cheeks told me she was a professional at that. Crying silently. Crying so no one knew.

"Come here. It's okay. I've got you."

I wrapped my arm around her and pulled her against me. And finally, Cecilia pulled her eyes away from the 'For Sale' sign swinging underneath our mailbox. Fear filled them. Wariness wafted behind them. Confusion wrinkled her brow and when she sniffled, there were twinges of anger riding on its coattails.

"I don't know how he can do this, Clint."

Her words were nothing but a whisper. But they felt as loud as a bullhorn. All my life, I'd been telling myself that same thing. Telling myself that I didn't understand how my father got away with some of the things he did. For a while, I thought it was his money.

The millions and millions he threw around only to come out on top, again and again. Never losing. Never failing. Always climbing higher. I wondered when his time would come. When he'd fly too close to the sun and fall to the earth.

And in my dreams as a child, I dreamt of that fall killing him somehow. So I'd be rid of him for good.

It killed me to see that same want in Cecilia's face.

"Do you have any idea of when he came by?"

She shook her head slowly. "I don't even know if he came into the house. I passed out hard around one. So, some time after that, I guess."

"Does Dad have any other property around here? A home or something I don't know about?"

She shrugged. "He's probably staying in some hotel or something. Or maybe he's placed a call from the hospital to someone. I don't know. It could be a million things."

"We should call the hospital today. See if he's checked out."

"I figured I would've gotten a phone call from someone."

"That's not always the case. Especially if he didn't want anyone calling you."

Her lower lip trembled. "What are we going to do?"

I thought back to the lawyer. To the doctor. The brochures and numbers they'd handed out for me. I knew they'd help me if I called them. I knew they'd talk me through this. Get me set up with resources. But I wasn't sure they'd help Cecilia. As far as I was concerned, we were a package deal at this point. Nothing happened to me without knowing there was a plan in place for Cecilia.

Because she was just as much a victim, too.

"Come on, we should get inside."

Cecilia stood her ground. "I want to rip that sign down."

I steered her toward the house. "We can't act irrationally any longer. We have to think this through."

"There's nothing to think through. Your father's about to sell this house out from underneath us and leave us homeless."

"Which means we should go inside and figure out a plan."

I guided her up onto the porch. Then I turned my head and looked down the road, toward the high school, where another day would be skipped. At least, the morning would be. My grades would slip. I might not be able to graduate. I'd be pigeon-holed into getting a GED or something and being the scum of the earth for the rest of my life. But seeing Cecilia cry was hell on earth. I couldn't leave her like this. If my teachers wanted to know what the fuck was up with me, they could call the house and I'd explain it all.

Maybe they'd let me repeat my senior year instead of expelling me for absences, if I begged them.

"That's it. Inside. One foot in front of the other."

Cecilia sniffled. "I'm sorry. Just—just give me a second to—"

I closed the door behind us. "You don't need to be

sorry. You've been the strong one throughout this whole thing. You're owed a moment, at least."

"Holy Hannah, what are we going to do?"

She broke down and I wrapped my arms around her. I patted her hair down and held her close as she cried into my chest. I kept telling her it would be all right. That we'd find a way out of this. That my father couldn't possibly legally do this. Not like he thought, anyway. But I wasn't sure who I was trying to comfort, her or me.

I wasn't sure which one of us would cave and not come back from it.

Her or me.

Get on the phone with your bank.

Figure out the status of your trust fund.

Figure out how much control your father has over that money.

Start stowing things away to sell.

My mind ran away from me the louder Cecilia cried. I felt her collapse and I scooped her close to me, refusing to let her fall to the floor. She was better than that. She was stronger than this. So I held her steady as I laid out a plan of action for my day. I clenched my jaw as she cried until she practically made herself sick. I walked her down the hallway and ushered her into the bathroom downstairs only seconds before she started puking.

I stood there with my back to her, giving her privacy but not leaving her alone. And as I listened to her sounds, I resigned myself to the plan. First, I needed to call my bank. Ask them questions about my trust fund and its contingencies. If I had any access to that money, I needed to transfer it into an account my father couldn't touch. Or see. Or dip into, if he had to. And if I didn't have control of it, I needed to start stockpiling things from around this house. Selling things off, right out from under my father's nose. I mean, if he wasn't going to come home, how the hell would he know I was selling his shit?

I could put the money into an account he couldn't touch. And since my father didn't make it a habit of keeping receipts, there was no way for him to prove this stuff wasn't my stuff to sell anyway.

I didn't know. That required more research from a legal perspective.

I could call that lawyer and ask.

I felt my stepmother's hand touch down between my shoulder blades. She pushed me softly, moving me out of the way. I turned around, watching as she wiped her mouth off with a washcloth. She tossed it into the sink. "We'll figure this out," she said.

And—just like I'd questioned earlier—I had no idea who she was really talking to.

10

RAELYNN

The school day crept by slowly. As I sat in the back of my morning classes, I got caught up on my homework. I worked so quickly that I finished a week's worth of work. Which meant no homework this weekend.

Which meant a weekend of sitting around and feeling sorry for myself.

Every time I checked my phone, I had a text message from my mother. Messages I deleted without even opening. Hell, she even called me a couple of times. And I thanked my fucking stars my phone was on silent. I had half a mind to block her. However, I settled on turning off my phone instead. While I was out to lunch.

With Michael and Allison.

"This is going to be great!"

I panted. "Keep running. If we're caught, we'll get in serious trouble."

Michael unlocked his SUV. "Come on, Allison. It's time for your first-ever lunch ditch."

She hopped into the front seat. "I feel so alive!"

I shook my head as a small smile crossed my cheeks. A small one. But one that helped prove I might come out of this all right after all. I'd gotten Michael's text about skipping out on lunch today just before I turned off my phone. And I was glad I got it. He cranked up his car as Allison giggled with delight. He sped out of that parking lot and we headed straight for the sandwich shop. Their tomato bisque was calling my name. Complete with their five-cheese grilled cheese and some homemade barbecue chips to go along with it.

Then Allison opened up the can of worms again.

"You feeling better from this morning?"

Michael tossed her a look before shaking his head.

I sighed. "I'm just… tired of him. I'm tired of D.J. always being around. Always trying to act like my father when I clearly see what he does to my mother."

Michael settled into his chair. "Does he know you recognize this?"

I nodded. "Yep. I even promised him the next time my mother came home busted up, I'd be calling the police. I reminded him of that promise this morning."

Allison shook her head. "I can't imagine being in a relationship like that."

"I've been telling my mom for years that she needs help. That she needs to get her life together and stop running around with men like this. And for a while, she was doing that. Applying for jobs. Trying to find a life of her own. I don't know what happened, though."

Michael snickered. "D.J. happened. As much as it sucks, your mother's had a hard life. She just wants things to be easy. And in her mind, a bit of physical pain is probably better than the heartache that comes with being alone, working a dead end job and struggling to make ends meet."

I paused. "Okay, Dr. Phil. Let's slow down there a bit."

Allison smiled. "Have you ever thought about doing psychology?"

He shrugged. "I may or may not like my A.P. Psychology class a little more than I figured I would."

Allison took his hand. "Well, anyway, the guy's a loser. Don't worry about him. One of these days, your mom's going to look at herself in the mirror and realize what we already know."

I rolled my eyes. "That D.J.'s a piece of shit that doesn't deserve to walk the earth?"

She snickered. "Yes, and that she deserves better."

I licked my lips. "I hope it's soon, then. Because I'm not sure how much more of it I can stand."

We pulled up to the sandwich shop and hopped out. It was busy, and I grew worried that we might not make it through our lunch before we had to go. By the time we got in line, placed our orders, and got our food, we had to get back in the car. Which meant eating on the go while trying not to spill shit on Michael's leather seats.

"Just be careful. I'll drive slow."

"Did you spill something? Hurry, get it with this."

"Speed bump. Hold your food up."

I swear, no one babied their car more than Michael babied this damn vehicle of his.

"Is there a long way around we can take? I won't be able to finish this with the regular route. And I'm starving."

Michael smiled at Allison. "Anything for you. I'll drive us through some neighborhoods."

And of course, the neighborhood with the easiest streets to drive was Clint's.

I gazed out the window as I sipped my soup. Instead of eating it with a spoon, I'd stuck a straw in it. My eyes lingered out the window while Michael and Allison talked with one another. And every once in a while, their laughter pierced the foggy haze of my mind. I was happy for them. I really was. But sometimes, I wanted to slap them both. Could they just put that shit on hold for one second? I mean, once we got back to school, it was game on.

Did I really have to be in the car for it, though?

I heard the smacking of their lips as they kissed. I caught a glimpse of Allison feeding a bite of food to Michael. I stared hard out the window, trying my best not to get angry or shut down. Trying my best not to seem like a bitch.

It wasn't easy, though. And it gave me a new respect for how they both felt when I first started dating Clint.

The closer we got to his house, the more silent they became. Until not a sound was made in Michael's car.

I finished up my soup and tossed it into the paper bag. I reached for my grilled cheese and unwrapped it, holding my drink still with my thighs. But the second Allison gasped, I whipped my head up. And when Michael cursed to himself, my eyes darted around.

Then I spotted it.

The sign hanging off their mailbox.

"'For Sale'?" I breathed.

What the fuck?

Allison drew in a short breath. "You think that's why he ended things?"

Michael shushed her. "Leave it alone."

"I mean, it's right there. Plain as day. Might give Rae some closure."

"That's not yours to determine."

I shook my head. "He would've told me about something like this."

Michael paused. "I mean, are you sure? Maybe he just didn't get around to telling you about it? Or didn't know how you'd react? Or something?"

"Drop me off."

Allison whipped around in her seat. "Say what now?"

"Drop me off. Now."

Michael shook his head. "Can't do that, Rae. We're going to be late for school if I have to wait for you."

"I didn't ask you to wait. I asked you to stop your fucking car."

Allison reached for me. "Just get through the school day. We can come back after classes are done."

I leveled my eyes with her. "Let me out of this

goddamn car, or I'm pouring my soda out on the leather seats."

Michael shook his head. "Fucking hell, Rae."

He came to a stop at the curb and I abandoned my food. I wasn't hungry anymore, anyway. I chugged the rest of my drink before I slipped out of the car, slamming the door behind me. Windows whirred down. I slid my purse over my shoulder. Allison handed me my backpack through the window as Michael stared at me with fire blazing in his eyes.

"Don't you fail school because of him. You've worked too hard for all this."

I scoffed. "Like it's any better watching the two of you neck and make eyes at each other."

Allison furrowed her brow. "Hey. What did we do?"

I shook my head. "Nothing. Get to school. I'll see you guys tomorrow."

Michael groaned. "Rae, you can't just—"

"Michael. Get back to school and leave me be."

Allison sighed. "Good luck, Rae. Really."

"Thanks."

Michael was getting on my fucking nerves, and I needed him to leave. His hands slammed against the steering wheel before he pulled away, leaving Allison watching me with worry on her face. Her head fell out of the window and she craned her neck back, waving as they faded away. I watched them leave before turning back to face Clint's house.

Please be home. Please be home. Please be home.

The chant seemed familiar as I drew in a deep

breath. With my things slung over my shoulder, I resigned myself to missing my last few classes. The only thing that gave my solace was keeping up with my homework. I wasn't sure how I'd fare come midterms. But I'd deal with that once it came around. Right now, I had bigger things to deal with. I needed answers. I deserved answers.

And I wasn't leaving until I got them.

I started up the driveway, making my way to the porch. I stared at the front door and couldn't help but pause. Listening out for his father. With every step I took up to the front door, I remembered that encounter. Only two or three days ago, but it felt like an eternity. It took my breath away. I stood on the porch, unable to move. I saw the front door, but my arm didn't move. I saw the doorbell, but my finger didn't extend.

The whirlwind of life hit me all at once, pushing tears to my eyes.

I held my breath as the still-life images bombarded my mind. The first time Clint ever picked on me. How I'd yelled at him and he'd grinned at me. The cascade of effects that came after it all. How he'd call me out in the cafeteria. Make fun of my clothes. Of my house. Of my mother. How he called me names and laughed at me with his buddies.

He's come such a long way.

I saw that night. Where he found me in the park. How angry I'd been that, of all people, he was the one that found me. I remembered how I vibrated with anger at the idea of him sitting next to me. Interjecting himself into my life like I wanted him there for some reason.

Then our first kiss.

That thing sent shivers through my body.

I closed my eyes and relived the first time we had sex. How magical it felt. How his hands felt against my skin. How waking up with him made me feel like a princess. Only, I couldn't stay. I thought about how he ravaged my thoughts. Occupied my mind after that moment. After understanding that he was like me. A boy lost in a world his parental figure had torn to shreds. Used and abused. And angry with the world.

He understands me.

I relived that night. Those boys. The chase. That crash. The ravine. It made me sick to my stomach to think about. And yet I couldn't stop it. It was as if the reel had been started up in a booth somewhere, designed to torture me. I blinked back tears and tried to move. But fear and anguish paralyzed me.

I feel helpless.

I saw Clint in the hospital. Hooked up to tubes. Filled with stitches and bruises. I wavered on my feet as I reminisced on his release. All those times we tried to do his homework, only for him to seduce me with his body. With his words. With his compliments and his eyes. How I wanted to be wrapped up in him again. How I wanted to be his again. How I wanted to tell him how much I loved him.

Does he love me, though?

Had someone asked me that question four days ago, my answer would be 'yes.' But now? I wasn't sure.

The reel spiraled me into silence. It held my voice captive. It choked off my tears and my ability to breathe. And it wasn't until I fell forward that I snapped out of it, gasping for air as I snapped out of my trance and slammed my hands against his front door.

Just in time for the front door to rip itself open.

11

CLINTON

"Howard, it's me. You really need to call me back. I've got a lot of questions to ask you that I deserve answers to."

"Howard, it's Cecilia. I don't know if you've blocked me or if you're dodging me, but where in the world do you expect Clint and me to go? Are you leaving me? What is your son going to do about school?"

"Howard, damn it. You pick up this phone right now or I'm hiring a lawyer. I'm serious. This is ridiculous. You started that fight!"

"Howard, it's me."

"Howard."

"Howard, pick up this damn phone!"

I sighed as I listened to Cecilia shriek her head off into the phone. She hung up and threw her cell phone across the room, damn near shattering it against the wall. I walked over to her and rubbed her back. She put her head in her hands and started sobbing, she was so angry. Or confused. Or scared.

Possibly, all three of them.

I knew she wanted answers to her questions. But I also knew my father would never give them to her. He didn't operate that way. Once he set his mind on a mission, he saw it all the way through. She shouldn't have threatened a lawyer, either. Because now, he'd go through with it and cut her off.

Like he'd apparently done to me.

While Cecilia had been blowing up his phone, I'd gotten on the phone with the bank. I mean, it took me a little while to figure out who the fuck managed my trust fund. A call to my regular bank led me to three other phone lines before they told me they had no idea. So I had to go poking around in my father's study. I pulled out drawers and sifted through files. I came across all sorts of random documents with monetary numbers on them that made my head spin. And finally, I came across a couple of names that looked promising.

So I called them both.

The first one told me they didn't manage funds like that. The second one told me I wasn't privy to the information. Which meant I was on the right track. I pulled out all the fucking paperwork for that place. And while my father was shit at a lot of things, keeping a paper trail wasn't one of them. He had records dating back to when he opened the damn account in the first place. I was able to trace that account from its inception all the way up to a few months ago.

When I had turned eighteen.

Cecilia sniffled. "What did the bank say?"

I sighed. "Not much."

"What do you mean?"

I shrugged. "According to the paperwork, that account became mine the second I turned eighteen. But the man I spoke to said that until I was twenty-two, I couldn't have unfettered access to it."

She turned around. "Has it always been that way?"

"Not from what I can tell. I went into Dad's study and read through the agreement."

"He's not going to like that."

"He's currently smoking us out of our own home by controlling the only thing he's got control over. I don't give a shit what he likes."

She paused. "Do you still have access to the money?"

"The man on the phone said I did. But I can't transfer any more than five thousand at a time without Dad's permission. So I initiated a transfer of $4,999.00 into my own bank account to see if I can actually get it to go through. And if I can, that opens up some doors."

She shook her head. "How in the world did it all come to this?"

"The second Dad realized he couldn't use his money and influence to yank our chains any longer."

"Can I admit something to you?"

"Sure."

"I'm scared, Clinton."

I nodded. "I know you are. But we'll find a way out

of this, okay? Come the end of the day, I should see a pending deposit in my account. And if that money's there in the morning, I'm calling that guy from the bank back and initiating transfers until Dad stops it."

"Is this what's going to happen now? Scrounging around for scraps?"

"With Dad, preparing for the worst is what you have to do. Let's hope there's a better outcome, but make a plan in case there isn't. Okay?"

She sighed. "Yeah. All right."

I knew my father would shut that money down. The second he caught wind of that transfer, he'd try to cancel it. I'd be lucky if I saw that money in my account in the morning. Cecilia went and retrieved her phone, poking away at the screen. And as she held it to her ear, I heaved a heavy sigh.

Before running down a plan in my mind.

I need to call that lawyer.

I didn't know how much I was really privy to in this house. What could I sell without my father getting me into trouble over it? Could he claim I was stealing from him? Extorting him, somehow? Those were questions for a lawyer. But I didn't know if I'd open another can of worms trying to ask those kinds of questions.

My eyes darted around the house. Everything expensive came into view all in one get-go. But if Dad was going to sell the house, then downsizing was reasonable. Right? I sell off his things, keep the money, and claim downsizing efforts in the process. I didn't know. It didn't make a lot of sense. I clocked the suede couches and the paintings on the walls. The sculptures standing on columns around the room. The projector television. All the fine china we had in a cupboard in the dining room. Legitimate silverware for days. Like it was plastic wear to us.

Even selling the small things would net me well over a hundred thousand dollars.

Could I get away with it, though?

A slam against the front door ripped me from my trance. Cecilia came rushing back into the room with her eyes wide as saucers. I held my arm out and stopped her in her tracks. I peeked down at her and mouthed 'stay put' before making my way for the door. I slowly approached it and peeked out the frosted windows to try and see who was out there.

But when I opened the door, the last person I expected to be there stood in front of me.

"Can you talk? Because we need to talk."

Rae's voice filled my ears and it wasn't a dream. It wasn't a fantasy. I ran my eyes down her body, clocking her crooked form. Her tired eyes. The bags underneath them that accentuated how pale her skin looked. Had she lost weight? Her cheeks looked a little sunken in. That could be from exhaustion, though.

Why is she so tired?

I looked back at my stepmother and she nodded, urging me to go outside and sit on the porch. I turned my eyes back to Rae and stared at her, our eyes connecting for the first time in days. My heart skipped a beat. My stomach exploded with butterflies. Hell, I felt my knees fucking go weak.

This isn't good.

"Are you all right?" I asked.

She glared up at me. "Outside, please."

"Rae, I can't—"

"The least you owe me is that."

I sighed as I stepped out onto the porch. Mostly because I knew she was right. Out of all this insanity and all she'd done for me, the least I owed her was an explanation. But would she accept it? Would she accept my words and leave with a lighter heart? I wasn't sure if she would.

I wasn't sure if *I* would.

I closed the door behind me and ushered her over to the rocking chairs. Her disheveled hair got tossed around in the wind as it whipped around the house. A smell crept underneath my nose, forcing it to curl up. And as I sat down next to Rae, the smell grew.

What is that smell, anyway?

"You look good, considering."

I focused on her. "You—you do, too."

She snickered. "You're a terrible liar. But thanks anyway."

"I'm not lying."

And when she shot me a look, I kept my mouth shut.

"Moving, Clint? Really?"

I shrugged. "I'm just as surprised as you were."

She paused. "Wait, you didn't know?"

"Not even Cecilia knew. We woke up this morning and the sign was out there. She's freaking out so badly that I didn't have the heart to leave her for school today."

"Have you heard from your father at all since…?"

I shook my head slowly. "No. We're not really sure he's the one who even came by to do it. She's been calling around all morning, trying to figure out where the hell he is."

"Has she tried the hospital?"

"I think she's doing that now."

"So, for all you know—"

"Dad's contacted a realtor to take over the sale of the house."

I leaned back into the rocking chair and closed my eyes. The wind felt nice. The harshness of the sun seemed to have finally abated. If the wind blew just right, I could smell the sea, its saltiness wafting in from a coastline I hadn't visited in months.

But, other times…

Is it Rae that smells like that?

"How are you doing?" I asked.

She scoffed. "Some question for you to ask."

"I'm serious."

I opened my eyes and looked over at her.

"How are you doing, Rae?"

She shrugged. "As good as I can be."

"Are you sure?"

"No, I'm not sure. All right?"

The harshness of her words wasn't like her. And I wondered who else had taken the brunt of her anger when it should've been me.

"Sorry. Sorry, Clint."

I shook my head. "No need to be sorry."

"So what are you guys going to do? I'm sure your father can't just sell the house like that."

I shrugged. "Honestly? It won't shock me if he tries anyway. I think this is payback."

"Payback for a fight he started?"

"How did you know he started it?"

"Your father is *always* the one to start shit."

I snickered. "True."

"Would he really do that to you guys? Just sell the house and leave you homeless or something?"

I shrugged. "I mean, I don't know. Dad's well… not a good guy. And neither one of us have heard from him since the other night. Since the paramedics took him to the hospital. Cecilia hasn't been to visit him. No one's called us to update his condition. I think he's on a warpath now. And it's a matter of riding it out."

"How do you ride something like this out, though?"

"I don't know. But I guess we'll figure it out."

"Do you have a plan for if he does sell the house?"

I sighed. "You mean 'when'? Because I'm betting money on the fact that he'll go through with it."

She rolled her eyes. "Whatever word you want to use, Clint. Just answer my question."

"Sorry. Uh, I'm trying to come up with some plans. Poking around at my trust fund. Trying to get money deposited into my account. Things like that."

"What about selling some of the stuff in the house?"

"I don't know what the legal ramifications would be from something like that. But it's crossed my mind."

"Well, you might not be able to sell stuff he's purchased and can prove he purchased. But you and Cecilia can sell things he's given to you or gifted to you. Because in the eyes of the law, those things are technically your possessions."

I paused. "How do you know that?"

She shrugged. "You're not the only one who's contemplated running away more than once."

"Rae, I'm so sor—"

She held up her hand. "Selling things like silverware and paintings might not be a good idea. But the furniture in your room? Your clothes? Jewelry or wallets or watches? Or any of Cecilia's clothes? You can sell those things and be just fine. Just in case you need that information."

I nodded slowly. "I appreciate it."

"Also, your father's a fucking jerk-off."

Like father like son, I guess. "Yep. He really is."

"Are you coming back to school?"

"I honestly don't know. Right now, I can't leave Cecilia. Not alone with my father, anyway. And something tells me he's waiting for that moment."

"Waiting for you to leave your stepmother here alone."

"Yeah. I mean, I don't know. It sounds paranoid. But it just doesn't feel right."

She drew in a deep breath. "Then you do what's best for your family and I'll talk to your teachers."

"Rae, you don't have t—"

She held up her hand again. "Will you shut up and

just let people help? You don't have to be fucking me in order for me to want to help."

Her statement tore my heart out. "Thank you, Rae."

"No problem."

But the more we talked, the icier her voice became. Her face etched itself into stone and her statements grew colder. Which told me we had many, many problems.

Despite her choice of words.

12

RAELYNN

Even though he answered my questions, I saw his walls up. His face seemed guarded and his eyes looked dead. He answered me, sure. But he wasn't opening up to me. I had to pry his answers to my questions out of him. He wasn't freely talking about anything. My questions were carrying this conversation. And I knew that if I stopped them, he'd stop talking.

Which pissed me off.

I heard my voice growing icier and felt myself becoming distant. I didn't want my anger to become the focus of this conversation. But I couldn't help it. I was hurt. Angry with his father. Angry with Clint for pushing me away and frustrated with my mother and the bullshit she kept pulling with D.J. I'd lost the only person in my life who understood me. The only person who seemed to get what I was going through. Talking with Michael and Allison didn't feel the same anymore because they came from great families. Parents that were still married. Two-income households with parents that worked jobs that made them happy. They didn't understand what I was going through. Clint did, though.

And it pissed me off that he'd taken that away from me.

He kept pushing me away. Pushing my advice away. Trying to get me to stop helping him under the guise that I didn't have to. I wanted to smack him across his face. Despite how much of a terrible person that made me. I wanted to grab his shoulders and shake him until he got it. Until he understood that breaking up with me was the worst possible thing he could've done during something like this.

I didn't have the energy, though.

I cleared my throat. "I'm serious. I'll talk to your teacher. I'll make sure you can still keep up."

He nodded mindlessly. "Thanks."

"And as far as your possessions go, I'm sure there are things you'd love to get rid of. Use that to your advantage."

"I will."

"Call the lawyer you spoke to as well. I'm sure he'd have some great advice on how to proceed next. Or even if what your father's doing is legal."

"I'm sure."

I sighed. "And if he doesn't, I'm sure he can point you in the right direction."

He blinked. "Yeah."

"Clint?"

"Hmm?"

"Are you going to even look at me?"

He slowly panned his gaze over to mine, and I found his nose wrinkled. Like something up above us stunk. There was this look of disgust on his face that made my heart sink. He didn't even want me there. He didn't want me near him. Talking to him. Interacting with him. It was as if our relationship had reverted back to its normal ground. Square one, with him being an absolute asshat and me getting stuck in his crosshairs.

Still, I pressed on.

"What your father's doing is wrong. What he's doing to you and your stepmom is downright despicable. Fight him. Fight him on it. And I'll be here if you need anything."

His eyes met mine. "Thanks, Rae. really. I'll take your advice into account. But Cecilia and I got this. We can handle it."

His words burned. I felt the crack of the imaginary slap across my cheek. He stood from his chair and my eyes followed him, watching as he rolled his shoulders back. I saw the last of his walls drop down. Like iron bars trapping him into his own little corner. His arms extended above his head and I hated myself for how my eyes lingered. The skin of his lower back came into view. Those cute little dimples that sat just above his buttbone greeted me. Called to my fingertips. I closed my eyes and shook the thoughts away. Clint wasn't mine anymore. I had no right to see him that way.

But I deserved an answer to the question running around in my head.

"Clint, do you really want things between us t—"

"Clinton? I need you. It's imperative."

Cecilia's voice interjected into my question and Clint whipped around. I stood up, facing his step-mother as she covered herself up. She held her silken robe closed, her hair a disheveled mess. She looked terrible, for lack of a better word. Like she hadn't gotten a lick of sleep in weeks.

Clint strode to her. "What's wrong?"

But her eyes fell to me. "I need to borrow him for a second. I'm sorry."

I shook my head. "No, no. It's fine. You seem flustered. I hope everything's okay."

The two of them looked at one another before Clint nodded for her to go back inside. I hated being on the outside like this. I hated no longer being a part of their lives. I mean, I'd always felt like an outsider. But I never thought I'd feel that way with Clint again. Truth be told, it hurt worse than anything else. Being privy to Clint's life and bonding with Cecilia only to see them completely shut me out felt like hell on earth. Like I'd ascended into Dante's Inferno and was living it for myself.

I snickered. "Yeah. I'll just—I'll head out."

Clint reached for me. "It's nothing personal. We're just—"

I waved my hand in the air. "If you need me, you know where to find me."

I scooped up my things and hopped over the railing of his porch. I fell to the ground and skinned my knees, but I didn't give a shit. I heard Clint rushing for me, but I held out my hand. Two could play his game. If he wanted to shut me out, then I'd shut him out.

No holds barred.

I glared at him before I walked across his lawn. With dirty knees and a hole where my heart used to be, I made my way down the road, slowly creeping toward the school. I knew something had flustered Cecilia. I knew something serious had gone down. But the way they treated me was unacceptable. Like I hadn't saved Clint's life, helped him keep his grades afloat in the hospital, and helped him transition back into school. Like none of that shit had occurred. At all.

Like it had all been erased from time.

You're being selfish, Rae.

"I know I'm being selfish," I murmured.

They're about to lose their house.

"Yeah, well. When do I get to be an important part of the equation?"

You are important.

"To who? Not Clint. Not my mother. Not Michael and Allison."

They're your best friends.

"Yeah, but I'm not their number one anymore. I'm no one's number one."

I felt like I'd blown a gasket in my brain, arguing

with myself. But who else was I going to talk to? Michael and Allison were sucking face every chance they got. I couldn't have ten uninterrupted minutes with Clint. Cecilia wasn't someone I could talk to. And my mother had lost her damn mind with D.J. coming into our home and trying to run it as he saw fit. I had no one. Nothing. No one to turn to. No one who understood me. No one who loved me enough to put me first for once.

I just want to be important to one person. Just one. Anyone.

Fucking hell, I'd take the stray cat in the neighborhood at this point.

I walked aimlessly until I found myself staring at the front doors of the school. I walked inside and looked at the clock before heaving a heavy sigh. I felt like that's all I did now. Sighed, cried, and turned in homework. I'd missed lunch. History only had about thirty more minutes left. If I walked in now, the teacher would berate me for sure. But if we'd had a pop quiz or something in class, she'd still let me take it.

So I headed into history class.

I walked inside and saw Allison turn around. Her eyes widened as I came into view, closing the door behind me. Our teacher leveled me with a stare. Students snickered at me from all angles. And as I made my way to my seat, the teacher asked me.

"Not the time to start slipping, Miss Cleaver."

I nodded. "It won't happen again."

"It better not."

There had been no pop quiz. But I had just enough time in class to read through the next chapter. Doing homework while not paying attention to the lecture.

That had become my signature move here recently. The bell tolled for classes to switch, but the teacher asked me to stay behind.

I couldn't stay long, though. Otherwise, I'd be late for my last class of the day.

"And where were you, Miss Cleaver?"

I packed up my things. "I had to go see someone."

"Is this someone your boyfriend?"

I winced. "Not technically anymore, no."

"Then why did you have to go see this someone?"

I stood. "Because he's going through a hard time and I wanted to know if I needed to keep bringing him homework or not."

"It's not your responsibility to keep up Mr. Clarke's grades."

"It is when his father is abusive and preventing him from coming to school."

My teacher paused. "What did you say?"

I shook my head. "Clint's going through a very tough time. And I'm sorry I was late for your class. But he's going through a lot right now, and if he doesn't have to fail his classes I'm not going to let him fail."

"Did you say 'abusive'?"

Shit. "If you want to know, visit him. But I won't be late for your class again. Even though it means possibly not helping out someone in need."

Then I turned on my heel and left my teacher in the room.

I sprinted for my last class. I only had three minutes to make it damn near to the other side of the school. The bell rang as I ran up the ramp, signaling that I was late. Fucking hell, late for another class. And because of a teacher chewing me out for shit I didn't deserve to be chewed out for! My grades wouldn't suffer. They never suffered. I was a straight-A student. Had been since middle school.

I leapt into the classroom just before the teacher closed the door.

"Nice save, Miss Cleaver. Stay after class with me, please."

I sighed. "Good thing I'm not a bus rider."

The class gasped and I froze.

"What was that, Raelynn?"

I closed my eyes. "I said, 'Okay. I'll stay behind.'"

"That's what I thought you said."

I swallowed a growl working its way up the back of my throat. It was like a damn catch-22. Late for one class, bitched out by a teacher. Only to be made late for another class so I could get bitched out by another teacher. As I dropped myself into my seat at the back of the class, my eyes found Allison. Michael. The two of them were staring at me as if I'd grown a third head. I nodded at them before pulling out my things, preparing myself to get homework done while my teacher rattled on about bullshit I didn't care about.

Because I'd gotten a small glimpse at Clint's world.

Teachers that didn't care. That didn't own up to when they made their students late for class. Teachers that didn't give a damn about someone's well-being. Or aptitude. Or test scores. This small debacle made me empathize with him more. Because while I'd only gone through it with a couple classes, he'd been going through it for years.

And as I started in on my homework, my mind fell back to Cecilia.

Her, and the emergency that had ripped Clint away from me in the middle of the most important question I needed to ask him.

13

CLINTON

I wanted to rush to her when she hopped over the railing. I saw the second she fell over a bit too far that she wouldn't plant herself on her feet. I moved for her, my arms outstretched. All pretenses gone out the window. I wanted to scoop her into my arms and apologize. Take it all back. Tell her I was sorry for my life turning out this way. But when she threw me a look that could've killed me where I stood, I stopped in my tracks.

And I watched as she made her way across the lawn.

The anger in her eyes haunted me. It made me worried that I had officially lost her. That I'd never be able to reconcile things once I could dig Cecilia and myself out of this hole. However much I might've dreamed about it, I feared the worst. That this was it. That this was the last time I'd ever see Rae, and I was watching her walk away from me.

For good.

I wanted to go after her. No matter how much I wanted to, though, I couldn't. There were so many things going on. I couldn't leave Cecilia like this. Too many things were at stake. Including this fuckery going on with my father. We needed answers, and we needed them quickly. So I kept my eyes on Rae until the horizon swallowed her whole.

Then I went inside.

"Cecilia?" I called out her name as I closed the door behind me.

"In the kitchen."

Her voice was so soft. Breathless. Worried. I made my way into the kitchen and saw her sitting there with a crystal glass of whiskey. She twirled it around in her fingertips. The sadness in her eyes was unbearable. I placed my hand on her shoulder and squeezed, knowing damn good and well that whatever she had found out wasn't good. I walked to the fridge and got me a soda. I wanted a glass of whiskey, too. But I figured Cecilia wouldn't allow it.

I sighed as I sat down in front of her, watching her glassy eyes find mine.

"What happened?" I asked.

Her eyes fell to her glass. "What time is it, again?"

I shrugged. "Sometime past lunch."

"Good." She put her whiskey glass to her lips.

She chugged. And chugged. She swallowed until the amber liquid was gone. And when she got up to get a second glass, I knew it wasn't good. Whatever she had to speak with me about would be life-altering.

That much I knew for sure. How badly, I didn't know.

But I braced for the worst.

Cecilia eased herself back down and leaned heavily into the chair. I brought my soda to my lips, mindlessly sipping as I gave her the space she needed to collect her thoughts. Part of me wanted to yell at her to spit it out. The rest of me knew how much she was struggling, though. The look in her eye. The sadness in her features. The way her eyes teared up and dried out. Like her body didn't know whether to be sad or angry.

Or both.

"Did Dad call you back?"

She nodded slowly.

"Did he answer any of your questions?"

And again, she nodded.

"Whenever you're ready to talk, Rae's gone."

She drew in a short breath. "You should really call that girl and apologize."

I nodded. "One thing at a time."

Cecilia reached for my hand. "Your father's already—"

I took hers, wrapping my fingers around her hand. "He's already what?"

Though I knew what was coming.

"Your father's already found a buyer for the house, Clinton."

I drew in a deep breath. Anything to keep my head from popping off. I had to keep my cool. I couldn't let loose on her. I couldn't become Dad in this moment. I squeezed her hand before I sat back. Her touch fell away and I replaced it with the cold soda in my hand. I brought it to my lips and chugged, wishing it were alcohol. Wishing it were something to wash away the pain and hatred and disdain I had circulating through my system. The carbonation burned. I let it burn, too. I didn't stop until the damn drink was gone. And even then, I wanted something stronger.

Something harsher.

Something more potent than a fucking Dr. Pepper.

"What else did Dad say?"

She sighed. "A lot. He blames you for what happened. Though I kept telling him it was his fault. That he started it after having one too many drinks. That you were only trying to defend me."

I shrugged. "Dad doesn't like chivalry unless it suits him."

She snickered. "So I'm figuring out."

"I'd really like to see the version of my father you've seen all these years."

"You know, I'm not so sure it was ever different. Just… masked. By presents, and clothes, and jewelry."

I nodded slowly. "You think?"

She sniffled. "Guess it's easy to get me to shut up with money."

"Don't say that about yourself."

"No, no. I'm serious. I mean, I grew up with nothing. I grew up with no voice. No things that were my own. No dreams or hopes of having a life I could live of my own volition. When I met your father, he promised me the world. Trips around the globe and nights spent in penthouses and fashion beyond my wildest imagination. I was so taken by all the things he could provide that I never saw the similarities between him and my father."

"You still can't blame yourself."

"I'm an adult, Clint. I can blame myself all I want. I can't control how I was raised. But I can control how I act as a result of it now. You'd do best to keep that in mind."

I nodded slowly. "I will."

"I guess I saw all the freedom of traveling with him and the freedom to eat whatever I wanted, and mistook it for actual freedom. An actual life. When really, I was still underneath someone's thumb. Unable to move or speak or think unless it was demanded of me a certain way."

"Sounds like Dad."

She wiped at her eyes, though her voice never cracked. "Anyway, this isn't about me."

"It's about us. You can talk about whatever you want to."

"I don't know how the fuck your father sold this house so quickly, but he did. We've got six to eight weeks until they close, then…"

I felt anger surging through me. "It's only been, like, two days. How the hell did he orchestrate all of this from the hospital?"

"He wasn't in the hospital when he called me."

"That makes more sense."

"Yeah. He's in a hotel on the other side of town somewhere. Said he got out that next morning and he's been there ever since."

I snickered. "Fucking bastard."

Everything was changing too quickly. Six to eight weeks? Where the hell did that man expect us to go? What did he expect us to do? I tried to figure out where I could start listing some of our things. We needed money, and quickly. I closed my eyes and tried figuring out all the jewelry I'd seen Cecilia in over the years. How much of it did she have in the house? She'd have to give up her luxury, but we could make this work. Even if we only sold—

"He wants me to go with him, Clint."

My eyes slowly opened. "What?"

Her eyes lined with tears. "He says he wants me to come with him."

"Go with him where?"

She shrugged. "I don't know. He said I'm his wife. And wherever we end up, I need to be there."

"Need to be? Or that he wants you there?"

"Do you really have to ask that question?"

"So he wants you to uproot, but you don't even know where you're going? Did he ask you to pack? Or anything like that?"

She shook her head. "No. Just to get ready. Which I assume means packing. Maybe."

I narrowed my eyes. "What aren't you telling me?"

"Clinton, it's not that simple."

"What's not that simple? Come on. Dad said something and I deserve to know what it is."

"I know. I know. Just... please. Just give me a second."

Don't explode like him. "He wants me to be some sort of rental tenant in this house, doesn't he?"

"No."

"He wants me to go live with Roy? Or Rae?"

"No, that's not it. He's just—"

"He's just what? Tell me, Cecilia. What am I supposed to do here? He's sold the house. You're going with him. Am I supposed to come, too?"

And when her eyes teared up, I fell back into my chair.

"You've gotta be fucking kidding me."

She sniffled. "I'm sorry. I tried reasoning with him. I'm still going to try and reason with him. Just give me some time, okay? He's still very angry."

"He doesn't want me coming with you guys?"

I slammed out of my chair. My fists balled up at my sides. I felt myself spiraling out of control as Cecilia yelped in shock. The kitchen table came off its fucking feet. It fell to the ground, raking across the marble of the kitchen floor. I felt my mind exploding. I felt my heart combusting. It felt like the pain and anger in my body was ripping me apart, limb for limb.

I had no words to describe the hurt coursing through my system.

"He said you're eighteen and you can figure it out. But I'm going to talk to him. You're his son. You're *my* son, Clint. And I'm going to do whatever it takes to talk some sense into him. To get him to back out of selling this house. Even if he puts it in my name. Even if he washes his hands of it that way. I'm not going to let him do this to you, Clint."

I heard her voice, but it seemed so far away. I felt her hand on my arm, but it barely rooted me to reality. Hot tears streamed down my cheeks. She eased me back into the kitchen chair. I sniffled as I stared at the wall, my chest jumping in anger. In hatred.

In defeat.

"He wants you to go with him, but not me."

Cecilia crouched down beside me. "Clint, look at me."

"Just say it. Just—just so I can hear it."

"Look. At. Me."

I slowly turned my eyes down to hers. She cupped her hands around my knee, steadying herself as her own tears flooded her face. I wiped mine away on my shirt, wishing and willing this life to be over. Hoping and praying I'd wake up from this fucking nightmare I'd been plunged into.

"I'm going to talk some sense into him. I've got weeks to do it. And I'm going to research legal avenues. See what I can do about fighting this. It isn't over. Okay? Can you hear me, Clint?"

I chewed on the inside of my cheek. "I just want to hear you say it."

"Say what?"

"Say, 'Your father wants me to come with him, but not you.'"

"I'm not saying that."

"Cecilia, just say it."

"I'm fighting this, Clint. Please, give me time. Give this entire scenario some time."

I gritted my teeth together. "Just. Say. It."

She sighed. "Why? What good is it going to do?"

It's going to help me let go of my hope. "Just trust me. Please. I'm begging you. If you give me nothing else, give me this."

And with a defeated sigh, she nodded.

"Your father wants me to come with him wherever he buys his next house, but not you."

Finally, after years of being bound to this hellhole, I felt the chains burst free. Any hope of ever finding the decency within my father popped off, leaving scars behind as the animal in me stood up. The animal he'd been starving and torturing and beating for years. The wounded animal he was more than willing to abandon out of sheer pride. Out of sheer anger. Out of sheer... abusiveness.

I was finally free of the dream of him. Of the dream I'd had ever since I was a little child. Of the dreams where my father loved me. Cared for me. Enjoyed my presence. Free of the expectation that I somehow had to make him happy. Make him proud. Do whatever he wanted simply because he commanded it. Weight after weight rolled off my shoulders. It felt easier to breathe. And as my tears dried up, I stood, helping Cecilia off her feet.

"Thank you for that."

She drew in a shuddering breath. "It hurts to say."

I nodded. "It does. But maybe it'll give you some perspective on what to do next, and show you that you always have a choice."

Then I pulled her into my arms and the two of us cried together, releasing emotions we'd been holding in for ages and finally freeing ourselves from the prisons my father had kept us in.

I only hoped she made the right decision for herself.

Because she was important, too.

14

RAELYNN

"Fucking teachers."
        "Giving me a hard time."
    "Once. I was late once!"
    "They're judging me because of Clint."
    "They shouldn't even be teachers!"
    "Prejudiced fucks."

I kept my head down as I walked home from school. I murmured to myself, pissed off that all my afternoon teachers kept me behind to give me a lecture. I'd been late to their classes once. How the fuck did that warrant pulling me aside and berating me? What the hell did they expect from me? Yes, if a teacher pulls me aside, I'm going to be late for my next class. That isn't my fucking fault!

That didn't even touch what I found with Michael and Allison, though.

Michael sent me a text, telling me they were waiting out back in the parking lot. The only damn bright spot to my entire day. But, when I walked out of the back school doors, I didn't see Michael's big-ass SUV. It wasn't until I squinted that I saw it at the back corner of the parking lot, parked underneath some damn trees. I should've known not to go near the damn thing. But I was naïve. I figured they wanted to get out of the sun while waiting for me.

Didn't take a fucking rocket scientist to explain why the windows were fogged up.

Gross.

I didn't even bother them. I simply turned around and headed for the road. The last thing I wanted to do was get in a car that smelled like pheromones and sexually-frustrated teenagers. This day had been a nightmare. Straight from the asshole of hell. And all I wanted was to get upstairs, get to my room, and close myself up for the weekend.

I didn't even want to bother with school tomorrow.

I deserve a long weekend.

I didn't know which to be angry about more: the fact that my teachers didn't give a shit that I was a straight A-student, or the fact that my best friends didn't give a shit about really waiting for me. I mean, why fog up the windows and perch yourselves for a make-out session if you know someone's going to be joining you soon? That's downright selfish! I would've never pulled that shit with Clint.

Are you sure about that?

I rolled my eyes and muted the voices in my head. I rushed across the road and tore into my neighborhood, because I wanted to get into the house as quickly as I could. I didn't know what to do with all this anger. All this hurt. All this betrayal I felt. I mean, rationally? I understood it was stupid. I knew my emotions were raging out of control and that I needed to pull them back a bit.

But I just couldn't.

I looked up just in time to see D.J. getting into his car. Fucking really? He was here? Just my luck. I moved quickly. I practically jogged into the driveway as he turned his engine over. It wasn't until he started backing out, however, that I realized he was leaving.

Finally, someone's having mercy on me.

"Hey, kiddo."

Spoke too soon. "Hey, D.J."

He rolled down his window the rest of the way. "How was your day today?"

I flashed him a bitter smile. "Getting worse by the second."

He snickered. "What did I ever do to you to make you hate me so much?"

I shrugged as I passed his car window. "I don't know, Deej. Breathed air? Opened your mouth? Set your sights on my mother? Sent her home with bruises? Pick one. They're all valid."

"Spoiled brat."

"Ignorant prick."

I looked back at him as I made my way to the porch. I glared at him as he sped out of the driveway, his tires peeling off into the distance. The smell of burnt rubber filled the air, and I grimaced as I made my way inside. I drew in a deep breath of fresh air. Well, fresh air tainted with something terrible my mother had obviously cooked. I closed the door behind me as tires squealed in the distance. Probably D.J. taking a tight turn out of the neighborhood. Because he thought he was cool.

Asshat.

I leaned against the door and sighed, closing my eyes. I dropped my purse. My backpack. I felt my knees weakening as I closed my eyes. I wanted this day to be over. Hell, I wanted this year to be over. I wanted to be graduated so I could get the fuck out of here and the fuck away from Clint. And everything that reminded me of him.

"Rae? You all right?"

Mom's voice hit my ears and I drew in a shuddering breath. The last thing I needed to do was break down. I was tired of it. Tired of feeling weak. Tired of feeling alone. Tired of feeling disposable. Like I was second-best.

But, when I opened my eyes, I saw Mom standing at the end of the hallway.

"Rae, what's wrong?"

I swallowed hard. "Do I smell cookies or something?"

She nodded slowly. "I tried making your favorite. But I think there's something wrong with the stove."

"Burning the cookies?"

"Which is saying something, since we both know I'm a slow baker."

"And a terrible cook."

She snickered. "I'll let you get away with that this time."

I nodded. "Sounds good."

She paused. "Do you want to talk about it?"

I shrugged, but I couldn't say anything. I felt the knot forming, my knees buckling. My entire world was crumbling around me as the loneliness in the pit of my black soul ignited. The light blinded me behind my eyes. It hurt to feel the heat of that searing anguish. My hand came up to my chest and I gripped my shirt. Tugged at the collar because it was now too close to my throat.

"Oh, Raelynn. I've got you. Come here."

I held my hand out. "No. No, no. No hugs. Please. I just—"

"Stop it. You have to let it out. You know better than that."

The second I felt my mother's arms around me, I collapsed. I threw my arms around her neck and my knees finally buckled. She gasped as she sank us to the floor, her arms holding me tight. And as I tucked my face into the crook of her neck, I sobbed. I cried like I did when I was a child. When I first skinned my knee, or when I first jammed my neck. When Allison first hurt my feelings, or when I got my first failing test in middle school.

"What's wrong? Talk to me, sweetheart. What's happening?"

My lower lip quivered. "I-I-I, Clint—he's mov—mov—school just—"

She kissed the top of my head. "Deep breaths, Rae. Even breaths. You're close to a panic attack."

"My chest. It hurts."

"I know."

"I can't—"

"Just do as I'm asking. Breathe in through your nose, out through your mouth. And focus on keeping the rhythm even."

I did as she asked. My chest kept jumping, but I kept at it. She murmured softly in my ear. She cradled me as if I were still a child. She rocked me side to side, groaning and grunting underneath my weight. She didn't let me go, though. She didn't push me away. She simply let me cry into her neck until my breathing finally stabilized.

Then the words poured from my lips like water from a backed-up fountain.

15

CLINTON

California state assistance for teenagers.
Jobs that require only a high school degree.
Cheap motorcycles for sale.
Places for homeless students to sleep in Riverbend
Can I sell my dad's stuff if he's selling the only place I live in?

I slammed my finger against the 'enter' key and watched the search engine whirl away. I picked up my third cup of coffee and chugged it back, groaning at the taste of rosewater. Fucking hell, I loved this coffee place. I'd miss it when I left. And I was damn lucky they didn't charge me for the usage of their computers.

Because my neck had grown stiff researching shit on my cell phone.

I typed in everything I could think of. Any search that might give me some sort of reprieve from the insanity coming down around me. Weeks. I had only weeks to figure out what my next moves were. Otherwise, I'd be homeless. I'd have to sleep on the streets. Possibly drop out of school. Make my way in this world scrubbing dishes for less than minimum wage in some food truck while I sweated my ass off.

"Come on, there has to be something."

I clicked around and sent myself articles. I highlighted things I jotted down in the notebook I carried around with me now. More and more, my notebook filled with ways to live. Ways to eat. Places that might take me in versus poems and short stories and novel ideas that came to me at the drop of a hat. My notebook had gone from creative to proactive. Artistic to sadistic. I felt like it mocked me some times, laughing at me. Like my father probably was right now.

Satanic.

The devil. My father was Lucifer himself. How he could do this to his own flesh and blood, I'd never know. How my mother could leave me with a man like this, I'd never understand. I didn't want to understand. I never wanted to be as cold-hearted and as desolate as the two of them were.

I just wanted to find a safe place to be myself.

After hitting dead ends and growing tired of frivolous searches, I broke down and called that lawyer. I found his card I had taped to the inside of my notebook, figuring I'd have to make an appointment with him. I reached his secretary and gave my name. The reason for me calling. And just when I thought she'd rattle off his schedule to me, she told me to wait.

"Clinton Clarke?"

I paused. "Uh, yes?"

"I was wondering if I'd ever hear from you again. How are you?"

I was so shocked, I couldn't even remember the man's name. "I'm good. I mean, well, I have a question. But, otherwise, I'm good."

"Are you wanting me to answer that question for you?"

I sighed. "No, no. I just—I want to pick your brain a second."

"About what?"

"I have a hypothetical for you."

"Question for a friend. That kind of thing?"

"You could say that."

"Got it. Shoot."

"Let's say there's a house up for sale. Just went on the market. And there's already a buyer."

"Nice. That happens sometimes."

I snickered. "Yeah. Anyway, the issue is that there are two people still living in the house. A high schooler of legal age and a woman."

He paused. "Uh huh."

"Yeah. And it's assumed the woman is going to move when the house sells. But it's not assumed the high schooler is going to move."

"Okay?"

"What rights does that high schooler have? Can he —I mean—can this high schooler somehow stop the sale?"

"Does this high schooler want to?"

I snickered. "I mean, the high schooler won't have anywhere to go."

"So, this kid not going with the move isn't a decision he's made."

I paused. "No. It isn't."

He clicked his tongue. "Clinton?"

"Yes, sir?"

"You want to drop the veil of pretense for a second and talk seriously?"

"That depends. Are you going to interject your services and make things worse?"

"Not unless you hire me. Otherwise, this is simply a phone consultation where I tell you the kind of rights you have and how I can help you."

I sighed. "All right. Shoot."

"Your father's sold your house, but has he explicitly said to you that he doesn't want you going with him?"

I cleared my throat. "He said that to my stepmother. Not me. I can't get him on the phone."

"Is there any way for you to get a copy of the sale contract of the house?"

"I have no idea."

"Okay. You need to try and do that first. I can place a few phone calls if you—"

I shook my head. "No. I don't want to make things worse."

He sighed. "I can leave your name out of it."

"Please, just—do I have a right to sell some of the things in the house to get some money for myself? Because I can't leave town right now. I need to graduate first."

"Kid, I know. That's what I'm trying to tell you. If you can get that sale contract on your hands to make sure your father hasn't sold the furniture and the possessions inside the house, then you can sell those off yourself."

I paused. "I can?"

"Yep."

"Even, like, the silverware and the furniture?"

"All of it."

"Seriously?"

"Yep. Dead serious. Even if he takes you to court and tries to prove that you 'stole his stuff' by selling it out from underneath him, the second you prove that he did it to you with the house, a judge is going to throw it out of court. It'll be seen as neglect, and that won't shine a good light on him."

I sighed. "I don't have proof of that, though."

"You said he said it to your stepmother, right?"

I nodded. "He did, yes."

"If you can get him to say it to you, too, or get it written down electronically somewhere, you're good. You can't record him without notifying him of the fact that you're recording. But what he says in emails or text messages…"

"I read you loud and clear."

"But even so, there are things in that house you're privy to that aren't specifically your belongings. Not sculptures and priceless art he might've gotten at an auction or anything. But neutral items the entire family uses, like couches, chairs, china. You have a right to that."

I sighed. "Thank you so much."

"And before we hang up, I just want to put this out

there. If you need me—for anything—it'll be pro bono work."

"You don't have to do—"

"Pro. Bono. Do you hear me?"

I swallowed hard. "I do. Thank you."

"Keep my number handy. Know you're not alone in this fight."

"I will. Thank you, sir."

"Call me in a few days and let me know how you're doing. All right?"

I snickered. "Why?"

He paused. "Because I care. And I get the feeling that idea is foreign to you. So let me start teaching you that."

It wasn't foreign when Rae was around. "Okay. Sounds good."

I hung up the phone with him and leaned back into the chair. I pressed the heels of my hands into my eyes and sighed with relief. Okay. That was a better outcome than I had hoped for. Now, how the fuck was I going to get my hands on a copy of that sale contract?

Time to start searching the internet again.

The more I searched, the more insane this scenario became. A few weeks ago, I'd been hanging out with Roy, biding my time until graduation, and dreaming about plans to get out of this place. And now, I'd loved. I'd lost. I'd almost died. Only for my father to come to the decision he was going to throw me out on my ass. Force me to survive alone, no matter what.

Wait. The bank account.

I picked my phone back up and punched in my information on my banking app. And when I saw that the $4,999.00 transfer had actually gone through, my jaw hit the floor. I pushed away from the coffeehouse computer as I sifted through the numbers I'd recently dialed. I called the guy back I'd spoken with at the beginning of the week, hoping to initiate another transfer.

But things didn't go as planned.

"Your account's been locked down, Mr. Clarke."

I sighed. "Figures. I take it my father did that?"

"I'm not allowed to discuss the specifics of—"

"A few days ago you could. I'm still a beneficiary on that account, right?"

He paused. "Actually, sir, no. You're not."

I blinked. "What?"

"Your name has been removed from the account."

"You're being serious right now, aren't you?"

I guess I shouldn't have been surprised. But it didn't lessen the sting.

"I'm sorry, Mr. Clarke. But if I can be of service to you at all—"

"You're good. Thanks."

And I hung up the phone before the tears crested the folds of my eyes.

I tried to focus on the good. If I could just get my hands on a sale contract, I might stand a chance at reaping a great deal of money before this six to eight week period was up. And until then, I still had things I could sell. I threw away my empty coffee cup and started out of the coffeehouse. I flagged down a taxi and got in, then rattled off my home address.

I needed to go home and start preparing things to sell off.

It didn't shock me when I found Cecilia at the kitchen table. She'd practically taken up permanent residency there. I had come downstairs this morning and seen her sitting there, staring into her mug of coffee. And when I left to skip school and come back to the coffeehouse, she'd still been sitting there. Now, as I walked back inside around three in the afternoon, I found her still sitting there. Still in her robe. Still with that same damn mug of coffee.

Had she even moved?

"Cecilia?"

The two of us hadn't spoken since yesterday. Since she told me the offer my father had made her. And that the invitation wasn't open to me. I walked into the kitchen and sat down in front of her, waiting for her to lift her eyes to mine. Waiting for her to acknowledge me.

But she didn't.

"Cecilia?"

She sighed, but didn't say anything.

"Cecilia, we can do this."

She licked her lips. But again, stayed silent.

"I know you think this is hopeless. I know you don't think you have a choice. But you do. You have a choice in all this. You have a choice to stay with me and not go with him."

She closed her eyes. Drew in a deep breath. And

still, she fucking stayed silent.

"I'm serious. I know you don't believe me, but I'm dead serious. You deserve better than him. Better than this. You won't be safe with my father."

"But I'll be safe with you."

I sighed. "I talked to that lawyer. Remember him? We've got some avenues we can take to get money."

She shook her head. "You and I both know how unpredictable your father is."

"And angry. Which is why you shouldn't be with him. Don't live alone in a house with him. You know it won't be better. Don't you? Can't you see how happy we've been as a familial unit every time he's been gone?"

She shook her head. "If we try something, he'll find a way to snuff it out."

I reached out for her hand. "Which is why we have to fight."

Her eyes fell to my palm. I wiggled my fingers, beckoning for her to take my grasp. She slowly moved her hand over mine and I closed my fingers, holding her trembling hand within my own. Tears slipped out from her eyes. It made me sick to see her crying so much. After everything this woman had done for me— after stepping up for me the way she had—it killed me to watch her go through this. To watch my fucking sperm donor yank her around like this.

"You have a choice, Cecilia. You just need to see that for yourself."

And instead of answering, she fell silent, refusing to answer as the tears continued to silently fall.

16

RAELYNN

The weekend came and went. As empty as my heart and as angry as my soul. Neither Michael nor Allison called me once the entire time. Probably because they were spending every waking moment doing everything but having sex. D.J. kept waltzing in and out of the house like he fucking owned the place. Which meant I had to listen to him and Mom fight all weekend. More of the same. More of him accusing her of shit she wasn't doing. More of Mom crying. More of him storming out. More of her getting drunk and bringing some random guy home from a bar before D.J. showed up with flowers and make-up sex.

The cycle made me sick.

I hated being at home. I hated being in this town. I wanted to graduate, leave it all behind, and get the fuck out of Dodge. The plan had been to move with Allison. Get a place together near her college campus. But I wasn't sure I wanted to do that anymore. How could a best friend forget about her heartbroken friend all weekend? And for a guy? If Allison's heart had been broken and I was still with Clint, I'd bat Clint off in a fucking heartbeat to go be with her.

Guess I didn't mean as much to Allison as I figured I did.

Monday morning couldn't come fast enough. But even then, it still sucked. I walked to school by myself, went to class by myself. I got out of one toxic environment and plunged headfirst into another. I didn't see Michael or Allison until I got to homeroom. Allison's face was flushed with a red I was all too familiar with. She smiled with a dopey smile I'd once had on my face.

She was in love.

And making out in the back stairwells of the school.

I didn't feel like facing Michael and her at lunch. It was too painful and I was too angry. Sure, maybe my anger wasn't warranted. But that didn't stop me from feeling angry. From feeling like they needed to tuck shit in a bit. So I took my lunch to the library. I bypassed the table I usually occupied and headed for the middle of the room. A table surrounded by rows and rows of books.

People had to navigate a labyrinth in order to come find me.

And that was how I wanted it.

I sighed as I tried studying. I opened my books and munched on some snacks I managed to steal from my pantry at home. But I wasn't hungry. I was tired. I needed caffeine. I needed a pick-me-up. I needed coffee, otherwise I wouldn't make it through the back half of my day. I looked up from my books, spotting a clock down one of the rows of books, hanging cock-eyed on the wall at the end. I squinted my eyes to take in the time. Only halfway through lunch before my studying period started.

I hadn't taken my study period lately.

But today I needed it to get some damn coffee.

I packed up my things and snuck out of school. I made my way out the back doors and sprinted for the main road. I had over an hour before history class started. So I took my time. I walked into town and crossed the road, heading straight for the coffee shop by my work. It still gave me the creeps to walk around in that parking lot. I stayed as far away from that dumbass tree as possible. I ripped open the door of the coffeehouse and sniffed deeply, drawing in its wonderful scent.

Then I got in line.

I pulled out my phone while I waited and scrolled through the pictures I had saved. The only thing that gave me any sort of distraction this past weekend was looking at prom dresses. I mean, I wasn't going. Not now, anyway. I wouldn't have a date. My two best friends would be tonguing each other down all night. Not something I wanted to endure for some 'high school memories.' Still, looking for dresses and saving pictures pulled me out of my nightmarish life for a little while.

Gave me something else to focus on.

"No. No. Too short. Why did I like this one again? Nuh-uh. Too expensive. Don't make it in my size, I don't think."

I deleted dresses I didn't like. Ones that were too sparkly after sleeping on them for a couple of nights. I eliminated them, one by one. Until I was left with dresses that were more simplistic. Elegant. Full-length dresses with soft, silken material. And definitely no fucking sparkles. Something green. Or blue. Possibly navy. Though not black.

A tapping on my shoulder ripped me from my trance.

"Can I help… you…?"

I turned around and gazed into Clint's eyes. I looked up at him, my brow furrowing in confusion. His eyes fell to my phone and I quickly closed out the pictures. Then I slipped my phone into my purse.

"He—hey, there. Hi. Hi, Clint."

He grinned. "Hi, Rae."

I cleared my throat. "How are you doing?"

He nodded. "Been better. Yourself?"

"I'm getting along."

"Study session time, I take it?"

"Huh?"

He nodded toward the door. "At school. Study session time?"

I snickered. "Oh. Yes. It is. I need a pick-me-up."

"Don't blame you. Sleep's hard to come by nowadays."

"Yeah. I suppose so."

The cashier sighed. "Can I get you anything?"

I whipped around and saw there was no one else standing in front of me. Just an impatient woman behind the cash register softly glaring at me. I scurried up to the front and placed my order. An iced caramel macchiato. With an extra shot.

Then Clint leaned over. "And I'll have a large rose-water and caramel coffee. Put it on the same ticket."

I looked over at him. "You don't have to do that."

But he didn't answer me.

Instead, he simply handed the girl his card, paying for my drink without so much as a glance down at me. I didn't know whether to be thankful or frustrated, irritated or flattered. Clint ushered me over to the side where we waited for our drinks. And I watched as the girl behind the cash register followed Clint with her eyes.

Making me very jealous.

"So, how's school?"

His voice pulled me from my jealous trance. "You'd know if you were there."

He shrugged. "Finding a place to live is a bit more important right now."

"So your father's really selling the house?"

"Got a buyer and everything. I'll be out on my ass in a few weeks, if I can't come up with something. Oh, those are our coffees."

I reached for mine. "Thanks."

Clint took a sip of his. "Anyway, it is what it is."

"Will you please let me help?"

"There's nothing you can do to help. It's just a shit scenario."

"All I'm asking you to do is let me back in. We don't have to date. We don't have to see one another. Just let me help you. When have I proven to you that I can't help?"

"This isn't your issue to deal with anymore, Rae."

I sighed. "Then why passive-aggressively bring it up like that?"

He paused. "What?"

"If it wasn't my issue and you didn't want me worried about it, then you wouldn't have brought it up at all. But you did. Which tells me you at least want to talk about it. So I'm here. You've already bought me coffee. Why don't we sit, or take a walk, and at least talk about it?"

His eyes danced between mine. "Are you taking a psychology class or something?"

"Michael is."

"Ah."

"That's beside the point, though. Are you going to let me back in long enough to help you? Or are you going to silently suffer and then proclaim the world's against you?"

He grinned. "Did you just call me out?"

"Yes. I fully and completely did. But only because I want to help."

"Rae, it's just—"

My glare shut him up. "You don't get to make choices for me, Clinton. If you push me away one more time, it's because you want to. Not because you're protecting me. Because the only thing you've caused me is heartache and sleepless nights. Don't you dare fool yourself on that."

And with a heavy sigh, I watched sorrow rush behind his eyes.

"Want to take a walk with me?"

I nodded. "I'm more than happy to. Come on. You lead the way."

17

CLINTON

I opened the door for Rae. "I don't really know where to start."

She walked out the door. "Well, you can start from the beginning."

"You already know the beginning. Kind of."

"Then, start from what happened after the last time I came to your house."

"You mean where you almost killed yourself jumping over the porch railing?"

She shrugged. "I would've done anything to get away from you in that moment."

Her words struck me hard. "I'm sorry."

She waved her hand in the air. "It's in the past. Talk to me, Clint. What's going on? What did Cecilia want to talk to you so badly about?"

I sighed. "Ah. That."

"That doesn't sound good."

"I mean, it's not. But it also doesn't shock me.

Cecilia finally got in touch with Dad. He confirmed that he was selling the house. That he already had a buyer for it. And that I wasn't welcome to come with them to their next destination."

She stopped in her tracks. "What?"

I nodded slowly. "Yep."

"Wait, can he actually do that? Just… abandon you like that?"

"I'm eighteen. I'm a legal adult. He doesn't have to take me anywhere."

"That can't be right. Clint, that just can't be right."

I sighed. "Well, it's the reason why I haven't been at school. I've been here every morning, giving the illusion I'm at school in case Dad randomly stops by the house."

"But Cecilia knows you aren't in school right now?"

I nodded. "She does. We aren't talking about it. But she does."

"Why are you coming here?"

I started walking again. "I'm using their computers to do some research. Figure out my options. Find my next moves."

Rae walked alongside me. "Have you come up with anything substantial?"

"I mean, not really. Some working theories. There are states where, if I live there and declare residency, community college is free. But that's assuming I can get out of school with the grades I need. Which we both know won't happen."

"You never know, Clint. If you get back to school

and let me help you, we can easily ace your classes. That'll bring your GPA up."

"Yeah, but even if I did that, I'm not sure more school is my route. I hate school. I can't stand it. I'll need money, and quickly."

She nodded. "So what kind of jobs can you get? There isn't much out there for someone without a high school diploma. Which means you'll still have to come back to school and graduate."

I paused. "How did you know that?"

And when she blushed, my heart went out to her.

"Who did you ask?"

She shook her head. "It was nothing. Just a passing question."

"Rae, what happened?"

"Just a rough conversation with the guidance counselor. That's all."

I reached out for her, stopping her in her tracks. "What did you say to the counselor?"

"Nothing that implicated anything was going on. It was just a passing question. Nothing more. Okay?"

"Are you sure?"

She scoffed. "Do I look like I'm lying to you?"

I searched her eyes. The last thing I needed was for someone at the school to be breathing down me and my father's necks. Things were bad enough. I didn't need them to get any worse.

"Why were you in the counselor's office?"

Rae shrugged. "Does it matter?"

"It matters to me."

"Well, maybe that'll be our next conversation."

I sighed. "You want me to talk, but you won't talk?"

"The focus isn't on me right now. We can put the focus on me after we're done with this conversation. Okay?"

"You promise?"

She gazed into my eyes. "With all my heart."

The look in her eye tugged at my gut. At my soul, really. How she still had care for me in her eyes, I'd never know. Rae was a mystery. Unlike any person I'd ever met in my life. And I had no idea how the fuck she still cared about me. I wanted to take her in my arms. I wanted to kiss those lips of hers. I wanted to taste her coffee on the tip of her tongue and erase any fear or pain or doubt from her mind.

I still care about you, too. Can you see it?

"Clint?"

I blinked. "Yeah. Sorry."

"It's okay. It's fine. Just—traffic's picking up. So we better cross the road now."

Without thinking, I took her hand. We jogged across the intersection, and the heat of her skin against mine sent tingles up and down my spine. But once we touched down on the side of the road, I dropped her hand. I couldn't stand to hold it. I didn't have a right to hold it.

Even though I wanted to thread our fingers together and lead her onward.

"What else is going on?"

Rae's voice forced me to speak. "I mean, that's

really it. I got in contact with a lawyer. You know, that one I went to talk to after my accident?"

"What did he have to say?"

I shrugged. "He gave me some good advice. Apparently, many of the things in that house are mine, though I didn't purchase them. He said something about 'common use,' or something like that. You know, the couches and fine china. Since we all used it in the house, it all belongs to us. Just like he can't force me to replace it if I break it, he can't sue me if I sell it."

"So you're thinking about getting money that way."

"Not thinking about it. Doing it. I put some things up for sale last night. Took pictures with my phone. That's the reason I was at the coffee shop today. I was meeting various people with things that already sold."

She looked over at me. "So you've got some money in your pocket now."

"More than 'some money.' Let's just say I'm itching to get back to the house so I can stash it away somewhere. It's making me nervous to carry it around."

She smiled. "I mean, I hate that you're having to go to those kinds of lengths. But I'm glad it's working out for you."

"It sucks, but it'll give me what I need to take my next steps."

"How much are you hoping to get?"

"If I can sell everything I want to? Three hundred thousand."

"Holy shit! Are you serious?"

I chuckled. "I don't expect to sell all of it, though.

That's a lot of money in a small amount of time. I'd be fine with even a third of that."

"Do you mind me asking how much you have right now?"

"Including what's in my bank account? About twenty grand."

Her jaw dropped open. "Wow. Then, yes. We need to get you to a bank or something."

"Not a bank."

"Why not? Don't you have a bank account?"

"I do, but my father can access it at any time."

She paused. "Wait, your father still has access to your bank account?"

I nodded. "He does. I'm working on that, though. I placed a call today to a completely separate bank. I wanted to open up an account and I've already got an electronic transfer in the works. Come tomorrow morning, the account I have right now should have all my funds transferred into this new account my father can't touch. Then I'll put this money in my account."

"Once you know your father can't access it."

"Exactly."

She puffed out her cheeks. "It makes me sick you even have to go to these lengths."

"My father's a control freak. Any amount of control I can rip away from him puts me in a much better position."

"Is it bad that I kind of want to wring his neck?"

I chuckled. "You and me both."

I worried that being seen with me would be bad for Rae. But she didn't seem to give a shit at all. We got to talking so much that we weren't paying attention to where we were walking. It wasn't until the smell of her neighborhood caught my nose and I realized I'd walked her to her doorstep that I understood why I had aimlessly walked here with her.

Because for days, all I'd wanted was to come over and lie down with her.

"I probably should've walked you back to school, huh?"

She snickered. "I'm kind of over school right now."

I furrowed my brow. "Why?"

She shrugged. "I don't know. Just not resonating with me right now."

"Rae, you can't let your—"

"I know, I know. Clint, my grades aren't slipping. I'm not behind on work. In the whole of my high school career, I've had four absences. I'm good. I promise."

I sighed. "Okay, then."

"I just don't want to be bad for you. And I feel like the more I'm around you, the worse for you I become."

She opened her front door. "I mean, if you want to get technical, none of this shit started happening until you broke up with me. So, I guess I have an argument for how *not* being with you is bad for me."

"Do you always have an argument for everything?"

"When people try to dictate what's best for me instead of letting me do that? Yes. Come on in."

I stood my ground. "I'm not sure if that's smart."

Rae snickered. "Stop denying yourself what you want and get the hell inside. No one's home."

"Which is the issue. I'm bad news, Rae. And the more wrapped up in me you get, the more of my life you get with it."

"And how is that bad? When did I ever give you the impression I didn't want to be wrapped up in it? You do get that, right? You do understand that you don't get to decide what's bad and what's good for me. Right?"

"I just want to keep you—"

Her face turned red. "Damn it, Clint. Cut the shit for a second! I want to *be* with you. Really be with you. How the hell is that a bad thing? You aren't your father. I know you *think* you are, but you aren't. You aren't a culmination of the bad things that have happened to you. You're just you. Why can't you see that? Why are you punishing me because *you* can't see that?"

I stood there, dumbfounded as she reached for my hand. She took it and threaded our fingers together. An action I hadn't had the balls to do myself. She softly tugged me inside. And after she closed it, she held my hand tightly, physically refusing to let go as I looked down into her gorgeous eyes.

Eyes I had missed.

"You're all I want, Clint. And whatever life comes with you, I'll weather it. Because that's what people do when they care about each other. And I care about you. I always will."

My eyes danced between hers. I felt so shell-shocked by her words that I couldn't move. She rose to her tiptoes and pressed her lips softly against mine. I froze. I didn't pucker my lips or flinch as her hand slid up my arms. I tried to stand my ground for as long as possible. I tried to resist her warmth and her loving demeanor and her perfect words.

Until I couldn't any longer.

"Just let me have you. That's all I'm asking," she whispered.

Settling my hands against her hips, I backed her against the door as my tongue invaded her mouth.

18

RAELYNN

My God, how I missed him. His kiss. His touch. His forceful nature. And when his hands fell to my hips, I opened my mouth for him. I felt his tongue slide across the roof of my mouth and I could have cried.

He ripped my shirt off and kissed down my neck. I managed to slip off his jacket and wondered where his leather one had gotten off to. Clothes came off in a flurry as his lips slid down to my chest. Kissing and sucking. His teeth sank into my skin and marked me as my hands slid through his hair.

It had grown so long, and I loved it.

I slid my hands down his back. He buried his face into my cleavage. His warmth encompassed me as his hands slid up and down the backs of my legs. I panted with need for him. I had to have him. And as he picked me up, he slung me over his shoulder, my eyes level with his lower back as he carried me into the living room.

But not before cracking his hand against my ass.

"Clint!"

He growled as he tossed me to the couch. I watched him with wild eyes as he slid out of the rest of his clothes. Those rippling muscles came into view before he ravaged my body, pulling off the rest of my clothes. I was bare, naked underneath him as his lips crashed back to mine. The heady feeling I got from his body settling against mine turned my brain to mush. I raked my fingernails across his skin. He kissed down my stomach before shifting me how he wanted me. And with my back melting into the couch cushions, he knelt between my legs.

Before diving into my body.

I moaned. "Clint, yes."

His tongue parted me and my back arched. My hands twisted into his hair as he stroked me to a constant high. He kept me on the edge. Teasing me. Filling me with his fingers. Stroking those wondrous parts of me I had ached for him to touch. My legs wrapped around his head. My heels dug into his shoulders. He drank from my fountain as I poured forth for him, ravenously bucking against his face. Feeling his stubble against my lower lips. Feeling his hands meander up my curves until he massaged my breasts.

"Clint. Clint. Clint. Clint."

His name fell from my lips like a desperate prayer. And as my body locked out, I spiraled into a darkened abyss. I felt like I was floating and sinking at the same time. Light burst behind my eyes before being swallowed up by the darkness. My toes curled as he buried his tongue between my lower lips and my nails raked along his scalp. He held me to him. Drank every ounce of arousal I offered him.

And when I collapsed, heaving for air, he kissed my inner thighs.

A trail of wetness followed his lips as he kissed up my body. My arms fell to the side, unable to move. I shivered with anticipation, puckering my lip as I waited for him to press against me once more, pick me up and mold me however he wanted, so long as it made him happy.

But he didn't kiss me with the fury he did before.

His lips softly captured mine and I tasted myself on him. He wrapped his arms around me and effortlessly picked me up. He swung me around, settling himself on the couch as I straddled him. I sank against him, resting my naked body against his muscles. My curves dripped into the divots of his strength. I gasped for air against the crook of his neck. His hands massaged my back. My thighs, my hips, until I was strong enough to lift my head.

"Please tell me this isn't a dream," I whispered.

His forehead propped up mine and my eyes fell open. I found him staring at me with a smile on his face. A genuine smile. One that reached his eyes. And my heart felt fuller than it had in days. I felt as if my broken heart were mending with every massage of his palms. With every stroke of his fingertips. With every kiss of his lips.

Then his cock pulsed underneath me.

"No. It's not a dream," he murmured.

His hands fisted my hips and he lifted me up. Like a rag doll, there for his pleasure, he slowly sank me down his girth. Inch by inch, until he filled me in all the ways I remembered. My head fell back. My eyes fluttered closed. His arm wrapped around my lower back, holding me to him as I adjusted. I felt him pulsing, his heat already filling me. My hands pressed against his chest, sinking him deeper into the cushions of the couch.

And as our eyes connected, his hands slowly pushed back.

"Let me guide you, Rae."

I captured his lips. "I'm all yours."

Our eyes held one another as he steadily moved my hips, showing me how to please him. How to stroke him in all the ways he wished. My arms wrapped around his neck and I clung to him as I slowly found my rhythm. His arms cloaked my back, holding me to him as I rolled and bounced, pulling groans and grunts from the back of his throat.

"Rae. Shit."

"That's it, Clint. Like that."

"Don't stop. I can't—you're—don't stop."

"I won't. I won't. I won't ever stop. Never."

Faster and faster, until our breaths became one. I breathed the air he afforded me as his hands explored my body. I bounced in his lap, feeling my arousal dripping against his skin and marking him, the way he'd marked me with his teeth. His hands slid around to my ass cheeks and gripped them tightly, rolling me deeper against mine. And as his face fell to my bosom, I felt him sucking deep, dark marks against my skin.

Until the two of us sought our end with one another.

"Clint, yes!"

"Fucking hell, Rae. You're perfection."

He pounded into me and my body jumped for him. His growls overpowered my whimpers as I spiraled out of control again. I collapsed against him, feeling him hold me as he thrusted quicker. Faster. Harder. He worked me through my orgasm. Jumping my bones and making my muscles twitch as I felt him mark my warm walls.

And as my head fell into the crook of his neck, he collapsed against the couch. Holding me. Splaying his hands across my skin.

As the evidence of our lust dripped from between my legs.

19

CLINTON

I stroked my fingers through her hair as her weight rested against me. Home. I felt as if I were home again. And I didn't know if I'd ever feel this way about anything again. A place. Or a person. Or a city. Or a state. I felt more confused than ever about my future. And yet, none of it mattered.

Not when Rae was in my arms.

"We should clean up."

I grinned as she slowly lifted her head.

"You think, huh?"

She smiled. "I know. I'm leaking."

I chuckled. "I thought you liked that feeling."

"No one likes that feeling."

I paused. "True. I don't like leaking, either."

She snickered. "So, shower?"

"Together?"

"Is there any other kind?"

I felt a renewed sense of strength rush through my muscles and I quickly picked her up.

"Clint!"

"Up the stairs, I presume?"

She kicked her legs. "We need our clothes, you idiot."

I dipped down. "I've got them. I can get them."

"Put me down. You're going to drop—Clint!"

I chuckled as I bent down, picking our clothes off the floor. I slowly made my way to the stairs with her tossed over my shoulder, her legs kicking and her hands gripping tightly to my hips. I walked up the stairs and found my way into the bathroom upstairs. And after kicking the door closed behind me, I dropped our clothes before settling her onto the bathroom counter.

"I didn't drop you."

She frowned deeply. "Don't you ever do that again."

I kissed the tip of her nose. "No promises."

"Clint!"

I captured her lips and felt her giggle against me.

"I missed you, Rae."

She sighed. "I missed you too, Clint."

"I'm sorry."

She nuzzled my nose. "I'm sorry, too."

"You have nothing to be sorry for."

"Just take the apology, crazy."

I snickered. "Not when it isn't warranted. I put us in this situation. Let me own up to that."

She cupped my cheeks. "Fine. You can make it up to me by washing me down in the shower."

"Doesn't sound like much of a punishment."

"It is when you realize I'm not letting you have sex with me in that shower."

"Oh, really. Is that a challenge?"

Fifteen minutes later, I had Rae pinned to that fucking shower wall. I rolled against her, feeling her cling to me as her muffled moans fell against my shoulder. I loved being encased by her. I loved the feeling of her pussy squeezing me dry. And as bubbles popped against my skin, I made love to her in that shower.

And I hope she felt it as much as I meant it.

We washed one another down, and it took all I had not to indulge in her a third time. We dried off and put our clothes back on, then made our way downstairs. The heat of the shower followed us. I couldn't take my eyes off Rae's glistening hair, damp from the shower and begging to be fisted. Begging to be wrapped around my wrist and tugged on as I took her from behind.

Focus, Clint. Don't fuck this up.

"So, you hungry?"

Rae's voice called to me from the kitchen, helping me focus.

"Starving, actually."

She giggled. "I figured. So how does a pizza and movie kind of night sound? I mean, you're here and we might as well make the most of the moment.."

"On a Monday night? Won't your mom be back soon? And you can technically make it to your last class of the day, if we leave now."

She shrugged. "I already finished up the homework

and read ahead. Plus, there's a note here in the kitchen from Mom. She'll be out for most of the night tonight."

I paused. "When did your mother come home?"

"I'm not sure. I guess it's a good thing we were quiet in the shower."

I furrowed my brow. "I wasn't quiet in the shower."

And her laughter filled the hallway that separated us. Drawing me down the corridor until I found her in the kitchen.

"What do you like on your pizza?"

I shrugged. "Anything you want is fine with me, so long as it doesn't have peppers on it."

"So, pepperoni, mushrooms, and tomato all right?"

"Sounds fine to me."

"If you want, you can go pick the movie while I get this ordered."

I grinned. "Just make sure you tell the delivery guy you're paying with cash."

Rae turned to me. "Why?"

I quirked an eyebrow. "Already forgetting our prior conversation? I've got money on me. I'll take care of it."

"You don't have to do that, Clint."

"I want to. Tell him you'll be paying with cash. And get whatever else you want."

She smiled so sweetly at me and it tugged at my heart strings. I didn't think this day could get any better. But I also didn't want to jinx it. I left the kitchen as she started placing our order, making my way into the living room. With the scent of us still lingering in the air, I blushed. Actually, truly blushed. Because holy fuck, her mother must've known something was up from the smell of this room.

Hopefully not, though.

I turned on their television and flipped through the few channels they had. Until finally, I settled on a movie just starting. It looked like a sappy romance movie. One of those kinds of movies where women cried at the end. But I didn't give a shit. So long as I got to stay with Rae, I was happy.

"Pizza's ordered. What'd you find?"

I tossed the remote control to her. "Just this romance movie, I think."

"Oh, no. Not that one. I'd rather watch the news."

I snickered. "Then, by all means, find something else."

She flipped through the channels for a while before rushing up the stairs. I heard her thundering around and my brow furrowed deeply. Until she came jumping down the stairs with DVDs in her arms. She sprawled them out on the floor for me to take in, then yanked me down to the floor with her.

"Here, take your pick."

I glanced at the titles. "These are all action movies."

Rae paused. "And?"

"You don't want to watch something more…?"

She snickered. "Girly? What? Girls can't like action movies, too?"

Fucking hell, I love you. "The Expendables, then. Definitely."

"Ugh, I love these movies. I hope they make a third one. Really."

"We can watch both of them tonight, if you want."

"Yes!"

The way she hissed with delight pulled a smile across my face. One that made my cheeks ache. I went and sat on the other couch in the room, the love sofa, so I could cuddle Rae close to me. She started up the movie and flopped down, pouring her legs over my lap. And as our hands found one another's, our fingers laced together.

It felt good, being back together with her.

"Thank you," I said.

"For what?"

"For fighting with me through all this."

She giggled. "You aren't getting rid of me that easily."

"Most days, I feel like you're the only reliable thing I have in my life. And I'm scared of fucking that up."

"Well, try not breaking up with me this time around. That might help."

I chuckled. "Yeah. I'll try that tactic this time."

I felt her staring at me and I turned my head.

"What?"

She smiled softly. "Say more sweet things."

My thumb stroked her skin softly. "You're amazing."

"Again."

"You're the best thing that's ever happened to me."

"Again."

"There isn't a night that's gone by that you haven't been in my dreams."

Her eyes welled with tears. "One more time, please."

I brought her hand to my lips to kiss. "I feel bad for people who don't have something like this."

And when she smiled, it filled my heart with sunlight.

"Me, too, Clint. I feel bad for them, too."

The ringing of her doorbell severed our moment. But it brought along a completely different moment. A set of moments forever seared into my memory. One where we gorged ourselves on pizza and rooted on the good guys in the movie. One where we watched back-to-back movies with full stomachs and barely-opened eyes. One where Rae tugged me upstairs, insisting that I stay the night with her in her bed.

Making memories I knew I'd never forget as I stripped her body down, kissed every valley she had to offer, and made love to her until we both passed out from exhaustion.

20

RAELYNN

My eyes fell open and, for once, my chest didn't hurt. My eyes weren't sore. My legs weren't trembling with exhaustion. I felt something warm draped over my waist and I sighed with relief, seeing Clint's hand splayed over my bare stomach. I reached for my cell phone slowly, not wanting to disturb him and the soft breaths that fell against the shell of my ear. And as I gazed at the time, I quickly navigated my phone to turn my alarm off.

Before it started blaring and woke him up.

"Mm-mm. Come here."

I giggled as he pulled me close.

"We have to get up soon, handsome."

"Mm-mm. No."

He buried his face into my hair and I smiled broadly. I slowly turned around, abandoning my cell phone for one last glance of his sleepy face. He peeked out of one eye before screwing it shut tight. I kissed his forehead. Then the tip of his nose. And finally, both of his cheeks.

"It's Tuesday morning. We can't skip school."

He groaned playfully. "I've been skipping school for days."

"Which is why you need to get up with me and come to school."

"I don't have a change of clothes."

"Are the ones you have dirty?"

"If I say 'yes,' will that get me out of school?"

I snickered. "You're insane, you know that?"

"And you're too comfy for your own good."

He buried his face into my breasts and held me close. I laughed softly as I stroked my fingertips through his hair. As I stared up at the ceiling, I felt life falling back into place again, my anger dissipating, my frustrations melting away. He kissed my skin mindlessly, allowing his leg to slip between mine. He trapped me underneath his body, pinning me to the mattress.

"I know what you're doing, Clint."

He slid on top of me. "No moving."

I wrapped my arms around him. "Clint."

"Just five more minutes of this."

"We don't have long as it is. School starts in an hour."

"It won't take me but about twenty minutes to get ready."

I scoffed playfully. "And what about me?"

He kissed my neck. "What about you?"

"What if it takes me longer than twenty minutes to get ready?"

He rose his head up. "Does it?"

"I mean, no. But that's not the point."

He snickered. "You're amazing to wake up to."

He kissed me, and I didn't even mind his morning breath. The sun shone through my window and my heart felt fuller than it had in, well, what seemed like forever. I wrapped my arms around him and let him slide between my legs. My hips ached in all the right ways and my body felt as if it had been run over by an eighteen-wheeler.

And yet I let him slide into me.

I gasped. "We have to be quiet."

He kissed my nose. "I know."

"Clint, I don't know if—oh."

And when he captured my lips, he swallowed my sounds.

Slowly, deftly, he rolled against me, pulling us both out of our hazy stupors. He swallowed my moans and I held on to his groans. My hands slid down his back as his skin prickled underneath my touch. I'd never get used to waking up to him like this. It would always be a treat. Feeling him fill me would always be a surprise encounter I hoped would never end.

He moved so easily my bed didn't even rock. He ground his tightly-wound curls against my body, shivering me to ecstatic heights. I kissed him, sucking on his lower lip. I relished how he felt first thing in the morning. I wanted to always experience this. Him. Inside me. Slowly waking us both up.

Whatever I had to do in my future to get that, I would.

Because Clint was my future.

We climbed up the precipice before throwing ourselves over the edge. And as he collapsed against me, I felt him filling me. Time and time again. His body quivered as I clung to him. I locked my legs around him, refusing to let him move. He growled against the crook of my neck, kissing and nibbling my collarbone. And once our bodies stopped shaking, I sighed with relief.

"We really do have to go to school, Clint."

He groaned. "You really know how to ruin a moment."

I giggled, kissing the side of his face. "Come on. Up, up, up."

"I don't want to go to school."

"You sound like a toddler. Get up and let's go."

"You're so mean, stupidhead."

His pouting voice made me laugh out loud.

"Come on, now. Don't make me scold you like a child."

He harrumphed like a toddler and I fell apart in laughter.

"Quit being the lazy son of a bitch you've turned into and get your ass to school."

He scoffed. "Wow, Mom. So harsh."

I smiled. "I know. But sometimes, you test me."

He cupped my cheeks and captured my lips. He rolled me on top of him and it took all I had to wiggle away from his grasp. I knew if he kept distracting me, touching me, and sliding between my legs, I'd stay there. All day. Enjoying him and feeling him as our bodies writhed together.

And we really needed to get to school.

I stood up. "Come on. School will help us get our minds off things."

He grinned. "You take my mind off things."

"It's not working, Clint. I'm not coming back to bed."

"Oh, really? Not if I… do this?"

He wrapped his arms around my waist and I clapped my hand against my mouth. I cried out into my palm as he picked me up and tossed me back onto the bed. I turned over and tried to scramble off the bed before he fell on top of me. But I didn't move fast enough and his body pinned me to the mattress.

Giggles fell from my lips. "I'm in the wet spot. I'm in the wet spot."

Clint kissed the back of my neck. "Should've thought about that before telling me no."

"Clint! We're going to be late."

"And if you keep yelling my name, you're going to wake up Mother Dear."

He tickled my sides and I pressed my face into my mattress. I wiggled around, trying to buck him off as laughter made my voice hoarse. I felt myself sweating. Growing red in the face. And if we didn't get a move on it, we'd both be late.

"Clint! Mercy! Uncle! I give!"

He chuckled. "Ready to give up and spend all day gazing into one another's eyes in bed?"

I sighed. "We really have to go to school. We have

to get you graduated. Your future depends on it, if you want a decent one."

Reality crashed back down around us and Clint wiggled off my body. He helped me to my feet and I turned around, readying myself to apologize. But he pressed his finger against my lips, silencing any plea I might have had. And as his hand slid through my knotted hair, his eyes danced between mine.

"I know you're right. I also want you to know how much I cherish these moments we have together."

I smiled. "Well, because of your antics, I now need a quick shower."

He grinned. "So do I."

"Care to take one together?"

"Do we have time for a distraction?"

"No, we don't. Because you spent it tickling me."

"Damn."

I swatted his chest playfully. "Consider it a lesson learned, then. Come on. We have to be quiet. Mom's still snoring, but she won't be for long."

Clint paused. "Wait, you can hear her snoring?"

My face fell and I walked over to the door. I felt him watch me, his eyes on my naked hips as they swayed. I cracked the door open and let the bombastic sound fill the room. I mean, my mother was sawing some fucking logs in her sleep. Pulling the damn curtains in from downstairs. I grinned as I watched Clint's eyes widen. But we didn't have any time to waste. I nodded my head down the hallway, motioning for him to follow me. And quickly, we crept down the hallway, making it into the bathroom with nothing but the sound of Mom's snores following us.

Then we hopped into a hot-ass shower.

Clint's hands wandered, but he didn't try to distract me. He washed me down like he had last night, taking great care with my inner thighs. I narrowed my eyes at him. I silently scolded him as he slipped to his knees. He kissed random parts of my body, causing my skin to flush as my eyes slowly closed.

Teasing me. Relentlessly.

A few minutes before we needed to start getting dressed.

"Clint."

He chuckled. "Just giving you a taste of what you could have had."

I moaned. "Please, we have to go—"

"I know. I know. We do. I know."

He punctuated his sentences with kisses, though. Against my hips. Inside my thighs. Against my lips.

My lower lips, at least.

I gripped his hair and pulled him up from his knees. I crashed our lips together, seeking some sort of a release. I needed it. I couldn't go to school like this. But I'd have to. I got out of the shower without washing Clint down. I wouldn't be able to touch him without forcing him back between my legs. He chuckled as he washed himself down, and I stewed in my frustration as I dried myself off.

It was good frustration, though.

Frustration I couldn't wait to relieve after the day was done.

Clint hopped out of the shower and I handed him a towel. He dried himself off and we crept back down the hallway, greeted with the sounds of my mother's awful snoring. How any man slept beside her with that nonsense was beyond me. And together, we quickly got dressed. I slipped my phone into my back pocket, threw my hair up into a ponytail, slipped my backpack over my shoulders and led Clint down the hallway, trying to maneuver around the creaky steps. I didn't want to risk waking my mother up. I didn't want to deal with any of her bullshit on such a perfect morning. After such a perfect evening.

With the boy I adored.

"Come on. We can still find Allison and Michael. If they're waiting for me."

He paused. "What do you mean 'if'?"

I sighed. "It's a long story."

His fingers threaded through mine. "Care to fill me in on the punchline?"

"They're together now and can't keep their hands off one another."

"Ah, the honeymoon stage. I like that stage."

I snickered. "I know you do."

"I mean, good for them. They seem like a cute couple. I take it they've kind of… set you off to the side, though?"

I shrugged. "I mean, I get it. Just kind of came at a shit time. Them making out all the damn time while I'm nursing a broken heart."

He kissed the back of my hand. "Well, no more of those."

"Promise?"

He kissed my cheek. "I promise with all I am."

I smiled. "Good."

"Is that Clint!?"

Allison's squeal made me smile.

"Guess they're waiting this morning," I said.

Michael waved at us. "Hey! Clint! Good to see you, man."

Clint squeezed my hand. "You think he's serious?"

I nodded. "I think Michael's loosened up a *lot* since he and Allison started officially dating."

Allison came running at me and I wrapped my arms around her in a massive hug. Part of me was still hurt, but the bulk of me was simply happy to have my friend back. I saw Michael walk up and give Clint a pat on the back. One of those dude hugs I saw around school. Allison released me and wrapped her arms around Clint's waist. And I saw a look of jealousy flash behind Michael's eyes. It was cute, really. How protective he'd become of her.

Clint made sure to do nothing but pat Allison's back, though.

"Good to see you, Mike. Aly. How you guys been?"

Allison pulled away. "Oh, my gosh. We have so much to catch you up on."

Clint grinned. "Like how you two are an item?"

Allison smacked her lips. "You told him already?"

My eyebrows rose. "Was I not supposed to?"

Michael grinned. "She wanted to tell him. Well, she wants to tell everybody. I'm assuming that also included Clint."

Allison nodded. "If he ever got his butt back to school. Really, it's good to see you."

Clint smiled. "It's good to see you two as well. And I'm happy for you guys. Congrats."

Michael clapped his back again. "Thanks, man."

Silence fell around us before Clint sighed.

"So I take it you guys know?"

I looked up at him. "They don't know everything."

Michael cleared his throat. "You know where you're moving to?"

Clint snickered. "Who said my father wants me moving with him?"

Allison sighed. "Oh, Clint. Really?"

He nodded slowly. "Really."

Michael's face fell. "Well, we've got an extra room at my place. My parents can fix you up. You can stay there until graduation. You know, finish out the school year and everything."

Clint shook his head. "I don't wanna put you and your family out."

Allison furrowed her brow. "Who said you are? I mean, you have to graduate. With us, you know?"

I linked my arm within his and looked up at him.

"Think about it, at least? Michael's parents are really nice. You'd like them."

Clint looked down at me. "You sure about that? My own father doesn't even like me."

Michael put his hand on Clint's shoulder. "I'm sure. You take my word for it. All you do is let me know, and I'll have it fixed up for you. Okay? If you need a place to stay, I've got you."

Clint sighed. "Why, though?"

Allison shrugged. "Because that's what friends do."

Michael nodded. "Yep. It's what friends do for one another. Though, if you break Rae's heart again, we're going to have to have a talk."

Allison's face fell. "No hurting my best friend again. Got it?"

Clint grinned. "I read you loud and clear."

Michael smiled. "Good. Now, let's get the hell out of Dodge before we're all late for class."

21

CLINTON

Aly linked her arm with Mike. "So I can help you get caught up in the classes we have. I mean, other than history. Out of all the subjects, I'm terrible at history. And Rae's great with dates."

Mike nodded. "Yep. I'll shoot my dad a text during class changes to see about you staying in the guest bedroom. I'll just let him know your parents are moving and you need a place to crash to get to and from school."

"Oh, oh! I can get you notes as well in your classes. I'm sure I know someone that can photocopy things for me. I'll get you copies so you don't have to worry about it."

"And you can ride with me to and from school. Since I'm assuming you haven't replaced your bike or anything."

"Are you going to replace your bike? I don't know if I could, after what you've been through."

"You're going to need some money, too. I mean, unless you've already got that worked out."

I paused. "Actually, I do. But that puts me in a bind."

Aly furrowed her brow. "Why?"

Rae gasped. "Oh, shit."

I rubbed her back. "It's okay. It's fine. Let's just get to school and we can figure it out."

Mike started walking. "What puts you in a bind? What's going on?"

I sighed. "I need to check something first. Hold on."

Him mentioning money reminded me of that damn bank account. As we continued walking toward school, I pulled out my phone, checked my email notifications and smiled. I went and checked my current bank account and laughed when I saw an account balance of zero. I threw my fists into the air and Rae started clapping. Then, she leapt at me and wrapped me up in a massive hug.

Leaving Aly and Mike in confusion.

"Yes! Yes! This is a great step in the right direction."

I snickered. "If only I had time to get to the bank."

Rae shook her head. "No, no. No focusing on the negative for now. Promise me."

I grinned. "I promise."

Mike paused the walk. "Someone want to fill us in now?"

Aly nodded. "Yeah. I want to celebrate with you guys, too."

I sighed. "So, this whole thing with selling the house? It's kind of a backlash from my father. You know, from what happened. I take it you told Aly?"

Mike nodded. "I told her some of it, yeah."

"Yeah. He's doing it out of spite. Because he's not in control anymore and that pisses him off. He's told my stepmother she's moving with him, but I'm not welcome. So I've been scrambling for money."

Aly held up her hand. "Wait a second. He actually told you that you can't go with him?"

Rae scoffed. "Yeah. It's been a massive thing. He's an absolute asshole."

Mike murmured. "You can say that again."

I held my hand up. "Anyway, long story short? I'm selling things off I have a right to in order to pick up some money. The good news is that I sold off a lot yesterday. But I haven't been able to get to a bank yet."

Mike narrowed his eyes. "So you have that money on you right now?"

Rae nodded. "He does, yeah."

Aly shook her head. "Do you have a bank account you can put it in?"

I smiled. "That's why Rae and I are celebrating. I opened up my own bank account that my father can't touch and transferred everything from my old account to my new one."

Mike patted my back. "Dude, that's awesome. But keep that money stowed away in your locker. You know, in case something happens at school today. And after classes I'll get you to a bank so you can deposit it."

"That means more to me than you realize. Thanks, Mike."

He squeezed my shoulder. "Anything I can do to help, you just let me know."

I felt loved again, like I had friends again. I didn't know what the fuck I did to deserve these people in my life. But I was determined not to fuck it up again. We all rushed into school and the girls darted off to go to homeroom. And Mike? Well, he did exactly as he said he would. He escorted me to my locker and stood guard while I stashed the wads of cash I had on my person. I placed it under a stack of books and shoved it all the way back. I piled some shit in front of it before grabbing my books. Then I slammed my locker closed and booked it to homeroom, getting there just before the late bell rang.

And as I dropped into my seat, I felt all eyes on me.

Even though people kept giving me funny looks, it felt good for things to be returning to normal. Well, not really normal. But a sort-of-kind-of normal. School felt familiar. Mike and Aly felt familiar. Rae felt very familiar. And I needed familiar in my life right now. I needed something I could count on. Depend on. Lean on.

Even if that 'something' was school.

The one thing on this planet I hated more than my own father.

My phone kept vibrating in class, so I turned it on silent. But the vibrations were good. People were snatching up these things I was selling left and right. If I could get Mike to drop me off at my house, I had the potential to make another seven grand before tonight was over. That had me smiling all throughout the morning. I had a pep in my step and slowly, things felt less and less overwhelming. I had money in a bank account my father couldn't touch. I had a little over fifteen grand in checks and cash in my locker, waiting to be deposited. And if I could get my hands on one last decent sale, I'd be set for a while.

At least, until I got back on my feet again after graduation.

I liked this kind of normal. The kind where Mike waved at me in the hallways and Rae rushed up to kiss me between classes. Roy and Marina weren't aimlessly laughing at stupid jokes and trying to rile me up over dumb, useless shit. This reality was much better. I had friends that gave a shit. I had my girl back. I had money coming in to help me once my father abandoned me for good.

And this time, I wouldn't fuck it up.

Or let someone else fuck it up, either.

I'm all in, Rae. One hundred percent.

The bell for lunch rang and I rushed to the cafeteria. I found Mike already sitting down with his food tray while Aly unpacked their lunchbox. I waved at them before hopping in the food line, finding myself standing behind Rae. I tapped her on the shoulder and she turned around. And very quickly, I captured her lips.

"Mmm, hello there."

I grinned. "Hey, beautiful."

"Ahem."

The lunch lady cleared her throat and she blushed. Which pulled a smile across my cheeks. We walked through the line and got our lunch. I even had the cashier charge Rae's lunch to my account. Despite her protests, I did it anyway, winking at her as we picked up our trays. We walked over to were Mike and Aly were already cuddled up, smiling as they gazed into each other's eyes.

As I sat my tray down, I leaned over to whisper in Rae's ear. "Is that what we look like?"

She shrugged. "I don't know. But if it is, I don't mind it one bit."

I smiled. "Neither do I."

I kissed the top of her head before we sat down with them. Mike and Aly paid us no mind. Which didn't bother me one bit. They deserved some time with one another, just like Rae deserved some time with me. So as I picked at my pathetic hamburger, I turned my attention to the beautiful girl sitting next to me.

"So are you free tonight?"

Rae sighed dramatically. "No, I have to work."

I quirked an eyebrow. "You sound overly thrilled at the idea."

"Really? Should I try that sigh again?"

And before I could stop her, she sighed and leaned against me. She placed the back of her hand against her forehead, causing me to chuckle. Wrapping my arm around her, I kissed the top of her head again. I breathed in the smell of her conditioner, letting it pull me back to the memories of last night. This morning.

Memories of having her whenever I wanted her and making love to her every waking moment she'd let me.

I held her close as she rested her head against my shoulder.

"I wish I was free, though. I'm having to close again tonight."

I nodded softly. "Well, that's all right. I'll come visit you."

"Yeah?"

"Yeah. I'll get a taxi or something. We can go get a milkshake afterward at the diner up the road from where you work."

"Mmm, that sounds like heaven."

I smiled. "Only if you're there, though."

I closed my eyes and let myself slip into another world. Another place. Another time. Where nothing existed except Rae and me, trying to make a way for ourselves in the world. I wanted her by my side. Always. Now more than ever, I understood how much I needed her. She was my rock. My shelter. My safe place to fall. The one person I felt I could be weak with and not be judged for it.

I needed her in my life for as long as she'd stick around.

Mike sighed. "So how are classes going for you two?"

I snickered. "As good as they can for now. I'm completely lost in them, though. It'll take me some time to catch back up."

Rae kissed my chest. "Don't worry. We'll help."

Aly smiled brightly. "Yep! Study sessions at my

place in the basement. We have all the good snacks, too."

Mike nodded. "They really do. I'm jealous. My parents are health freaks. You'll have to watch out for that."

I shrugged. "I can go and buy myself some ice cream and chips whenever I need them. That's not an issue. And with this stuff I'm selling off, I can help with—"

"Oh! That reminds me! I sent the text off to my dad and he said he wanted to talk with Mom before they made a decision. But he also said it shouldn't be an issue. I should know by the end of the day today. We can talk about it while I take you to the bank."

I nodded. "It's appreciated more than you realize. Seriously."

Aly leaned against Mike. "It's really not a problem. We just wish you would've talked to us sooner."

Rae nudged me. "Yeah, Clint. You should've talked to us sooner."

"Yeah, Clint. You should've talked to us sooner."

The mocking voice made me swivel around, although I already knew who it was. I'd never forget the voice of Marina. That piercing, tinny, Valley girl voice. There she was, chomping on that banana like she was sucking down Roy's dick. I eyed her closely before I looked over at Roy, watching him practically hover over the four of us.

"Enjoying lunch, losers?"

I shrugged. "Of course. Are you?"

Marina snickered. "We always enjoy lunch until you assholes show up."

Aly rolled her eyes. "Nice one, Marina."

Mike nodded. "Yep. Very creative. A-plus for effort."

Marina glared at them. "At least I'm not a pathetic loser that goes around helping charity cases just to feel better about myself."

Rae cleared her throat. "I'm sorry. Do you mean 'charity cases' as in us? Or 'charity cases' as in you? Because I'm pretty sure the two of you can't be helped."

Marina jumped at Rae and she stood out of her chair. Like lightning. I'd never seen her move so quickly, and I shot up from my own seat to step in front of her. To shield her from the nonsense of the crew I used to run these halls with. I stared Roy down, refusing to look over at Marina. Because I didn't believe in intimidating a girl, no matter how much I figured she deserved it.

"What? The two of you are back together now? Rumor had it you dumped her for another piece of ass."

Marina grinned. "Yeah. People are talking about how you're fucking your stepmom now. That how you roll over there in the Clarke household? Fucking family members."

Rae growled. "I'll claw your damn eyes out."

Marina stepped forward. "You want to try that statement again?"

I moved with her and felt her shove me in the

chest. I slowly looked over at Roy, but all he did was fold his arms over his chest.

"What? You got your girl fighting your fights now?"

He smiled wickedly. "She can handle her own. Question is, can you?"

I nodded slowly. "I don't swing at girls. I'm better than that. Rae won't hesitate, though. And I wonder who's going to win in a battle of women? The one who knows how to fight, or the one who tips over in her own heels?"

Roy shoved Marina out of the way in order to stand toe to toe with me.

"You think you can come into this cafeteria and stand up to me? Huh? After fucking around with pathetic assholes like these three? You think you can still rule this school and get away with bullshit like that? With abandoning the only friends you could count on?"

I grinned. "You really thought you were my friend?"

He shoved my chest. "You deserve everything your father fucking hands you."

My eye twitched. "And I've had about enough of your shit, Roy."

22

RAELYNN

I rubbed Clint's chest. "Hey, hey. It's not worth it. They're not worth it."

I saw his nostrils flaring, and I knew he was only half paying attention to me. I had to calm him down. The teachers weren't in the cafeteria yet, but they would be soon. And the last thing Clint needed was to get expelled just as he'd gotten back into the groove of things here. We needed to get him graduated, and this wasn't the way to do it.

"Clint. Listen to me."

Roy snickered. "Yeah, Clint. Listen to her."

I eyed him hotly. "You shut the hell up before I punch you myself."

Marina jumped in front of him. "You lay one hand on my man and I'll—"

Allison's voice came from behind me. "Or you'll what, you snide little bitch?"

My jaw fell open and I whipped my head around.

Michael laughed as he rubbed her back, and Clint started chuckling. I smiled and winked at her, then turned my attention back to the two goons in front of us. And I noticed something.

None of the other guys from the table across the cafeteria had joined them. They all just sat and watched. With smirks on their faces before rolling their eyes and turning their backs.

Seemed as if Roy and Marina were losing their position with those assholes as well. So I decided to use that to my advantage.

"You know, I figured more of your friends would be here to back you up."

Roy grinned. "I know what you're trying to do. And trust me, they're backing us up."

I shrugged. "Then where are they?"

Michael piped up, "You know, other than sitting over there and not paying one bit of attention to what you're doing over here."

When Marina and Roy looked over, I saw their faces falter. Their confident, cocky smiles slowly begin to fade. I looked up at Clint, ready to relish the victory. Because we might actually get out of this without some sort of a fight.

But the look on his face hadn't changed. His nostrils still flared with anger, his shoulders rolled back. He was still on guard. Still watching, waiting for something to break out. I hated seeing him so riled up like this. I rubbed his arm and moved it to his chest. I patted his heartbeat softly, trying to talk him down from his heady high.

It didn't work.

Roy snickered. "Anyway, now that the distraction's over—"

Marina smiled wickedly. "Want to settle this? Woman to woman?"

I rolled my eyes. "When you show me a woman, sure."

"What did you say?"

She lunged at me and Clint stepped in front of me again. She started beating her fists against his chest, but he didn't move. Roy stood behind his girl like a fucking coward, letting her wail on my man. But, even though Clint's fists were gripped tight, he didn't swing one punch.

He simply let her get it out of her system before she backed away.

"Yeah. And that'll be your girl's face if she ever talks to me that way again."

Clint shook his head. "You won't touch Rae."

Roy narrowed his eyes. "You threatening my girl?"

I snickered. "No. He's not. He's simply telling you Marina won't touch me without consequences."

Roy licked his lips. "And what kind of consequences are those?"

Clint sighed. "The kind of consequences that get you both expelled and thrown in jail for all the underage drinking parties you throw."

Marina hissed. "You mean the parties you helped us throw? The parties you got drunk at? The parties where you hooked up with random bitches and boasted about it later? Yeah? Those parties, you damn drunk?"

Michael came to my side. "Doesn't matter what he did in his past, so long as he's moved past it."

Allison came up to Clint's other side. "Yeah. We don't care about that stuff. We only care about what he does now."

I nodded. "Which is why you two aren't worth it. Clint, they aren't worth it. Let's just sit back down, okay?"

I looked up at him, hoping he had relaxed. But he hadn't.

"I'm good. I'll sit down once they leave."

I tried to tug him into the seat, but he shrugged off my touch. He looked down at me and winked, but it didn't provide me with any solace. I didn't like where this was going. I just wanted everyone to go back to their respective places so we could eat and get the hell back to class.

Roy snickered. "You got something to say, asshole, then say it."

Clint nodded. "Fine. I will. I'm tired of you and Marina pushing me around. Pushing us around. I'm tired of you thinking you're a big shot when the only reason you got into your position is because I took pity on you. Befriended you when I didn't have anyone else. It's time someone taught you a lesson. It's time you were reminded of who's better with their fists."

"Oh, you want a fight. Is that it?"

I placed my hand on his chest. "Clint, don't do this."

He shook his head. "I don't want a fight. But, sometimes, that's the only way people listen. Getting the ever-loving shit beat out of them. If that's what it takes for you to get the picture, then I'm all for it."

Marina stood behind Roy. "Get him, baby. Break that fucking jaw of his."

Roy put up his fists. "Fine, then. Come on. Hit me."

Clint shrugged. "You first."

Roy didn't hesitate. He swung at Clint and he shoved me out of the way. Michael caught me and pulled me away from the scene as I watched it unfold. Allison ducked and Michael rushed for her, clamoring over the lunch table to get to her. He picked her up and climbed back across the table as Clint caught Roy's fist mid-swing and twisted his arm. He backed Roy against the wall. Marina cried out and whipped around, looking for some sort of support for Roy.

But everyone at their table kept their backs turned.

"Someone help him! Where the fuck are you guys!?"

Her cries echoed across the cafeteria and I saw students turning our way. With each punch Roy threw, Clint caught them. Not once did that asshole land a punch. Clint brought his knee up into Roy's gut and took him to his knees. The stupid boy heaved for air as Marina fell down beside him. Clint hovered over them, a dark look on his face. Not once had he swung a punch, though. All he did was warn. And promise.

Then he made good on that promise.

Roy pushed Marina away again and lunged at

Clint. He shoved Clint down, back first, onto the table. Into the food we had just purchased. I reached for Clint, wanting to pull him away. But Michael held me back.

"He's got this. He knows what he's doing. Let the teachers see him defending himself."

My eyes widened as Roy's fist came up in the air. I cried out Clint's name, watching as he caught it. He rolled Roy over and straddled him, pinning the boy's hands to the table. Then, Marina came up behind him and gripped his shirt.

And my vision dripped red.

"Oh, no you don't."

I tore away from Michael's grip and rushed toward Marina. I wrapped my arms around her and picked her up, moving her away from Clint. I set her down on her feet and glared at her, and she cocked her hand back to slap me. But out of nowhere came Allison, who jammed her heel down into Marina's toe. Marina bent over and grabbed her foot.

I grinned. "Good one."

Allison frowned. "We have to get out of here. The teachers are coming."

By the time I got back to the table, I saw Roy's elbow come up into Clint's jaw. He stumbled back into the wall and Roy pushed himself off the table, heading straight for Clint. His fist connected with Clint's jaw. Clint wrapped his hand around Roy's throat, and just as Clint pushed him away, teachers came around the corner.

"Clarke! Emerson! Principal's office, now!"

Teachers pushed us out of the way and wrapped their arms around the boys. Roy kept clamoring for Clint, cursing and yelling as Clint backed away. He didn't fight the teachers or try to pull out of their grasp. Roy, on the other hand, bucked and kicked and cursed like a toddler not wanting to go into time out.

It was pathetic to watch.

Even though Clint had come out on top, it also looked as if he'd started the fight. I knew damn good and well those teachers hadn't seen Roy attack him. And I wasn't sure how all of this would go down. I saw them haul Clint down the hallway toward the principal's office. He peered over his shoulder at me and winked again. Like he somehow had everything under control. I went to walk after him, but both Michael and Allison grabbed me, wrapping their hands around my wrists and pulling me back as teachers hauled a kicking and screaming Roy out of the cafeteria.

With Marina in tears, following behind them.

"I have to go after him."

Michael sighed. "Let the teachers sort it out."

Allison stroked my arm. "Yeah. You know the principal will get to the bottom of it. He knows Clint's trying to turn over a new leaf."

I pulled out of their grips. "You know they'll throw Clint under the bus in a heartbeat."

Michael nodded. "Yes. But there are plenty of people here who will say Roy started that fight. Not Clint."

Allison smiled softly. "Yeah, it'll be okay. Plus, there's us who can attest to that, too."

I sighed as I turned back to the entrance of the cafeteria.

"I don't know, guys."

They rubbed my back, but I felt more over-whelmed than ever. I couldn't fucking catch a break. Every time I made a step forward in my life, two steps were taken away from me. For all I knew, this would lead to Clint's suspension. Or expulsion. And we'd all be back at square one. Me, with my broken heart. Clint, dealing with shit at home by himself. And us, graduating without our newfound friend.

I hate this so much. "Why does he have to be like that all the time?"

Michael patted my shoulder. "What do you mean?"

I shrugged. "I just—why did he have to egg Roy on like that? Why did he have to instigate things?"

Allison took my hand. "I have to say, I'm with Clint on this one."

I furrowed my brow. "What?"

Michael squeezed my shoulder. "Me, too."

I paused. "Wait, what?"

Allison giggled. "You see a fight. You see Clint slipping back into his old ways. But if there was ever a fight to engage in, that was the one."

I shook my head. "I don't get it."

Michael snickered. "Of course you don't. He was standing up for you, Rae. That asshole had it coming. And Marina, too. I'm sure it felt good for Clint to blow off a little steam and to be the bigger person in the process."

I rolled my eyes. "Fighting doesn't make anyone the bigger person. It makes them a bigger target."

Allison came into my vision. "Even when he's standing up for his girl?"

Michael rubbed my back. "Even when he's big enough to defend himself and not start the fight in the process?"

I shrugged. "I don't know. I don't know anymore. All I know if that if this fight leads to him getting suspended—or worse—we're right back to where we started."

Allison paused. "How do you figure?"

I cracked my neck. "I mean, think about it. He'll be back home dealing with this shit by himself. Caught up in his father's whirlwind instead of here, where he should be, trying to graduate. He can't make a life for himself without a degree. And once we graduate, who in the world is going to help him do that? Because I don't know about you, but I don't see anyone else jumping up to defend him or help him. Do you?"

And when they both fell silent, I knew I had them.

"That's why I'm scared right now, guys. Because if we graduate without Clint, he doesn't stand a chance."

23

CLINTON

I picked at my fingers and fidgeted in the principal's office. I kept stealing glances at Roy, who sat there with a holier-than-thou grin on his face. I still heard Marina crying outside. Like she'd somehow been wrapped up in all this. The little bitch. I wanted to stick my head out into the hallway and tell her to shut the hell up. The principal was calling all of our parents. First, Marina's. Then Roy's.

And when he hung up the phone, I slowly lifted my eyes.

"Please, sir. I didn't start this fight. There's no reason to call my father."

Roy snickered. "You start every fight you're in, Clarke."

The principal held up his hand. "Who started the fight and who didn't isn't my concern right now. Mr. Clarke, you're clearly not in any condition to be in school right now. By the looks of your nose and the accident we all know you've been in, you should be home. Resting."

Roy rolled his eyes. "Can I go now?"

The principal glared at him. "You can sit right there until your mother gets here. I just called her. Then you can explain to her how a boy who's just been in a life-threatening accident suddenly has a bruise on his jaw and across his face."

He stood from his chair. "I didn't do that to Clint's nose! It was probably his fucking father or some—"

The principal slowly stood. "Sit down and stop that language in my office. Now."

Roy flopped back down into the chair and I sighed. If that man called my father, he was sealing my fate. I'd never recover. I'd never recuperate. Because my father would beat me until I was dead. I drew in a deep breath and closed my eyes, trying to settle my heartrate. I thought of some way to try and get myself out of this. Anything that didn't force me to own up to what was happening in my own home.

Because if my father got arrested because of me? And he paid his way out?

He'd chase me to the ends of the earth if it meant retribution.

"Sir, please."

The principal held up his hand. "I'm sorry, Mr. Clarke. But you know the rules. No matter who throws the first punch, all parties are to be picked up so they can cool down. We can start fresh tomorrow. I'll make sure your teachers get your homework to you somehow."

I shook my head. "Sir, you don't understand. If you call my father—"

He blinked. "What happens if I call your father?"

I felt Roy grinning at me. Marina's crying stopped as footsteps came into the front office. I swallowed hard, watching as the principal leveled his eyes with mine. All I had to do was say it. Tell him these bruises were from my father. Tell him what he was doing. How my father was about to abandon me and never return.

But I was also eighteen. The hell was some principal going to do?

I sighed. "Can't you just trust me on this?"

The principal picked up his phone. "You know we don't compromise rules. It sets a dangerous precedent."

I wanted to strangle Roy when I heard him chuckling at my side.

His mother came and collected him as I sat there. No explanation of how I got my bruises. No having to grovel to his mother. She cooed at him and checked him over. Made sure he was all right before tossing me a disgusted look. I ignored it, though. I had larger worries on my plate.

Like the words coming out of the principal's mouth.

"I'm sorry, Mr. Clarke. But I'm going to need you to come pick up your son. Yes, sir. Immediately. A fight with another student. Though, one I'm not sure he— no, I'm not sure he start—Mr. Clarke, your son didn't start this fight. But he does have to be picked up from school. Yes. Uh huh. He'll be in my office."

It wouldn't matter, though. Not to my father. The

only thing that mattered was the word 'fight.' The fact that I was probably interrupting his day. I pulled out my cell phone and quickly started texting Rae. Spitting out everything I could before my father stormed through those doors.

"Mr. Clarke, you need to put your phone——"

I whipped my eyes up. "I've got things I need to take care of. Things that are beyond the scope of your reasoning and what I want to tell you. Now, you can either let me send a message to Rae so she can take care of it, or you can throw me out. But I'm not putting up my phone until I send this message. Are we clear?"

The principal sighed. "Tuck in that attitude."

"Let me send one message to make my life just a little easier, and it'll be put away."

My eyes fell back to my phone and my fingers flew across the screen. I didn't bother editing it. Because any second now, my father would walk into this office with steam pouring from his ears and I'd be dead.

Or, at least wish I were.

Me: Rae, I need something from you. The money, it's in Mike's locker. Make sure it stays safe until I can get to it. Dad's about to pick me up. It looks bad. I won't be here after school. Don't come check on me until you hear from me. I don't want you hurt. I'm sorry you have to deal with me all the time.

And just as the principal's door whipped open, I slid my phone back into my pocket.

I slowly turned around and saw my father's angry eyes. I swallowed hard as I stood up. I took one last look at the principal and I could've sworn I saw regret in his eyes. But it didn't matter now. The smoke blowing from my father's ears had nothing on the daggers flying from his glare. He watched me as I walked out the door, then left the principal's office without a second thought. The heat of his body worried me. The fact that he hadn't laid a hand on me yet only put me on edge. What would he do to me once we got home? Were we even going home?

I slipped into his car and neither of us spoke a word as he drove us back to the house.

He didn't say anything as we got out of the car and walked inside. Or even as he slammed the door behind him. Which gave my mind more than enough time to theorize what might happen next. I felt my body already crumbling. I didn't know if I'd be okay after this. I jumped when the door slammed shut. But dread filled my gut when I heard him flip the lock.

"You are a mystery to me, Clinton."

The growl of his voice kicked my body into over-drive. I whipped around, but not soon enough. His hand came down against my neck and he slammed me into the wall, pressing my cheek against the pristine white walls. I pressed my hands into the plaster, struggling to breathe as his fingertips closed down against my pulse points. Tears welled in my eyes, but I refused to give him the satisfaction of seeing me cry.

Although I felt the little boy within me screaming out for help.

"Did you really think I'd punish you for some stupid little fight? Hmm?"

He ripped me away from the wall and tossed me against the banister of the stairwell.

"Did you really think I'd let you get away with what you've done to me? To our lives? After that stunt you pulled last week?"

He fisted my shirt and pulled me up to his face, and my body fell limp. I didn't have the strength to fight him any longer. I didn't have the ability to push him away. I hurt in so many places. My muscles ached for death. My mind went blank and I found myself traveling to my happy place as my father's voice melted away into nothingness, growing further and further away the deeper I sank.

Like the river waters that almost swallowed me whole.

"Well, rest assured, Clinton, I don't give a flying fuck what you do at school. This is going to be for putting ideas into my wife's head. For trying to take her from me, you pointless little bastard. She's mine, and you will do nothing more with her. Do you understand?"

As he tossed me to the floor, I closed my eyes. And the last thing I remembered was his foot jammed into my lower back. I let the tears fall as my happy place swept me away. Back into the arms of Rae. I saw her face smiling at me, felt her lips pressing against my cheeks. Her soft fingertips brushed my tears away, making me smile. Making me feel better about things.

Making me feel loved.

"Come. Follow me."

Her voice filled my ears. Drowning out my father's

rage. I felt my body being tossed around, but I didn't register the pain. Only the intensity. Only the pressure. Like my body had been filled with morphine and was numb from head to toe. Rae took my hands and pulled me into a beautiful wildflower meadow. Fraught with colors that warmed my soul. Yellows and pinks and blues. Purples and reds and so much green. A sparkling lake with fish jumping out caught my eye. And as the wooded landscape backdropped all around the meadow, a cabin magically appeared.

A cabin, in the middle of a meadow, situated on a crystal clear lake. A massive three-story behemoth, with a wrap-around porch. It was gorgeous. It called to me as Rae pulled me closer. She pulled me past the lake. Past the fish that called to my fingertips. To my hungry stomach. She pulled me up the porch steps and inside, showing me its glorious majesty.

And it left me stunned.

"Welcome home, handsome."

Rae kissed my cheek, and I knew this had to be heaven. She threaded her fingers within mine and guided me through the cabin. The massive kitchen with marble countertops. The roaring fireplace with microfiber furniture, ready for me to flop against. She walked me up the stairs, showing me the bedrooms. The bathrooms. The hallways and the library.

Until finally she stopped at what looked like an office.

"What is this place, Rae?"

She giggled. "You've been gone too long, sweetheart. I take it the book tour went well?"

I paused. "Book tour?"

"Yeah. For your latest novel. Are you feeling all right?"

I blinked. "Yes. No. I'm fine. Sorry. I guess I have been away too long."

"You got any ideas for your next book? Or are you taking some time off to hunt?"

"To hunt."

"Yeah. And fish! Though, if you ask me, we don't have anywhere else to put any more meat. The deep freezer in the basement's already full."

I stared at Rae, dumbfounded. I had no idea what the fuck she was talking about. And yet, I wanted to. It all sounded magical. Like utter perfection. Her, in this house that was clearly ours. With a lake to fish in and woods to hunt in and food to feed ourselves with and money from books I wrote to keep us afloat. I smiled as I wrapped her up in my arms. I walked her into the wall as her giggles filled the space around us. My lips pressed against hers and I drank her in. The sweet concoction of her tongue as it slid across the roof of my mouth.

"Mmm, I guess things did go well on this latest book tour."

I nodded softly. "And oh, how I missed you."

We sank to the floor of my office space and I kissed her body, peeling her clothes back and sucking marks against her skin that I wanted to see for the rest of my life. She scratched her nails along my back as I pounded into her, diving deeper into the life I wanted. The life I needed. The life that ripped me away from my current reality. The image shook from time to time, and I tried to keep it still. I lost myself in her curves and buried myself between her legs. I took her from room to room, marking the house with her scent as she fell weak against me.

And I found myself hoping to never wake up from this amazing dream.

Even if it killed me to stay there.

24

RAELYNN

Clint's text made me fucking sick. I couldn't concentrate for the rest of the time I was in classes. Allison and I went around to his teachers after school, explaining to them that he had a family emergency he was dealing with. That he needed his homework. Tests. Any reading assignments he might have missed. Pop quizzes he needed to take. The teachers seemed less inclined to work with him after today's little spat, and I wanted to slap them all. How dare they judge him when they didn't know shit about him?

Still, they gave us what we needed.

Michael jogged up to us. "All right. I've got the money out of his locker. I don't feel comfortable keeping it there. Should I take it and stash it at my place?"

I nodded. "If you could, please. I don't know when he's going to be able to get it, but I want it somewhere safe that isn't here until he can get back to it."

Allison swallowed hard. "Should we call the cops or something?"

I paused. "I honestly don't know."

Michael shook his head. "Have you heard from him at all since that text?"

I closed my eyes. "No, I haven't. And I have to work tonight. So I can't drop by."

Allison put her hand on my shoulder. "Michael and I can just do a drive-by, if that makes you feel better."

Michael piped up. "And if you want to give me his number, I can call him. You know, keep at it until he picks up."

I drew in a deep breath. "I'm really hoping he makes good on his word. He said he'd come by after I was done working and we'd get a milkshake or something tonight. If he doesn't come by, I might need a ride home."

Michael hugged me. "Consider it done. Just call, okay?"

I opened my eyes. "Please tell me everything's going to be all right."

Allison rubbed my back. "One way or another, we're all getting out of this. I promise."

After coming up with a plan, I headed back to my house. Michael had his money, Allison had his homework, and I had the task of trying to get Clint on the phone. But it wasn't any use. Every time I called him, his phone went to voicemail. Every text I sent went unanswered. I stood in front of the small mirror on the wall of my room, trying not to cry. I wanted to put on a bit of makeup for work, make myself look more presentable, in case Clint did come around.

But I kept crying it off.

"For fuck's sake, come on."

I hissed at myself as I wiped at the mascara running down my face.

"Lip gloss. Lip gloss and some powder so my face isn't so red."

It would have to do, because I had to be at work within the hour.

Just as I swiped on a layer of lip gloss, I heard something crash downstairs. Mom started screaming and I heard D.J.'s voice rising above the commotion, which sent me running. I ripped my door open and made my way to the top of the steps. I heard them yelling at one another as more things crashed against the wall. I heard tears in Mom's eyes. I heard blood in D.J.'s voice. And as I turned the corner, heading for the kitchen, I saw a plate crash against the wall.

"D.J.! Stop!"

"Stop? Stop? You want me to stop when I hear my girl's been fucking other men around town?"

Mom sniffled. "D.J., please. Calm down so we can talk."

He roared. "I'm not calming down when I've just learned my girl is nothing but a fucking whore!"

I ducked as a glass went flying. Shards of the damn thing scattered all over the place as I shielded my head. Anger rushed through my veins. I wanted this man dead by the end of the night tonight. I saw my mother crouched down in a corner, her face in her hands while she sobbed. And D.J.? Well, he just kept destroying our stuff and yelling bloody murder. As if that might help things.

"How many men, huh? How many men did you let inside you?"

Mom sobbed. "I don't know. Please, it was just when we were broken up. I'd never cheat on you, D.J."

He snatched her arm. "Like hell you wouldn't. You already did! We never broke up. We just had fights. And we always made up."

"Let me go!"

"I'm not doing a damn thing you ask of me. You can't even keep your fucking pants on, you bitch."

"Stop!"

I came around the corner and picked up a glass filled with water. I chucked it at D.J.'s head and hit him square in the jaw with it. He released my mother and glared, lunging at me. But Mom threw herself at him and tackled him to the floor.

"You won't lay a finger on my daughter. Do you hear me?"

D.J. snickered. "And that's the issue. Like mother, like daughter. You're an ungrateful bitch, just like she is."

Mom screamed out as she raked her nails across D.J.'s face. I rushed over to her and pried her off his body, praying for all of this to stop. I couldn't take it any longer. The chaos. The confusion. The insanity. It would drain my next paycheck just to replace all this shit in the house he'd already broken.

Because God knows Mom couldn't afford it without D.J. funneling money into her purse.

"She's just as fucked up as you are, Lucy."

Mom shrieked. "Don't you talk about my daughter that way!"

I shook my head. "Mom. Stop. It isn't worth it."

D.J. grinned. "Yeah, Lucy. It's not worth it."

I pushed my mother behind me and leveled my eyes with the bullshit excuse of a man on the floor. He stood up and dusted himself off, but I saw his arm and the side of his face bleeding, where the little shards of glass he had splintered all over the ground had come to wreak havoc on his body. I snarled at him and picked up a knife off the kitchen table. He chuckled at me as his eyes fell to the dull instrument in my hand. Then he quirked an eyebrow.

"I have to admit, your mother wouldn't have the guts."

My eye twitched. "Get out, or I will."

Mom hissed. "Raelynn."

I held my hand up to her. "Get the hell out of this house and don't you ever come back."

D.J. grinned. "I take it you're not calling the police, then?"

I shook my head. "I never said that. I only said to get out. I'm more than willing to give you a headstart."

Mom panicked. "She's not calling. D.J., I promise she's not calling."

I rolled my eyes. Mom sounded pathetic, but I wasn't afraid of this loser. I hated him. Every ounce of him. And I didn't care if I had to carve his fucking eyes out with a spoon.

I'd do it just to get him out of our home.

D.J. chuckled. "Think your mom still loves me."

I nodded. "Maybe so. But she won't be getting back with you. Not this time. You've got five minutes before I call the police. Whether you're here, or there, it doesn't matter."

He narrowed his eyes. "You don't have the balls, kid."

I dropped the knife, reaching for my phone. "Want to bet?"

I felt my mother's hand around my wrist and I had to resist the urge to smack her. To push her down. Because she had endured enough of that in her life. Instead, I wrenched away from her grasp. Stepped away from her and held my finger against the red button on the front of my phone. D.J.'s eyes darted from my finger to my eyes. Again and again. Almost as if he were testing me.

Then I pressed it.

"No! Rae!"

D.J. backed up. "Fuck you both. I'm out."

"No, D.J. Come back. We can talk this out, please!"

"9-1-1, what's your emergency?"

I held the phone to my ear as Mom collapsed on the ground. She sobbed against the glass, not caring that it gouged her knees. Her shins. The palms of her hands. I stared at a carcass of my mother. Unlike the woman I used to know.

Or maybe the mother I thought I had never existed. And I simply grew up.

"Hello? Is anyone there?"

I sighed. "Yes. Hi. I'm not really sure if it's an emergency, but there's been some domestic issues at my house and I think my mother needs medical help."

"Sounds like an emergency to me. What's going on?"

"Her ex boyfriend stormed in and broke a lot of our things. Mom's bleeding from some glass shards. I also think she might need some mental help."

Mom slowly looked back at me, and the daggers she shot from her eyes were forever etched into my memory.

"Is the assailant still there?"

I shook my head. "No."

"Do you have a name for him?"

"D.J. I don't know his last name."

Mom snarled. "You hang up that phone now."

I licked my lips. "No, Mom. You need help."

"What was that?"

I cleared my throat. "Sorry. Are you ready for my address? I won't be here, I have to go to work and I can't be late. But I'll make sure someone keeps my mother here until you arrive."

I rattled off my address to the 9-1-1 operator. Then I hung up the phone. Mom picked herself up off the floor, but every time she dusted herself off, she created more cuts. My feet crunched over the glass as I wrapped her arm around my shoulders and guided her to the couch, easing her down. She refused to look at me as hot tears burned their way down her cheeks.

Then I spoke my own truth.

A truth I'd wanted to proclaim the last time she pulled this.

"Mom, I need you to stay here."

She snickered. "No, thanks."

I sighed. "I know you hate me now, but once you get the help you need—"

"I'm not fucking crazy, Raelynn."

"No, you're just depressed, anxious, and addicted to any man who will give you attention because you never healed from Dad leaving."

And when she didn't say anything, I brushed her hair back.

"You're going to stay here and wait for the paramedics to get here. They're going to offer you help and you're going to take it. Okay?"

She leaned into the couch, away from my touch. "And if I don't?"

I stood upright. "Then I'm moving in with Allison and never coming home."

She snickered. "So you'd leave. Just like your father."

"If anything, I'm the only one who's stayed and fought for you. Fought with you. But I can't fight against you any longer. I'm tired. I'm eighteen years old. I'm at a point where I'm about to go live my own life. And you expect me to dig you out of your messes and pay your bills and watch you tramp around with men coming in and out of this house at all hours of the night. What kind of life is that for me?"

She refused to meet my stare. "I can change, you know."

"I know you can. With help, Mom. So you'll take their help once they get here. Or I move out. Your choice."

"You're more like your father every day, you know."

I shrugged. "And if that means fighting for my own life when you won't even fight for yours, then so be it."

I left my mother to her choice and walked back upstairs. I gathered my things, shoving them into my purse. I packed a change of clothes and my phone charger. A few toiletries. I packed down my purse in case I got the opportunity to stay somewhere else. Then I grabbed my backpack for good measure. I reached for the bike Allison had loaned me and walked it up the driveway, listening to sirens roar in the distance. And as I walked up the street, I turned to look back. To take one last look at my house before I went to work.

Committing it to memory, in case I never saw it again.

I felt numb. As I peddled out of the neighborhood, I felt the rest of my body grow numb. An ambulance and two police cars raced by me. I didn't even stop to watch them as they made their way into the neighborhood. I didn't even debate on whether or not to skip work and stay with Mom. Because I knew my time was better spent earning money to get me the hell away from this place. I peddled faster. I broke a sweat getting to work. I let my worries about Clint and my mother and D.J. and my future fall to the wayside as I cycled into the parking lot.

I chained up Allison's bike and walked into the grocery store, leaving my proverbial baggage outside as I went to put my backpack and purse underneath my register.

25
CLINTON

I hissed as I moved the ice packs. Three of them, to be exact. Sliding around my body as bruises kicked up, grew hot, then subsided into nothing but a dull ache. As I lay on my bed and stared at the ceiling, I laughed bitterly to myself. It was a wonder no bones had been broken. That, miraculously, I wasn't bleeding all over the place.

Because judging by the state of things downstairs, Dad had really tossed me around.

Pictures crashed to the ground and dents were impacted into the walls. The banister was crooked now, cracked in three separate places. Now, I didn't know much about moving. But I figured the new tenants of this place wouldn't be happy with the destruction. Which meant that my beating had bought me a little more time in this place.

Unless Dad dropped the price of the house for them substantially.

That was the furthest thing from my mind, though. The only thing I focused on was the ceiling while Cecilia and Dad yelled at one another downstairs. Hearing her angry voice waft through the floor was definitely a treat. One I thought I'd never hear again. But I supposed she had gotten her footing. Found the courage to stand up to my father after waking me up in my bed.

How I got here, however, I still didn't know.

All I knew was that when I opened my eyes, I saw her. Cecilia. The image of Rae faded away and was replaced by the face of a woman that had been more my mother than my own had ever been. And even though concern was etched across her face, anger flooded her eyes.

Anger she now unleashed against my father.

"You've gone too far, Howard. You should be jailed for this!"

"And you'd go back to living on the street. What are you going to do, huh? Have sex with men for money? You're not even good at it, Cece!"

"And you're even more abusive than my father, you pretentious asshole!"

They argued for a little while longer. Then the front door slammed. The only reason I knew that Cecilia had stayed behind was because I heard her still screaming downstairs. Still yelling at nothing as my father peeled out of the driveway. I tossed the ice packs off to the side. I needed a shower. Something to flood rejuvenation back through my pulsing muscles.

Anything to get my mind off the shitstorm of my life.

I eased myself out of bed and stripped out of my clothes, leaving them in a pile on the floor as my phone continued lighting up in my back pocket. I saw it flashing on the floor. Notification after notification. People wanting me to meet them as soon as possible to pick up the things I was selling. I cast it off to the side, though, as I turned on the water as hot as I could stand it and eased myself underneath the waterfall stream.

"That's it."

I groaned as I settled down onto the floor. With my legs outstretched and the water pouring over me, I opened myself up to a stream that hurt before it cleansed. And as I sat there, my mind swirled with so many things.

All the things I had to get done.

I had to get those people their items. Collect my money. Damn it, I still needed to get to the bank. What did Rae do with that money? I had to call her and figure out where it was so I could pick it up. I didn't want anyone feeling responsible for that kind of money for very long. It came with a heavy burden and a constant paranoia I didn't want anyone else experiencing. I had to figure out what kind of deal I could strike with Mike's parents. Because I didn't want to freeload off them. And with the damage done to the downstairs, I wondered how much free time that bought me to sell off more things.

"Shit."

The hot water made me feel clean again. But the

dirt settled back in the second I turned off the water. I heaved myself off the floor and out of the shower, settling back into a life my father had carved out for me. The dumbass bathroom he'd renovated two years ago for my birthday. Before he left for a month to be anywhere else other than here, celebrating it with me. A bedroom he'd decked out with expensive items, gifts to apologize for every bruise I'd grown up with. This bedroom had become a museum to the pain he'd caused me, the pain I lived with every day. And as I stared at my mahogany bed frame and matching dresser, it made me sick to think about.

"I'm selling it all."

I wrenched my phone off the floor and started snapping pictures. Then I started responding to those who had already claimed items online. I made appointments for tonight, telling them I'd knock fifteen percent off the price if they met me between eight and ten o'clock on the corner of my street. I watched them respond with fervor, taking me up on my offer and thanking me for this reason or that.

I didn't care about the reasons. I only cared about the money.

I slipped into a clean pair of sweatpants and a T-shirt. The hot water loosened my body up a bit, though I was still very bruised. I slipped my cell phone into my pocket and put my sandals on. I needed to start gathering things in my duffle bag for later. However, a knock came at my door. A small, soft, subtle knock.

"Come in."

The door eased open. "How are you feeling?"

I snickered. "Uh, good considering?"

"I suppose that was a stupid question."

I sighed. "It's not stupid. We're just in a hard situation. How are you doing?"

And when she let out a shuddering breath, I looked over at her.

"I've decided to leave him, Clint."

I rushed over to her and wrapped her up in my arms. I held her close, rocking her softly side to side. She sniffled against my chest and patted my back. I closed my eyes and silently thanked my fucking stars she'd come to her senses. I knew this was a turning point for us. A moment in time we'd never forget. I knew she was trembling with fear. But I also knew how strong she was. How far she'd come in life. What she had survived.

"We're going to make it. I swear to you, Cecilia."

She sighed. "After what just happened..."

She shook her head as she pulled away from me.

"I can't forgive him. I'll never forgive him, Clinton. I mean, look at you. Just—just look at you."

I nodded slowly. "I know. Trust me, I've lived with it my whole life."

"I'm so sorry I didn't intervene sooner."

"No, no, no. Don't you start doing that. Don't you start blaming yourself for things we can't change. You've done a hell of a lot for me. More than any other adult in my entire life. I won't let you feel guilty for anything else."

She sniffled. "I love you. I hope you know that."

I grinned. "I know. I love you too, Cecilia. Now,

come on. I'll help you pack. Because you damn well know we aren't keeping this house."

"I wouldn't want to stay in it anyway."

"Honestly? I feel the same way at this point."

We walked out of my room and down the hall-way, heading for the double doors. I'd only ever been in my father's room once. One time, in my entire life. She threw the doors open and it was even bigger than I remembered. A sprawling room, easily three times the size of my bedroom. Cecilia walked through it as if it didn't faze her. As if the grandeur of it all didn't shock her in the slightest. She walked over to a door in the corner and opened it up, flicking a light on that seemed to cascade down sprawling corridors.

I walked over to her and peeked inside as my jaw dropped to the floor.

"This is my closet. It's a lot to pack up, but I figure I'll have to sell some of it anyway."

I scoffed. "All of this is yours?"

She nodded. "Your father's closet is on the other side. The other door in the corner. The petty part of me wants to burn his clothes in a bonfire tonight. But I know better than that."

My cheeks puffed out with my sigh. This would be a long night, packing all this shit up. But she was right. If she wanted to leave my father for good, he'd cut her off. Completely. Which meant she'd have to sell a lot of this stuff just to keep herself afloat.

I cleared my throat. "All right. Where are your suitcases?"

Cecilia walked inside. "I definitely don't have enough to pack up all this stuff right now."

"Do you want to sort it first, then?"

She paused. "I suppose I could make a pile of clothes I'm willing to sell now. What's that site you're using?"

"Facebook?"

She giggled. "Oh."

"Yeah. Their marketplace is fantastic. I'm targeting just this area to get things sold quickly. But if you broadened your selling area even twice that, you'd sell this stuff like lightning."

"How do you price it?"

I shrugged. "I just look up the listing price for things like this in the store, take ten percent off the top for wear and tear. Then drop it another hundred bucks. It's worked for me every time."

"That's actually not a bad price."

"We can sort, then take pictures of everything. If you get even a few items up tonight, by morning you'll have an inbox flooded with people waiting to buy your stuff."

"Is that what you've been doing?"

I paused. "It is."

She grinned. "I noticed some things missing."

"Is it that obvious?"

She shook her head. "No. It's obvious because I've been around here for more than a week at a time. It wouldn't have been had I been dipping in and out like your father."

I breathed a sigh of relief. "Okay. Good."

"Are you using a separate account? Or, just your regular Facebook?"

"Oh, no. I'm not that dumb. I created a separate account. Which is why you only post a few items at a time this first time around. If you post too many, the site flags you as a bot and shuts your account down."

"How many did you post the first time?"

"Five. I got those items sold first. And now, I've got eight more people I'm meeting tonight to sell things."

Her eyes bulged. "Eight more people? Really?"

"Yep. So come on. Let's get sorting and start taking some pictures."

"Will you help me make an account? You know, on this site?"

I threaded my arm around her shoulders. "I'll even help you post the pictures and come up with neat ways to sell the items."

"Thanks, Clinton."

"Of course."

I kissed the side of her head, then we got to work. In the midst of sorting her dresses and shoes, accessories and bags, I took breaks to pack up things of my own. Silverware I'd sold and a set of fine china I'd found in the attic. Dusty from being up there for years. Never touched. Never seen. Never used. I found a shitton of things in that attic to sell, actually. Old Armani suits. Genuine leather Gucci shoes. All sorts of things that hadn't seen the light of day in at least a decade.

I packed it all away in my duffle bag, preparing it to be sold.

There were moments where I saw Cecilia tearing

up over items. Things she tossed into the 'sell' pile I knew she didn't want to get rid of. And my heart ached for her. But I kept reassuring her this was the right decision. That she was taking the right strides to try and get away from my father. I rubbed her back and listened to her stories. Romantic tales of my father that were almost too much to believe. The man she'd once known was foreign to me. It was as if she were speaking about another person entirely. But, I still listened. I still cried with her. I still held her and helped her through the pain.

Of course, until it was time for me to make my way to the corner.

So I could make some money of my own.

26

RAELYNN

I kept an eye on the door as I checked people out. And every time there was a lull in customers, I started cleaning down my area. I went through my usual duties as work, watching as the cashiers I worked silently with slowly phased out for the night. Until no one was left except myself and the night manager. I closed in an hour, and Clint still hadn't shown up. Which worried me. Not that I hadn't been concerned since that fucking text in the middle of the school day.

But, now I had more of a reason to be concerned.

Me: It's okay if you can't come to the grocery store. I understand. Just let me know you're all right. Please.

I sent the text off to Clint in the middle of customers. My manager gave me a look and I slid my phone into my back pocket and continued on with my duties, hoping I'd feel my phone vibrate against my ass cheek. I didn't, though. Which made me even more worried.

What did his father do to him?

I feared the worst. Clint was back in the hospital. Unable to communicate. Maybe he had packed up his stuff and run away. Or, maybe his father had finally beaten him to death.

Tears rushed my eyes and I had to take a bathroom break.

I turned off the light on my register and raced to the back of the grocery store. I slammed through the door of the women's restroom with my hands trembling. I splashed cold water on my face, trying to calm myself down. I wiped off the little bit of makeup I'd managed to paint on my face before leaving, and my mind bounced from Mom to Clint. Mom to Clint. Mom to Clint.

Why couldn't my life just settle the fuck down?

I pulled out my phone and crafted a message to my mother. One I hoped she responded to. I asked her if she was still at home or at the hospital. Though I wasn't sure of the hospital's policy on phones for their patients. I sent it off before checking on Clint again. He hadn't seen my message yet, and I felt bile creeping up the back of my throat.

Please be okay. Please be okay. Please be okay.

I drew in a deep breath before heading back out to my register. And after checking out seven more people, it was time to close down. I wiped down my register, as well as the remaining ones that looked terrible. I swept, making sure to get up and down the aisles where people waited. Then I cashed out my till and took it to the manager, who proceeded to count it and tally it up before we left.

He stood and watched me as I hopped on my bike.

"You get home safe, okay?"

I heard the tremor of his voice and I sighed.

"I will. I promise. Okay?" I asked.

I took off into the night, peddling back home. What I needed to do was call Michael and ask him to give me a ride home. But what I did was exactly the opposite. I pumped as quickly as my legs would let me go. I felt my backpack and my purse weighing me down as I made my way back toward the school. I didn't head home, however. I headed straight for Clint's house.

I needed to know if he was all right.

I pulled into the driveway and came to a screeching stop. My eyes danced over the lights that lit up the windows of the house. Nothing looked out of place. Or broken. I didn't hear screaming or crying. No one burst out on the porch with bodies flying in every other direction.

So far, so good.

I placed my bike down on its side in front of the porch steps and shifted my bags onto my shoulders as I walked up the steps. I knocked softly on the door, but no one answered. No footsteps. No voices. Nothing.

And with each knock, the silence grew.

"Clint?" I called out.

I reached for the doorknob and found the door unlocked. With what felt like a brick of lead in my gut.

I slowly opened the door and listened for yelling. Or screaming. Or crying. I didn't hear any of that, though. I heard nothing, which was worse. Was anyone even home?

Because if no one was home, why were all the lights on?

"Clint? Cecilia? Anyone here?"

"Rae?"

Hearing Clint's voice rushed relief through my body. I heard thundering footsteps upstairs as I dropped my things to the floor. I closed the door—and locked it—behind me. And as Clint came rushing down the steps, I found him in one piece.

Bruised, but in one piece.

"Clint," I breathed.

He wrapped me up in a massive hug and picked me up.

"I'm sorry. I'm so sorry I couldn't make it. It's been a whirlwind of a night."

I buried my face in his neck. "I'm just glad you're okay."

He kissed the side of my head. "I'm sorry I worried you."

"What happened with your father?"

He set me down on my feet and cupped my cheeks. The smile on his face lit up my insides. He crashed his lips against mine, weakening my knees. And as he caught me in his arms, he smiled against my lips.

"Come upstairs. I'm helping Cecilia pack her things."

I paused. "What?"

He snickered. "Cecilia's leaving my father. Finally. Come on. Upstairs, with me."

"What do you mean, 'leaving him'?"

"I mean, she's leaving him. Filing for divorce. Not going with him to this new house."

He tugged me up the steps behind him like a kid at Christmas time.

"I mean, that's great. But I don't get why that's good news for you," I said.

He laughed. "It's not, but it's great news for her and I'm happy for her. I'm proud of her, Rae!"

I still didn't understand. But, I rejoiced with them all the same. He pulled me into the massive master bedroom and I gawked at its beauty and size. I looked up toward the vaulted ceilings and slowly turned around. It was beautiful. This one room was half the size of my fucking house alone.

"It's good to see you, Rae."

Cecilia's voice hit my ears and my eyes whipped over to her. She smiled at me and held out her arms, prompting me to hug her. I rushed over to her and held her close. The room felt different. Her aura felt different. Even her smile looked different.

I giggled. "Divorce looks good on you."

She barked with laughter. "I'm not divorced yet. But I'm getting there."

Clint piped up. "We've still got a lot to pack up. You in?"

I nodded. "I'm in for helping, yeah."

Cecilia drew in a short breath. "Oh, by the way. If you see anything in the 'discard' pile you or your mother might like, feel free to take it. It's all going to a donation place anyway."

I smiled. "I appreciate that. Thanks."

Clint took my hand. "Here, I'll show you what we're up to right now."

Clint led me into a closet that was easily the size of my bedroom. Probably bigger, to be honest. There were drawers pulled open showcasing sizzling diamonds. Ruby red gems. Bright gold and rose gold jewelry. An entire wall of sunglasses. Purses tossed onto the floor. It looked like a bomb had gone off in this place. And in its wake, designer clothes for people to rummage around in.

Cecilia definitely had great taste in fashion.

"This is the packing pile. And believe it or not, it's only half the size it was. Everything else is kind of scattered around, but they are the 'discard' piles. We're going to sort all the discarded stuff by accessory and clothing type before boxing it up."

I blinked. "Wow. there's a lot of stuff here."

Clint chuckled. "Yeah. And we've been at it for three hours."

Cecilia called out. "Except for that break you took!"

I furrowed my brow. "What break?"

He grinned. "I sold more stuff tonight."

I threw my arms around him and rejoiced with him. Even though things felt more disconnected than ever, I knew they would fall into place the way they needed to. I felt it in my bones. The chaos was slowly coming to a close, this chapter of all of our lives coming to an end.

Finally.

After struggling for weeks.

I jumped into the sorting and packing. Cecilia handed off some used luggage she didn't want anymore, and I snickered when she handed it to me. Louis Vuitton luggage. A beautiful brown with creamy tan logos emblazoned onto it. Clint ended up tossing all sorts of things into the luggage. Random purses he thought I might like. Sunglasses that looked absolutely ridiculous on me. Jewelry Cecilia didn't want to lug with her that he thought my mom might enjoy.

There had to be at least two hundred thousand dollars' worth of stuff in one of these suitcases.

"No, no, no. I can't take any more. This is too much."

Clint smiled. "Oh, come on. This dress still has the tags on it. And you don't think this would look great on you?"

I snickered. "I'm flattered you think it might fit."

Cecilia rubbed my back. "I think it would fit you. The material stretches. It's supposed to mold to your body. You're, what? A size twelve?"

I paused. "How did you pinpoint that?"

She winked. "It's a gift. Hold on."

I watched her walk into the back of the closet as Clint folded that dress up. He shoved it into one of the suitcases before zipping it up, and I heard him struggling with it. The damn thing was almost bursting at the seams. And I didn't know what to do with—well—

any of this. The jewelry they wanted to give me. The designer sunglasses. The outfits.

I'd never worn stuff like this before.

Nor my mother.

"Here we are. Take a look at this."

Cecilia came around the corner with the most beautiful dress in her hands. A hunter green dress, with silken fabric that sparkled in the lights of the closet. She held it up, and my eyes followed it. A full-length dress with off-the-shoulder straps and a built-in bra laid into the corset top.

"It's—it's beautiful."

Cecilia smiled. "A ten-twelve. Which I think will fit you just fine."

She handed it to me, and the first thing that flashed through my mind was 'prom.'

It was the perfect prom dress.

Before I knew it, I had matching shoes in my hands. Dainty white gold jewelry that matched. Even a clutch purse that went with that dress, and that dress alone. Clint took it all out of my hands and packed it away. They continued filling those bags with things they thought I might like until there was no room left in the luggage. Tears rushed my eyes. I didn't know what to say, or think, or do.

"Thank—thank you. I don't—I wouldn't—how do you even wash stuff like this?"

Cecilia smiled. "I'm sure Clint can talk you through that."

I paused. "Clint?"

He chuckled. "I'm not completely inept in the ways

of cleaning expensive clothes. I am my father's son, after all."

My face fell. "But you're nothing like him."

Cecilia shook her head. "No, he's not. He's much better than his father could ever be."

He slipped his arm around my lower back and I realized we hadn't gotten much packing done at all. They'd taken their time to fill up luggage for me, and not one ounce of time had been devoted to packing her things. I felt guilty. But they didn't. Which made me feel a bit better, but only a bit.

"Well, I'm going to go have myself a glass of wine downstairs. I have some things I want to pack up down there anyway. We can give the clothes a rest."

Cecilia's voice caught my ear and pulled me out of my trance.

"Do you need any help?" I asked.

She waved her hand in the air. "I'll be fine. Clint's been packing with me for the past three hours. And I know you came over to see him."

"But I'd like to help. If you'll let me."

Clint chuckled. "And we will. After she's had her glass of wine."

Cecilia nodded. "Exactly. I need a break. And if you're still here after my break, you can help. How's that sound?"

I grinned. "Sounds good. I'd like to repay you somehow for… all of this."

Cecilia snickered. "Nonsense. You're more than welcome to it."

27

CLINTON

I watched as Cecilia winked at me, then left us in the closet by ourselves. I felt how overwhelmed Rae had become. I felt her tensing next to me, and I wanted to help her relax. I guided her to my bedroom and closed the door behind me, locking it for good measure. In case Dad decided to storm the house again. Rae stood in the middle of my room, her eyes locked onto a spot on the ceiling.

Then she let out a heavy sigh. "I can't take all of that stuff."

I walked over, taking her hands in mine. "You can, and you will."

She shook her head. "It's too much. It's too nice. I don't know what to do with it."

"You dry clean it. Any stain, just take it to a dry cleaners."

"I don't have the money for that."

I shrugged. "Sell the jewelry. Then you will."

"That jewelry is beautiful, though."

"Then, sell some of the purses and sunglasses to afford the jewelry cleaning and dry cleaning."

She snickered. "So this is how the rich live."

I licked my lips. "Trust me, it's not as nice as some people think."

Her fingertips reached out and fondled a bruise against my jawline. Her eyes flickered over to worry, and I didn't want her to feel worse. I wanted her to feel better. I wrapped my hand around her wrist and brought her fingers to my lips, kissing the tips of them. All of them. Watching as she softly relaxed.

"It's okay, Rae. I'm okay."

She sighed. "I could've sworn your father had—"

I nodded slowly. "I mean, it wasn't pretty. He was angry. He lashed out. He did what he usually does. But it didn't come out as bad as I figured it would."

Tears rimmed her eyes. "I hate him so much."

"Come here. It's okay. I promise, I'm all right."

I wrapped her up in my arms and felt her cling to my clothing. She shook against me, and it made me silently spit fire at my father. Once he was finally out of my life, things would be so much better. For me. For Rae. For us, and my future.

Our future, if we had one together.

I walked her slowly into my bathroom and closed the door behind us. We both needed to unwind, and I needed to wash the stench of sweat off my body. Packing up Cecilia's shit was a big job. Because she had a lot of stuff. She certainly had access to my father's money over the years. But, she wasn't as materialistic as I'd taken her to be.

Especially after watching her easy generosity with Rae tonight.

I reached into the shower and turned on the hot water. I tempered it with some cold, then stripped myself of my clothes. Rae's eyes roamed over my body, clocking the bruises as tears continued to slip from her eyes. And as I helped her out of her own clothes, I ran my hands along her curves, stealing her warmth and her softness. Prepping a soft landing into the one person I called home.

"Come here, beautiful."

I pulled her into me for a voracious kiss. One that stiffened my cock almost instantly. I accepted the effect she had on me. The electricity she pushed through my veins. I pulled her into the walk-in shower and turned the hot waterfall into a wet mist. The entire stone shower turned into a wet sauna, coating us in a sheen of sweat and water vapor as our teeth clattered together.

"Oh, Clint."

I growled. "I'll never get tired of hearing you say that."

I pressed her against the wall and kissed down her neck. She opened herself up for me, and I took my fill of her. I marked her breasts. Sucked on her nipples. Tugged them to painful peaks with my teeth as her hands threaded into my hair. She pushed me further down her body. Aching for me to be between her legs. And as I fell to my knees, I slipped one of her legs over my shoulder before slipping the other.

"Clint, no, no, no. You're going to—drop—fuck!"

"Mmm, what was that?"

I gave her all my strength. All my devotion. I gave her all of me as I hoisted her off the ground. My hands pressed into the stone wall to steady me as her nails raked along my scalp. I opened my mouth and devoured her. My tongue slid up and down her slit, readying her for my assault as her heels dug into my back. Her body hovered above the shower floor.

"Shit, Clint."

"Mmm, that's it."

"Don't let me fall."

"I'll never let you fall, Rae. Not on my watch."

My tongue found her swollen nub and I flicked against it. Over and over, feeling her tremble against my face. I had her right where I wanted her. And I never wanted her to leave. I drank every droplet she had for me as she poured into my mouth. Opening herself. Relaxing herself. Offering herself up as my dinner.

A dinner I'd never forget.

"Clint! Yes!"

"Be as loud as you want, beautiful."

"Oh, fuuuuck. Please, don't stop."

I lapped harder against her. Deeper into her body. My fingers curled into the stone wall as my cock leaked from its tip. I felt her trembling and shivering against me. I felt her hands wrapping themselves around the tendrils of my hair that had grown far too long. She bucked against me, ravenously chasing her release on the tip of my tongue.

But when she unraveled, I didn't stop.

"Clint! Clint! No, no, no, n—yes. Oh, right there, yeah."

I chuckled as I continued my assault, following her every command. A little to the right. Back to the left. Down. Down. No, no, no, up. I smiled against her. Every chuckle I filled her pussy with made her jump. She hissed with delight and moaned my name. Until her words became choppy and her gasps became groans. I felt her unraveling again, losing control. Her arousal dripped down my neck as I coaxed her over the edge again, feeling her grow weaker against my assault.

Which still didn't stop, even as my body shook with exhaustion.

"Clint, I can't. I can't. You have to—oh, fuck, what are you doing to me?"

Her moans fell from her lips with ease. I felt her juices dripping down my chest. My cock leaked thick threads of precum as it pooled on the shower floor. Sweat dripped down my brow. Mist flooded my back. I rocked my face against her, digging deeper and keeping a steady rhythm as she slowly began bucking against me again.

"Oh, yeah, Clint. Yeah, yeah, yeah, yeah, yeah."

Her pleasure choked off her sounds. I heard her gasping as her body spun out of control. It was the most beautiful sound I'd ever heard in my life. And I never wanted a day to go by where I didn't hear it. I slowly slid her to the floor, my muscles trembling with exhaustion. I lay her down on her back, kissing softly up her stomach. Her breasts. Her neck. All the way up to her lips. And as our mouths met, I felt her legs spread apart.

"Fill me, Clint."

She didn't have to ask me twice.

I slid deep inside her as the mist of the sauna-shower cloaked us from the rest of the world. I threaded our fingers together, pinning her wrists above her head. Her pussy swallowed me whole. Her walls clamped down tightly around me. I felt her shivering. Quaking, for my viewing pleasure. And with every thrust I afforded her, I watched her breasts jump and her eyes roll back. I watched her jaw unhinge in silent pleasure as she entrusted me with her most vulnerable form.

A gift I'd never take for granted.

My growls met her moans. Her glance met my stare. I kept my eyes on her, unable to pull away as her face contorted with pleasure. She was a shaking mess. Dripping with sweat, flushed with ecstasy, and dripping with cum. And yet, she'd never looked more beautiful. Writhing beneath me. Helpless to my pleasurable assault.

I love you. I love you. I love you, Rae.

I pounded into her. I dug my knees into the stone and bit back the pain. I gnashed my teeth together as she lifted her hips, offering them to me as a sacrifice. Her walls squeezed me as her legs locked around my calves. Her fingernails dug into the tops of my hands as her pussy pulled me deeper, trapping me within the confines of its warmth. I dropped my lips against hers and hovered over her as my cock pulsed once. Twice. Three times, inside her body.

And then I burst.

Bringing her along with me.

Her moans filled the back of my throat as my grunts filled hers. I rutted against her, like a wild fucking animal, my threads of arousal filling her to the brim. Her pussy pulsed so hard it pushed me out. And with it came our intermingled juices, shooting against my pelvis. I grinned against her lips and chuckled as our teeth clattered together. What a mess we were. The two of us.

A perfect mess made for one another.

I love you, Rae. With everything I have.

I hoped she felt it, too. Because one of these days, I'd have the balls to say it. One of these days, I'd have the guts to tell her myself.

One of these days, if she kept me around long enough, I'd have the courage to look her square in her eyes and tell her.

But for now, I settled with holding her close, pulling her against me as we lay there, our bodies intertwined at the bottom of my shower. I kissed her shoulder and she jumped, giggling as I nuzzled her and threaded our fingers together as she slipped her shaking leg between mine.

I settled for feeling her press against me, wanting to get as close to me as she could.

In the hopes that one day soon, I'd tell her how I truly felt.

And hear those words from her in return.

28

RAELYNN

*Raelynn*One Week Later

I smiled as I tried on my prom dress for the fourth time that week. I still couldn't believe all the stuff Cecilia had simply handed away. I ran my hands down the silken fabric, watching as it molded to my touch. To my body. To the curves I apparently had. I even held the clutch in my hands to get an idea of what I might look like at prom.

If Clint ever asked me to go.

I felt much better than I did last week. And not just because Clint and I were back together. I mean, yeah. That played into some of it. We were spending a lot more time together, especially since we were working on catching him back up with classes. Getting his overdue homework turned in. Things like that. But work was also going well. I'd gotten a small raise. Only twenty cents more than I was making, but every little bit helped.

And selling off some of the jewelry Cecilia had passed to me helped cushion my bank account.

After Mom got back from her stint in the hospital, I gave her some of the clothes. Not all of them, but some. A couple of the sunglasses and a few of the purses. Some tops and pants and dresses that definitely didn't fit me. She ogled and swooned over them. She even put on a little fashion show for me as she twirled around in them. I hadn't seen my mother smile like that in years. And it warmed my heart to see her that happy.

Without D.J.

"Rae!"

I opened my bedroom door. "Yeah, Mom?"

"I'm off to my therapy session. I should be back in a couple of hours. I was thinking of picking up lunch for us."

"Don't worry about it. I'm graduation dress shopping with Allison today. I'll see you for dinner!"

"Sounds good."

"Love you! Have a good time at therapy!"

I heard Mom snickering as she walked out the door. That was another new thing, too. Because of our income status, she qualified for free therapy lessons through the hospital that had treated her. So, twice a week, she was scheduled to go in and talk with someone to help her sift through these issues she clearly still struggled with. I was so proud of her for finally pulling away from all the abusive nonsense and getting her happiness back and starting down a path to find her way in life.

Though another decision would be coming soon. Because eventually, she'd have to get a job.

That's when the real test would come.

Don't think about that now. Focus on the present.

I smiled as I slipped out of the dress. It still needed to be hemmed, since Cecilia was a good four inches taller than me. But I had the money to get that done now. Most of the money from selling off that jewelry was stashed in a savings account. But I'd kept a little bit of the money in my own checking account. You know, to have it there in case Mom and I needed something.

Or if I really did need to move in with Allison until graduation.

I got dressed into some jeans and a T-shirt. Then I peeked at the back of my closet. That luggage was still piled up, still half-full of things I knew I'd never use. I did grab a pair of the sunglasses, though. The one pair I did like. They were black, swirled with brown. And the frames were large. They almost covered my face. They were muted, not like the sparkling ones that twinkled at me every time I opened the small suitcase.

These I'd keep for myself.

I gathered my things then headed out the door. Allison had convinced her parents to let her borrow the van for today. So off we went. She pulled into my driveway just as I locked the door behind me. I was excited to go dress shopping with her. I rushed to the van and hopped in, with her exclaiming over my sunglasses.

"Oh, my gosh. Where in the world did you get those?"

I pulled a sparkling pair out of my purse. "Want a pair?"

She gasped. "Rae. Do you have any idea what kind of sunglasses these are?"

I shrugged. "No clue. But I know they're expensive. So treat them with care."

"Wait, are you giving these to me? Where on earth did you get them?"

"Oh, do I have some shit to fill you in on."

"Okay, okay. Hold on. Let me get us out to the main road first."

She slipped on the sunglasses and giggled like a little girl. I clapped my hands as I laughed, watching the way she enjoyed them. I had a pair set aside for Michael, too. Sunglasses that could easily pass for a men's pair. All black. A beautiful matte black. With sharp edges and a red streak going down either side of the arms.

I couldn't wait to give them to him Monday at school.

Allison pulled out of the driveway and headed toward the opening of the neighborhood. She drove like an old woman, though. Five under the speed limit, no matter what. I grinned as we made our way onto the main road, getting ourselves into traffic that made Allison white-knuckle the damn steering wheel.

I held off on my storytelling until we got to the mall. But the second she eased into a parking space and turned off the van, I whipped my head around to hers.

"So, last week after I got off work, I went to go check on Clint. You know, his first day back?"

Allison turned to face me. "Yeah? I mean, I take it he was fine. He's been back at school all week."

I nodded. "Yep. He was just fine. Apparently, Cecilia's leaving his father."

She gasped. "Nuh-uh."

"Yeah. She's really leaving him. They were packing up all her stuff when I went by. Her closet is massive, Allison. I mean, easily the size of my bedroom. If not bigger. She was packing away all the things she wanted to take and donating what she didn't want to keep."

"Let me guess. She let you pilfer through the donation pile."

"More than that, she and Clint loaded me down with stuff. You wouldn't believe the kinds of things I've got in my closet right now. Stuffed inside brown and tan Louis Vuitton luggage."

"What!?"

I laughed. "I know, right? It was insane. I've actually sold some of the jewelry she gave me just to put some money in my savings. You know, for after graduation. I gave a few pieces to Mom. I kept a few for myself—including my prom dress."

"Wait, wait, wait, you have your prom dress and I haven't seen it yet? What gives?"

"You can come inside after you drop me off and I'll put it on for you. Cecilia gave me matching heels and a clutch and everything."

"So, you got these sunglasses from her?"

I nodded. "Yep. I've got a pair for Michael, too."

"What will you do with the rest of the clothes?"

I shrugged. "I don't know. I mean, I've already got the things I want to keep folded away at the bottom of my dresser drawers. I guess you can come take a look at what you might want. But I figured I'd hang onto the things and sell them if I needed the money."

"Oh, that hurts my heart. I bet they're gorgeous clothes."

"Well, then come upstairs after we're done shopping and you can take a look. There's purses and dresses and shirts and pants and jewelry still up for grabs."

She threw her arms around me. "Your life is so insane."

I giggled. "Yeah. I know."

She released me from the hug. "So, what about the house? Is it actually being sold?"

I sighed. Because this was the one bad thing that happened this past week.

"It's actually sold, yeah. They have to be out in a little over two weeks. And according to Clint, neither of them have heard a word from his father since he came to pick Clint up from school that day."

She snickered. "What a butthead."

I giggled. "Yes. He's definitely one of those."

"Oh! Michael said Clint stopped by to pick up his money. Did he ever get it deposited?"

I nodded. "Yep. And he's still selling things off. I think he'll have a nice little nest egg going for himself."

"Has he given Michael's parents' place any thought? I mean, he'll need a place to go."

"If he has, he hasn't mentioned anything to me. And honestly, I'm trying not to press so much. I know he's overwhelmed, and we just got him caught back up with school. The last thing I want is for him to stop coming again because he feels like he's drowning and has to cut something out."

"That makes sense."

"So, ready to get this shopping done?"

She giggled. "You're just ready for the food that comes after."

I unbuckled my seatbelt. "You know I hate shopping."

"Which is terrible, because you look good in so many things. I'd kill for the curves you have. I'm nothing but a stick."

I rolled my eyes. "I know. Such a burden being thin and beautiful."

The two of us linked arms, then headed into the mall. We walked through store after store, with Allison turning her nose up at most everything she came across. I mean, I had planned for an entire afternoon of shopping. But, usually, shopping required trying things on.

And after walking through four stores, she hadn't tried on a damn thing.

"Are you okay?"

Allison sighed. "I think I should be searching for prom dresses instead of graduation dresses."

"You still haven't found yours yet?"

She shook her head. "No, and I'm still not sure if I'm even going. I mean, Michael's hinted at it. I think he kind of asked me, but I'm not sure."

"What do you mean, he kind of asked you?"

"Well, we were having this talk about it on Wednesday. And he started talking about his suit and all the colors he wanted to wear. And then he looked at me and asked me what color my dress was. I told him I didn't know because I hadn't gotten one yet, and that was that. He didn't formally ask or anything. Just... assumed? I think?"

I nodded. "It sounds like he assumes you guys are going together."

"I want him to ask, though. That's the fun part of prom."

"Well, maybe start dropping some hints. You know, like you did back before you two were dating."

She rolled her eyes. "Are guys always this clueless? Why do I have to do all the legwork?"

I snickered. "Trust me, you will *always* have to do all the legwork."

"Great."

"If you want to look for prom dresses instead, I'm all for it. Means I don't have to try on shit."

She snickered. "Yeah, you'd like that part, too. Oh! Wait! Has Clint asked you to prom?"

I shook my head. "No. Not yet."

"You think he will?"

"I really hope so. I mean, I've got that dress his stepmom gave me. I'd like a chance to wear it for him."

"For him? Wow, who are you and what have you done with my best friend?"

I laughed. "Oh, shut up."

"You've got it bad for him."

"And this is news to you?"

She giggled. "Nope. Just cute, is all. Love looks good on you."

"I never said I was—"

"Yeah, yeah, yeah. You're in love, whether you want to admit it or not. And it looks good on you. Take the compliment and come on. I see a dress I want to try."

And before I could fight her any more on the matter, she tugged me into a store. Headed straight for a pale yellow and purple gown that screamed Allison's name.

A gown I knew would look fabulous on her, even though it still hung on a rack.

29

CLINTON

The strip of tape made a bombastic sound as I pulled it across the cardboard boxes. I'd done everything I could. Sold everything I could without throwing red flags up to my father. And now the time had come. Cecilia and I had two weeks to get our asses out of this place before the new owners were due to move in. And I still had yet to figure out where the hell I was headed. I hadn't even talked with my stepmom about it. Were we sticking together? Was she leaving to do her own thing? Did I need to take Michael up on the offer from his parents?

Stay focused. Just keep packing.

As I dug through my room, I set aside a few more things I didn't mind selling. A genuine leather belt I hadn't touched once. Shined leather shoes that still smelled new. An entire tuxedo tailored to me I never planned on wearing again.

Well, after prom.

Shit, I have to ask Rae to prom.

My phone rang in my back pocket and I tossed my tuxedo onto the bed, which had been stripped of its sheets. If I really was being forced out of this house, I'd take with me anything and everything that could even possibly be mine. Towels. The decorative bathroom set. The sheets on my bed. Hell, I was still in the process of trying to arrange a storage facility so I could take my bedroom set, too. The mattress. The bedside tables. All of it. I'd gotten so much money from selling off the small things in this house that I had no need to sell that shit. Which meant I could start my new life off with some furniture of my own.

Though, part of me wanted to torch every bit of it and start from scratch. Erase the painful memories that came with the pieces of this bedroom set.

I pulled my phone out and saw an unknown number calling, so I ignored it. I got back to taping up boxes I already had packed. Then that number called back again. No voice message. No text. Nothing. It was our area code, though.

Just pick it up, Clint.

"Hello?"

The woman cleared her throat. "Is this Mr. Clinton Clarke?"

I paused. "Who's asking?"

"My name is Rena Nichols. I'm a lawyer in the area."

I furrowed my brow. "What can I do for you, Miss Nichols?"

"I'd like to speak with you, in person, about the

charges against the three kids that ran you off the road last month. Do you have some time to come in?"

"On a Saturday?"

"Yes, sir."

"You don't have to call me that."

"What do you prefer to be called?"

"Clint is just fine."

She paused. "All right, Mr. Clint. Yes, as soon as you can get in here, I'd like to speak with you. Preferably with an adult present."

I snickered. "I'm eighteen. I can come by myself."

"I know. But it might behoove you to have an adult here. To help you absorb what I have to say."

"Has something happened? How did you get my number?"

A knock came at my door. "Clinton? Everything okay?"

I turned around and looked at Cecilia. I pressed the phone to my shoulder as I tried gathering my thoughts. She walked over to me, her eyes filled with concern. And just as she went to reach for my phone, I drew in a sharp breath.

"There's a lawyer on the phone for me. Says she's got information on the charges against the boys that ran me off that bridge."

Cecilia nodded. "You want me to speak with her?"

"She's saying I should come into her office today with a legal guardian or something. Says it's not required, but I should anyway."

"Let me get my things. Get her address and we can head out now."

"Are you sure?"

She backtracked out of my room. "Positive, Clinton."

I put the phone back to my ear. "You still there?"

"I'm ready to give my address whenever you are."

I searched around for my notebook and pen before scribbling down the address she rattled off. I didn't know what this was about, but it sounded urgent. And not good. I hung up the phone and turned around, finding Cecilia standing in the doorway with her purse slung over her shoulder and her hair piled high on top of her head. We made our way out of the house.

"Did she say what this was about at all?"

I shook my head, closing the front door behind me. "All she says was it was important. I don't even know how she got my information."

She nodded slowly. "All right. Well, let's go figure out what this is all about. Then, we can get back to packing."

"You think she might be able to help with this house thing? You know, prevent the sale from happening?"

She sighed. "It's already happened. There's nothing we can do about that. And honestly? I'm not sure I'd even want to stay here, given the chance. Would you?"

I shrugged. "Where else am I going to go?"

She nodded slowly. "We'll figure that out. Together. Okay? I promise. But, right now, let's focus on what's in front of us. Which is the lawyer."

"Mr. Clint, it's nice to meet you."

I shook the lawyer's hand before reaching for Cecilia.

"This is my stepmother, Cecilia Clarke."

Miss Nichols shook her hand. "Thank you for coming in on such short notice. Please, make yourselves comfortable."

It was clear from the size of her office that she was a prominent lawyer. A successful one. The bookshelves were lined from floor to ceiling with all sorts of law textbooks and reference materials. Binders were open on her desk. There were filing cabinets tucked into every corner of the room. Miss Nichols walked with poise and grace, dressed to impress but not dominate.

She ushered for us to sit down in front of her desk.

"To answer your questions, I received your case file from a colleague of mine. A colleague that might have promised some pro bono work?"

I nodded slowly. "So, why are we in your office instead of his?"

She sighed. "My colleague's schedule has become filled. But he didn't want your specific situation falling through the cracks. He'd been keeping tabs on the police investigation, but once a major case fell into his lap, he wanted to make sure yours got passed on to someone he knew would take care of it."

Cecilia cleared her throat. "Which he feels is you."

Miss Nichols nodded. "Yes. And I have to admit, your case has caught my eye. It's an easy open-and-shut case. The police charged them for the speeding and reckless driving. I'm curious as to why you haven't pressed formal charges yet."

The women looked at me and I sighed.

"Just—a lot has happened lately. A lot is going on that needs my attention."

The lawyer nodded. "Something more important than putting bars around the boys that almost killed you."

Cecilia butted in. "You said pro bono, right?"

Nichols nodded. "Correct."

"And you think this is an open and shut case?"

"Once we go to court, I can prove within the day what these boys are guilty of and have them slapped in handcuffs."

I sighed. "Look, we're in the process of moving. And—"

The lawyer held up her hand. "My colleague gave me quite an interesting hypothetical over the phone."

Her eyes met mine as Cecilia looked over at me.

"Okay. Great," I murmured.

Nichols sat against her desk. "I'll answer any questions you want. I'll help in any way I can. But these kids can't walk. They need to be taught a lesson. And as far as this house situation goes, I'm more than willing to help you navigate it."

I snickered. "The house has been sold. It's a non-issue at this point."

"Then I can help the two of you get back on your feet. Get you established in the area. And if you don't want to stay here, I can reach out to colleagues I have up and down the West Coast. Have them help you get settled where you need to be without that man's influence ruining everything."

Cecilia drew in a shuddering breath. "You can do that?"

Nichols nodded. "I'm more than willing to, yes. The position you two have been put in sounds almost impossible. You're going to need someone on your side."

I felt so overwhelmed. And yet, so relieved. Cecilia started firing off all sorts of questions. How this woman could help. What court might feel like. Whether or not we'd have to get up and testify. How long the process took. I sat there, thankful that I'd brought her along. Because had she not been there beside me, I wasn't sure I would've come up with half the questions she had asked.

Cecilia took my hand. "How are you feeling about all this?"

I drew in a deep breath. "It's a lot to process."

Nichols stood up. "I want you to take your time and think about it. The police will push forward with charges, one way or another. But they can't charge the boys with attempted murder without you filing those formal charges. Which I'm more than willing to do."

I nodded slowly. "And, you're willing to help with the rest of this stuff, too?"

Her eyes met mine. "Anything you need. Pro bono."

I looked over at Cecilia before I stood up. I walked over to the lawyer and stared straight into her eyes. I search for any lie. Any manipulation. Any fault in the programming of what she was saying. And when I found none, I offered her my hand.

"You have a deal," I said.

Nichols took my hand. "Wonderful. The first thing I'm going to do is file the formal charges on your behalf. I'll need a written account of what happened that night for my own records. I know you've already written one for the police, but I'll need one, too."

Cecilia shot up beside me. "I'll get him back some-time this week. And thank you for answering all my questions."

She shook my stepmother's hand, too. "Anytime. I'm going to give you my information so you can contact me any way you wish. Phone. Email. Stopping by. You're welcome anytime."

"I'm confident my stepson's in good hands with you. Just make sure those reckless kids can't ever get behind the wheel of a car again and hurt anyone else."

Nichols nodded. "Don't worry. My firm and I will take care of it. Cases like this are easy ones."

After exchanging information, we left the law office. And I felt another massive weight roll of my back. It became easier to breathe. My legs didn't feel as sore. It was as if some of the chains had fallen away, allowing me a few inches closer to the exit of this terrible dungeon I'd been stuck in for years.

Cecilia wrapping her arm around my waist pulled me from my trance. "So, I know this is terribly irre-sponsible of me to ask. But, how do you feel about me picking us up a six pack of cold beers for the night?

There are some things I want to talk to you about. Things we have yet to discuss."

I snickered. "Beer? I thought you were a wine person."

She shrugged. "I have my surprises every now and again. Do you have a beer you prefer?"

"I'm honestly not really a beer person."

"I shouldn't be shocked that you know that."

I chuckled. "How do you feel about a wine and whiskey night?"

She unlocked her car. "Sounds like the only thing I need to pick up is food, then."

"Oh, what about that Indian place across town? Their curry and naan is fabulous."

"The little place with the bright pink roof?"

I slipped into the car. "Yep! That's the one."

She dipped in beside me. "Indian food with some wine and whiskey sounds fabulous. What do you usually order, other than the curry?"

"Their curry, extra jasmine rise, and garlic naan. You?"

"I love their chicken tikka masala. Extra spicy. With two orders of rosemary naan and their mango milkshake."

"They have mango milkshakes?"

"Oh! You haven't lived until you've had one of those. I'm going to get you one."

And as she cranked up the car, a smile crossed my face. I was in completely uncharted territory with her right now. But I loved it all the same. My stepmom was a lot cooler than I'd given her credit for. She was a completely different person from what I had assumed her to be.

I enjoyed spending this time getting to know her. Having her open up to me. Feeling as if I could rely on her.

I just hoped this conversation she wanted to have tonight ended with us sticking together instead of splitting apart.

30

RAELYNN

"I can't wait for Michael to see you in that dress." Allison pulled into my driveway. "If he ever asks me to prom. And I still didn't find a graduation dress for myself. Mom's going to kill me."

"Oh, boo. You needed a prom dress anyway. And that thing looks perfect on you."

"You think?"

I smiled. "The dark purple with the pale yellow under the tulle? You're going to look like the next Disney princess."

She smiled. "I'd like to find some yellow shoes. You know, to keep the continuation of the colors going."

"But do purple jewelry, if anything. Small items. You definitely want people focused on that dress."

She giggled. "Look at you, getting into fashion and all that."

I rolled my eyes. "Don't get used to it. Clint's stepmom can only rub off so much."

I reached over and gave Allison a tight hug. Then I gathered my things. I'd ended up finding myself a nice casual dress for graduation. I mean, I had the money in my account. It was already marked down on sale anyway. Why not? It fit me nice. It didn't have to be altered. And I already had a pair of flats that would go well with it. It wasn't a color I wore regularly. The pale blue and white swirls were definitely brighter than my entire wardrobe put together. But the cotton dress would breathe, according to Allison. And it was sleeveless. Came just above my knee. So, it would be light enough for the California summer heat.

"Are you seeing Clint at all tomorrow?"

I opened my door. "I'm not sure. But, if I don't, want me to give you a call?"

Allison paused. "Actually…?"

I waved my hand in the air. "Tell Michael I said hey. And have fun. I'll see you Monday."

"Love you."

"Love you, too."

I slipped out of the van and made my way for the front door. I went on inside, knowing it would be unlocked. Allison and I had stayed out far longer than I had anticipated. It was nearing dinner time, and I smelled something simmering on the stove. I closed the front door behind me and made my way for the stairs, ready to hang up my dress.

Until Mom's voice piped up.

"Where have you been all day?"

I furrowed my brow. "Dress shopping with Allison, remember?"

She paused. "Dress shopping?"

"Yeah. I shouted it down to you this morning before you left for therapy. How did that go, by the way?"

"Prom dress shopping, or graduation dress shopping?"

"Graduation dress shopping. I already have a prom dress."

She coughed. "Wait, you do?"

I nodded. "Mm-hmm. Cecilia gave it to me."

"Who's Cecilia?"

"Clint's stepmom?"

"Since when have you been over at Clint's? I thought you two were broken up?"

I shrugged. "Not anymore. We worked things out."

I went to go up the steps, but Mom stood up.

"Wait, wait, wait, wait. Hold on."

I held back a sigh. "I have an exam to study for, Mom."

She walked over to the stairs. "Can I... see you in your prom dress?"

"Maybe later. I really have some studying to do."

"And you didn't want to go dress shopping with me?"

I paused. "No."

I looked over at my mother and saw her eyes swell with hurt.

"I wanted to go shopping with you for that dress. Graduation's been a long time coming. I thought you wanted to go with me?"

I licked my lips. "Mom, I just—don't know how to have quality time with you anymore."

"What do you mean?"

I shrugged. "Just, with everything that's happened."

"You mean with D.J.?"

"I mean, in general. But, yes. That includes D.J. I couldn't spend time with you without being around him. And it's been so long since we've hung out that I don't even know how to do that anymore with you."

She placed her hand over mine. "Honey, why didn't you tell me you felt this way?"

I snickered. "Because I was too busy telling you to leave someone who kept smacking you around."

"Will you at least take out your dress so I can see it?"

"You don't just want to see it on me later?"

She eyed me carefully. "Why haven't you asked me about my therapy appointment yet?"

"Okay. How did it go?"

"No, no. That's passed. Why aren't you curious about it?"

"Mom, you're reading too much into things. It's fine. Things are okay."

"Things aren't okay. If there's anything I learned at therapy today, it's that things haven't been okay for a while and I simply haven't seen it."

"Well, keep up with your therapy sessions and maybe we can start to pick through some of it."

She paused. "Is that it?"

I rolled my eyes. "Is what it?"

"Do you feel like I'm not going to stick with my therapy sessions?"

"Mom, I don't have time for this. I have a test I really need to study—"

"In a minute. Right now, we need to talk."

"No, we don't. You're blowing something you've always known completely out of proportion. And now, you're getting in the way of my studies because *you* want to do something. It's selfish."

Her eyes welled with tears. "I'm sorry I can't seem to do right by you."

I swallowed my rising anger. "I just need some time. You need to heal, and so do I."

"Things are over between me and D.J. For good. I swear to you. We've had our last fight, Rae. I mean that."

I nodded. "Then time will tell. Okay?"

She squeezed my hand. "I'm getting better. I already feel better. My therapist and I talked about a lot today. Started unpacking some of the things I never let go of regarding your father leaving."

"I'm glad. I'm really glad to hear that."

"I feel like a new person, almost."

I smiled weakly. "Yes. So, let's just keep taking it week by week. Okay?"

She squeezed my hand harder. "You don't believe me."

"Mom, it's only been a week. And if you really want me to be honest? I've seen you go longer spans of time before accepting D.J. back. No doubt he'll come up to this door someday with money and flowers and

262 | REBEL HART

promises of a future together, and that will be your real test. Surviving without him. Making something of yourself instead of being so scared of the world out there."

She sniffled. "When did you grow up on me?"

"I did it while you were arguing in your room with D.J. and out at the bars on the weekends with mysterious men."

I knew that comment smacked her across the face. She physically stumbled away from me. Tears streamed down her cheeks and it killed me to hurt her. But at the same time, I had a right to express how she'd made me feel. How much she had abandoned me over the years. How very unlike my own mother she had become the further she slipped into this mania of hers. I shifted my bag into my other hand, giving her the silence she needed to dry her tears. I felt my heart breaking. But, at the same time, she needed to hear it.

Maybe if she finally heard the truth, she'd stick with this new path she had carved out for herself.

"You really believe that little of me?"

I snickered. "Mom, I don't want to fight tonight."

She scoffed. "I'm not fighting. I'm asking a question I want an honest answer to."

"I don't think you're little. I think you're lost."

"I'm not lost, Rae. I was hurt. And I never recovered from that."

"And you lost who you were in the process. Don't you lie to me."

She looked at me pointedly. "I'm not lying. And

don't you dare take that tone with me. No matter how you view me, I'm still your mother."

"And no matter what you choose to do with your life, I'm still the daughter you've neglected in the process."

"How have I neglected you, huh? Tell me. You've got a roof over your head. Food in your belly. Clothes in your drawers. Tell me how you've been neglected."

I shook my head. "I need to go study."

"Oh, no you don't. You wanted this fight, we're going to have it."

I spun around. "I didn't want any fight, okay?"

Mom stood in front of me as I slowly backed up the steps.

"I didn't want to fight with you! I just didn't want to lie to you! But, that's what I get when I tell you the truth because you don't like it. You don't like your truth. Which is why you need therapy. And I'm proud of you. I really am. But you broke my trust a long time ago when you continuously let an abusive man into this home where I live without asking me how I felt about it once. You broke my trust the second you started relying on that man for money and then preaching to me about how I had to stand on my own two feet and rely on myself. You broke my trust the second you tried to mold me into the kind of girl I am today while denying yourself that same strength because the world out there is too scary and too hard and too judgmental. Well, you know what, Mom? It's going to take more than a week for that trust to come back. So take it or leave it. Because that's all I've got for you."

"You don't believe a word coming out of my mouth, do you?"

I turned my back. "I'll believe it when I see it."

I started up the steps, leaving my crying mother to wallow in her own self-pity. On the one hand, I felt like an utter bitch. And on the other hand, I felt relieved. Now that the truth was out there and she knew exactly how I felt, I didn't feel like a stranger in my own home. Yes, it was a harsh truth. But, speaking my truth helped me to breathe a little easier.

Even at the expense of my mother's tears.

Hearing her cry downstairs broke my heart. But I didn't let it deter me. I closed my bedroom door behind me and hung my new dress up in my closet. I tossed my purse onto my bed, went into my closet and pulled out my backpack. And as I started pulling my books out, exhaustion washed over me.

I had no more pity to give out to anyone.

I tossed my books onto my bed. But staring at them made me tired. The test wasn't until Wednesday. I could study in the morning. I turned my eyes back toward my closet. They fell to the luggage at the bottom. And one by one, I pulled them out and dumped everything onto the bed.

I picked out the few things I figured Allison might enjoy. I set aside the sunglasses for Michael. Then I picked out one specific piece of jewelry I wanted to give Mom for her birthday. It had her name written all over it. Big. Beautiful. Loud. Just like her. I sighed as I set it off to the side. Her birthday was next month. I would wrap it up and give it to her. Something nice she could be proud of. A piece of real jewelry, instead of that fake shit D.J. always bought her. I wanted her to have something to remind her of what she deserved. To remind her of the beauty this world had to offer if she simply strived for it.

And after picking out a few more things for myself, I started taking pictures.

I wanted to post everything else online for sale. Because it made me nervous to have all this expensive stuff at the bottom of my closet. I had to look up the pieces of clothing in order to estimate how much to sell it for. And the prices boggled my mind. A few of the less expensive things I set off to the side. I slipped the items into the smallest luggage case I had as a back-up reserve of money. The big things, though, I posted immediately. The more expensive the item, the more nervous it made me.

The more I heard my mother cry, the more I wondered if she could stick with this. I kept posting pictures and getting hits on them. People who were interested. Who were asking for verification of the jewels and diamonds. I worked to answer their questions as more pictures uploaded. Because in the end, I needed a fall-back plan. If Mom fell through with all this—if Mom took him back—I needed enough money for an exit plan. Enough money to run my own life and completely disconnect myself with her. Because I meant what I said.

If he came back, I was gone.

And I needed to be ready for the worst.

31

CLINTON

I sipped my whiskey as I leaned back in the chair. It softly rocked, and the fall breeze kicked up. I swear, I smelled the fucking ocean in it. I closed my eyes and relished my full stomach. Lunch had been fantastic, which left us with more than enough to heat up for dinner. And after two rounds of Indian and whiskey, I was feeling limber. Light. Carefree. Relaxed.

Especially with Cecilia.

Things were just comfortable with her. I enjoyed having her in my life. Having her support on things. I never had evenings like this with my father. We either ate in separate rooms or I ordered take-out simply because he wasn't home. Never had we shared a meal like this. Not even during the damn holidays.

I wonder what holidays would be like with her.

"So, how are you feeling about today?"

I sighed. "You know, I feel good about it."

Cecilia nodded. "That lawyer was generous with her offer."

"She was, yeah."

"It's nice to know good people really do exist."

I snickered. "Maybe she'll help you with your divorce."

"I've actually already called her about that. She can't, but she's referring me to another one of her colleagues that has a really good win rate."

I nodded. "Good for you. Seriously. I'm proud of you."

She smiled softly. "But there's still the matter of you."

"What about me?"

"You'll need to stick around here and finish out high school."

"I'll figure a way around that. I've got a friend at school whose parents have already offered to let me use their spare bedroom."

"Oh?"

I nodded slowly. "I still don't know if I'm going to take them up on their offer. I mean, I'd have to find a storage unit. Store all my things. Only take what's necessary. Then, there's still the plan of what to do after high school. It would make more sense for me to keep selling things, or finding a part-time job now, so I can get a place of my own."

"What kind of job would you get?"

I snickered. "Hell if I know. Maybe a cashier some-where. A sandwich maker or a barista."

"Mmm, I don't think I can see you in an apron and a hair cap."

"It would definitely be a sight."

I sipped my whiskey as night time slowly fell upon us. The beauty of the sunset faded, leaving us with cars rushing by in the distance. The glow of the city rose above our heads, muting a lot of the stars. The ones that did twinkle seemed to almost be laughing. They flashed and blinked. Flickered, as if they were waving down at me.

But suddenly, I heard a chair scraping across the cement.

I looked in front of me and saw my stepmom pulling up her chair. She sat with me, knee to knee, before digging out her cell phone. She set her wine glass down on the ground, and I couldn't help but notice the glow on her face. She looked radiant. Happier than I'd ever seen her before.

Everything about this night was refreshing.

"So I've been taking your advice over this past week with selling some things off."

I paused. "Oh?"

She nodded. "Mm-hmm. I mean, I'm entitled to half of what your father owns, but—"

"Wait, wait, wait, wait. You guys don't have a prenup?"

She shook her head. "Nope. We don't."

I blinked. "Are you serious?"

"Yep. Dead serious."

"That doesn't sound like my father at all."

She snickered. "Like I said, the man I've come to

see now and the man he used to be when we first got married are two incredibly different people. He didn't want me signing a prenup. That's how much he believed in us at the time. I don't know if he was that generous or I was that stupid. But, given your history with your father…"

"You're not stupid, Cecilia."

"Well, I definitely wasn't this strong of a woman when I first met Howard. I was his puppy. I spoke only when he spoke to me and I was more than happy to accept his expensive handouts in exchange for loyalty. It was masked as love. But I don't think we ever really loved each other."

"What do you think happened then?"

She shrugged. "He provided me with a life I never had. Opulence. Expensive things. Wealth. All those concepts that were bad in my childhood he gave freely, and without me even asking. To me? It was romantic. And I fell head over heels for it. But not him."

I nodded slowly. "Why are you telling me all this?"

"I don't know. I guess because you have a right to know. Or maybe I don't want you thinking badly about me. Or maybe I just need to talk about it."

"I could never think badly of you. Not after all you've done for me."

She smiled. "Well, you've done me a great deal of good. You helped me find my voice. Find my strength with your father. And when that happened, I saw the angry side of him. The side that wanted to control me. If I stayed his little toy, he was fine. We were happy. The presents and traveling kept coming. But, in the end, I had to stay that way in order for him to love me. And that isn't love at all."

"No, it's not."

She drew in a sharp breath. "At any rate, I must've been so silent and airheaded in the beginning that he didn't think I'd ever change. Or leave him. So, yeah. I'm entitled to half of what he has. I'm sure he'll rake me over the coals to make sure I don't get it. But all of the things he's gifted me with are mine. That's what Miss Nichols told me over the phone today, anyway."

"So your car?"

"I can sell it."

"I take it you've already sold the clothes you were going to donate?"

She nodded. "And the ones that didn't sell got taken to the donation place. I want to wait until I get moved out of here to sell the car. But that's easily sixty grand in my pocket. I still have a ton of jewelry I can sell off. Shoes I know I'll never wear, even though I've kept them for now. And there are some things I insisted we have in this house that your father can't stand."

"Like…?"

"Some of the artwork on the walls. The decorative vases. There's artwork in the attic that should be on display that isn't. Even three or so of those paintings sold at auction would set me up in this city for almost a year. And that's if I wanted to keep living as opulently as I am right now."

My jaw dropped open. "Dad's got shit like that in the attic? All I found was the china stored up there."

She giggled. "That attic is expansive. That's my

next project, actually. I won't take anything off the walls. But, in exchange for that, things that have collected dust in the attic for years are mine to sell. That's how I'm going to frame my argument. The lawyer advised me to cut up my credit cards, too. Take dated pictures of them. It's all about covering my ass now in court. Proving that I'm not taking him for all the money in the world."

"And cutting up your cards to his bank accounts would start to prove that."

She nodded. "Exactly."

I sighed. "It's insane we even have to go to these lengths."

Her hand settled on my knee. "It is. But I want you to see something."

She pulled out her phone and started scrolling through it. I furrowed my brow as I watched her. When she handed it to me, I looked at the pictures. Beautiful pictures of what looked like a condo. Or an apartment of some sort.

"Is this what you wanted to talk about tonight?"

Cecilia nodded. "Yes. This is a two-bedroom condo for lease not far from here. Just on the other side of the high school. It's in a nice area. Has some nice amenities. And they have yearly leases that aren't going to break the bank."

"Twelve hundred a month? That's pretty reasonable."

"I thought so myself. It's two-bedroom, two-bathroom, with a shared kitchen and living space. Open concept. Around fifteen hundred square feet. And, it's got a pool with a deck as well as a gym and a yoga room."

I grinned. "And you'll love that yoga room."

I kept scrolling through the pictures and was amazed at the quality of the place. The building itself was only six or seven years old. The pool looked outstanding. There were tennis courts. A playground for kids. A pool, as well as an indoor hot tub. I couldn't believe a place like this in California only went for twelve hundred a month. I kept looking for the catch. I kept waiting for the other shoe to drop.

"Why is this apartment so cheap?"

Cecilia smiled. "I'm glad you asked. Apparently, we aren't the only two people your father has pissed off. I got to chatting with the front desk manager as I was calling around to places the other day, and it turns out your father's gotten into a pretty decent spat with the man who runs it."

I sighed. "Of course."

"I didn't ask for details. All I said was that I was looking for a place to stay. He asked if Howard was coming with me. I said 'no'. And I guess he read between the lines. The apartment dropped seven hundred bucks on the spot, making it affordable for me."

I handed her phone back. "Well, I'm really happy you've found a place. It really is nice. It suits you."

She took her phone. "The bathrooms are ensuite, too. So, ultimate privacy."

"That's nice."

"And they're big. About the same size. So, no one's

sacrificing room size because one of them is a 'master' or anything like that."

"Sounds like you'll really enjoy the place."

She smiled. "I do. I'm going to look at it Monday. I have a scheduled tour at four-thirty in the afternoon."

"You deserve this, Cecilia. You really do. Just make sure this front desk manager isn't giving you this kind of a deal because he's into you. I'd hate for you to get caught up in that kind of scenario."

"I promise, he's not. He and his husband have been proudly married for six years."

I barked with laughter. "All right. Good. Well, then make sure you check the appliances. Make sure they all work so you aren't liable for damage you didn't incur."

"Well, you could check them out for me. If you're worried about that kind of thing."

I shrugged. "I don't mind going with you after school."

"You're really not getting this, are you?"

I paused. "Getting what?"

She settled her hand on my knee. "I don't want you to just come look at this place with me, Clinton. I want you to move in with me."

"Wait, what?"

"I want you to come with me."

"You do?"

"Yes. This is what I wanted to talk to you about. You might have to help me with some things. Depending on how selling off this stuff goes, I might need help with food and stuff. But, yes. I want you to move into the second bedroom. I want you to have a place to go that at least remotely feels like home."

I blinked. "Are you being serious right now?"

"We're family, Clint. Maybe not blood related. But we're family. And we're going to need one another. Yes, I'm completely serious. I want you to come with me. If you want to, that is."

And as I sat there, completely dumbfounded, tears burned behind my eyes.

32

RAELYNN

"Welcome to Grady's Groceries. If I can help you, please let me know."

"Welcome to Grady's Groceries!"

"Raisins are on aisle four."

"No ma'am, we don't sell peppermint ice cream this early in the year. That hits the shelves two weeks before Thanksgiving."

"We do have some Halloween decorations! All the way back in the corner, near the bathrooms."

Even though Sunday afternoons were the busiest, I was glad they called me in. I needed out of the house. Mom had been moping since I came home yesterday. And every time I looked over at her, she started crying again. It was exhausting, and I was running out of sympathy. I couldn't handle her stuff anymore. And it shouldn't be my responsibility. I needed to focus on school and keeping my grades up.

"Ma'am?"

I turned at the sound of the voice. "Yes?"

"Where do you keep paper products?"

"I'm so sorry, we only have reusable products here. But if you're still looking for plates and silverware, that's on aisle nine."

"Is it more expensive?"

I nodded. "It is, yes. But, you'll only have to buy it once. Unless you back your car over it."

She giggled. "Well, I don't plan on doing that. Though I can't say much for the grandkids."

"Well, you could make them eat off paper towels. We have earth-friendly ones on the same aisle. Toward the back of the store. That side of it."

"Thank you for your help, dear."

"Any time. I'm here to help as much as I can."

I kept myself busy as the hours ticked by. The sun started to set and my dinner break was coming up. It wasn't a long break. Thirty minutes, as opposed to the ten-minute breaks I was usually afforded after school. Still, I thought about working through it. Keeping myself busy and keeping my mind preoccupied with other things. But the automatic door opening pulled me from my thoughts.

"Welcome to Grady's Groceries! My name's Rae. And if you need anything—"

"Just ask?"

"Clint?"

I looked up and saw him walking toward me, a smile on his face and pep in his step. I furrowed my brow as he came over to my register, then leaned over to kiss me. Captured my lips right in front of everyone without a care in the world.

It made me blush.

"Wow, what's gotten into you?"

He smiled. "Any chance you've got a break coming up soon?"

"If you give me fifteen minutes, I'm about to hit my dinner break."

"Perfect. Fancying some coffee?"

"'Fancying'? Who are you and what have you done with my boyfriend?"

He chuckled. "I'll hang around outside while you finish up."

I kept stealing glances at him out the window as he stood there. Whistling. With his hands in the pockets of his jeans. Every time he peeked over his shoulder, he winked at me. Like he didn't have a care in the world. It made me smile, and puzzled me at the same time. What the hell had put him in such a good mood?

"Rae!"

"Yeah?"

"Time for your dinner break. Wrap it up and shut it down. You've got thirty minutes."

I rang up my last customer and turned off my light. I made my way outside and threaded my arm through Clint's, watching as he smiled down at me. A playful wink, a nod of his head, and away we went. Toward the coffee shop next door that he had practically claimed as his second home.

"Dare I ask what's got you in such a good mood?"

He chuckled. "Let's get some coffee first. You hungry?"

I sighed. "Starving."

"What can I get for you two this afternoon?" the cashier asked.

Clint nodded. "Yes. I'd like two large caramel coffees made with rosewater, two of your ham and cheese sandwiches, two cinnamon rolls, two apples, and two packages of chips."

The girl behind the counter smiled. "What kind of chips?"

I looked up at Clint. "Doritos for me."

He nodded. "And salt and vinegar kettle chips for me."

The cashier rang it all up. "Will that be all for this evening?"

Clint slid his wallet out. "Yes, it is. We'll be sitting here, too. Thank you."

We paid and got our stuff, then he escorted me over to a table in the corner. Near the window. Where the sun shone and lit up the table in front of us. He divvied out the food, pampering me in ways I'd never experienced with him. He opened up my chips and handed them to me. Passed me my sandwich, but unwrapped half of it first. I narrowed my eyes at him as he hummed to himself. I'd never seen Clint this happy in all the time I'd known him.

"Okay. Spit it out."

Clint's eyes met mine. "What?"

I snickered. "What do you mean, 'what?' Spit it out. What's happened? What do I not know?"

He grinned. "Cecilia's moving out."

I blinked. "That's it?"

"That's it."

"You're happy Cecilia's moving out."

"I am, yes. She's found a great place on the other side of the high school. About ten minutes down the road. The front desk manager gave her a great price on the place."

"And that's why you're whistling."

"What's wrong with whistling?"

"Other than the fact that I didn't know you could do it? Nothing. I just figured—"

"I mean, she's asked me to move with her, but you know. Semantics."

I paused. "She's what?"

He started laughing as my hands flew to my mouth. I shot out of my chair and threw myself at him, wrapping him up in the biggest hug imaginable. I kissed his face. His neck. His shoulder. Tears rushed my eyes and I swallowed them down.

"She really asked you to go with her?"

He nodded against the crook of my neck. "She really did."

"Oh, Clint. I'm so fucking happy for you."

I felt him sniffle and it broke my heart. I slid into his lap as he wrapped his arms around me. I stroked my hand through his hair, which seemed to be growing longer by the second. I was so overwhelmed with happiness. With relief. I almost couldn't contain myself as I blinked back batches of tears.

I kissed his ear. "I'm so happy for you."

"She really asked me to go with her, Rae. Like, legitimately."

I rested against him as he held me close and shook underneath me. I was so thankful for Cecilia. Thankful that the two of them had grown so close over these past few weeks. Clint needed a fucking adult in his life that gave a shit about him. Who genuinely wanted him around. I knew how worthless he felt on a day-to-day basis. How pointless and unloved he felt by the adults around him. His father. The teachers at school. The principal, for crying out loud. He deserved Cecilia's love, and so much more.

"When do you guys move?"

He lifted his head. "I don't know. We're going to look at the place tomorrow after school. I guess we'll sign the lease there if we like it well enough."

"And you say it's not far from here?"

"Nope. I'll still be able to finish out my senior year here. Though I'll have to ride the bus or something."

I snickered. "That's crazy talk. I'm sure Allison and Michael and I can start picking you up or something. I'll talk to them about it."

"I don't want you guys to go out of your—"

I cupped my hand over his mouth. "We're your friends. We love you. Hush."

He furrowed his brow. "You... you love me?"

I nodded. "We all do."

And as his eyes searched mine, I felt my heart stop in my chest.

"Well, I love you guys, too."

I grinned. "All of us?"

He captured my lips in his before he slid me to my feet. His hands held my hips as our lips sat languidly together. A soft, genuine kiss. One that preached our truth even though we still couldn't say it.

Though, I hoped one day I'd build up the courage to tell him how much I loved him.

He patted the back of my thigh, then I went to sit back down. He kept grinning at me as I ate my sandwich, sipped my coffee and crunched on my chips. His feet slid against mine underneath the table where we sat. And I felt like one of those girls in the movies Mom always watched.

I finally understood how they felt.

"So, how's your weekend been?"

I sighed. "Pretty good, considering."

"Considering…?"

I shrugged. "I mean, things with Mom have been… interesting."

"Interesting, how?"

"Well, she's started therapy."

He paused. "Wait, she did?"

I nodded. "There's been a lot that's happened that I haven't told you about."

"Why not? Why haven't you told me?"

"I mean, things have been pretty chaotic in your world."

He put his food down. "That doesn't mean I can't be there for you."

I shrugged. "It's nothing bad. Just all happened at once, that's all."

He took my hand in his. "What happened, Rae? Talk to me."

I drew in a deep breath and told him everything. The fight with D.J. Him shattering things against the walls. Me telling him to get out. How hard my mom was crying. I told him about me finally calling the police on him and Mom's cuts as she fell to the floor trying to go after him. And the more I talked, the more Clint squeezed my hand.

With rage flying behind his eyes.

"I'm so sorry I wasn't there, Rae."

I shook my head. "It's fine. I mean, it really is okay. That happened the day your father came to pick you up from school."

"The same day?"

"Yeah. Like I said, it was a lot. And I just didn't want to talk about it, I guess? We were dealing with your stuff and—"

He looked me square in my eyes. "I want you to hear me. Are you listening?"

"I am, yeah."

"There is never going to be a point in time where my shit overshadows your shit. All right? The next time something like this happens, you speak up. Let me be there for you. I think I've proven to you how much of a big boy I am. Let me be a support to you like you've been to me."

I blushed. "Okay. I'm sorry."

"You don't need to apologize, Rae. But you don't need to protect me, either. That's my job."

"Hey, now. I can protect you just as much as you protect me."

He grinned. "I suppose you can. If you open up enough to let me protect you."

"I know, I know."

"So she went to the hospital?"

I nodded. "She did. She got help. With our income issues, she qualifies for free therapy through the hospital that treated her. And she had her first appointment with them yesterday morning."

"How often will she go?"

"Starting next week, twice a week. Wednesday and Saturday mornings. She said everything went really well and that they already started unpacking some things. But time will tell."

"You don't think she'll stick with it?"

I sighed. "I've seen my mother go without D.J. for almost a month before he comes swooping back in. Wanting her back. Coming with flowers and make-up sex and money to smooth things over. I'll believe her when I see her actively turn him down."

"I don't blame you on that."

"She's upset with me for that, though."

"What do you mean?"

I threaded our fingers together. "We kind of got into a fight last night. She was upset that I went dress shopping with Allison and not her. And it kind of spiraled into this same conversation. She was upset that I didn't believe she had changed, and I told her that she had broken my trust so much after promising to not go back—only to go back again and again—that I'd believe it when I saw it."

"Ouch."

"Yeah. It felt good to get off my chest, but Mom hasn't been okay since. And the worst is, I don't even fully feel bad."

"Because you're numb to it."

"I guess."

He grinned. "What kind of dress shopping did you do?"

Time to drop the hints. "Graduation dress shopping. Though Allison ended up picking up her prom dress instead."

"Has Mike asked her yet?"

"Not according to Allison."

"Let me guess. He's doing the whole 'assuming they're going together' thing?"

I paused. "How did you know?"

"I've been talking to him about it. I've told him that formally asking her is what girls like. Assuming things is only going to upset her in the short term."

I narrowed my eyes playfully. "What else have you and Michael been talking about?"

He winked. "Does it matter?"

"Yes, it matters. I didn't even know the two of you talked outside of school."

"I guess we've been getting along, yeah."

"So are you wanting to go to prom?"

He smiled. "Are you asking me to go with you?"

"No. Just wondering if that's your scene."

"And if it is?"

Just ask me already. "I don't know. Just wondering."

"Uh huh. Just wondering? That's all?"

"Yeah. Why?"

He shrugged. "No reason."

"Now, you're just being frustrating."

He chuckled. "And even when you're frustrated, you're gorgeous."

33

CLINTON

Rae still had three hours to go on her shift before she was done for the day. And I decided to stick around. I stayed at the coffee shop and did some writing in my notebook. I checked my bank account. Started on a budget. I wanted to have what finances I did have in line for my trip with Cecilia after school tomorrow. I wanted her to know exactly what I could contribute and what I wanted to take care of once we moved.

Because I'd certainly move with her.

That much I knew. Well, almost. I stopped banking on things a while ago. Nothing in my life was guaranteed, so that's how I saw everything now. Including this apartment, even though my stepmom wanted me to come with her. I would, too. If the offer still presented itself tomorrow.

But, if my life had taught me anything, it was the fact that twenty-four hours changed a hell of a lot.

Still, having a budget was good. So, for the first time in my life, I started jotting one down. I kept track of everything and rounded to the nearest dollar. I placed some calls. Like to the phone company my father used for our phone plan. Truth be told, now that he no longer had access to my bank account—and I no longer had my trust fund—the only thing connecting the two of us was the phone. I had no more bike. So no more insurance. Once I figured out how to separate myself and get my own phone bill, that was that.

No more strings to Daddy Dearest.

The phone call was long. Much longer than I had anticipated. And I was painfully honest with them. No use beating around the bush. I was moving out. Away from my father, and I wanted a new phone plan. One that didn't have my phone under his name. There wasn't much I could do other than open another phone plan under my name and have him eventually disconnect my line. Which I didn't have an issue with at all. They rattled off their available phone plans and I circled the two in my budget. Then I thanked them for their time.

Seven o'clock came around quicker than I had anticipated. I packed my things up and waved at the girl behind the cash register, thanking them for letting me take up a space. Then I stood in front of the main window of Grady's Groceries. I smiled as Rae came around the corner, purse in hand and fresh off of work. She rushed outside and laughed, throwing her arms around me.

It felt so good to hold her close.

"What are you still doing here?"

I snickered. "Can't a guy wait for his girl to get off?"

She grinned. "Cheeky, cheeky."

I quirked an eyebrow. "I see what's on your mind, beautiful."

"Are you going to whisk me home and help me decompress?"

"While that's a tempting offer, I'm craving ice cream. Care to go get some with me?"

"Trying to make up for the lost milkshake date?"

"Depends. Want to split some fries with me, too?"

She smiled, and it gave me all the answer I needed. She slipped her hand into mine and we walked toward the main road as I tried flagging us a cab. It took a few waves. But eventually, someone pulled over. I opened the door for her and told the driver where I wanted to go. And six minutes later, he pulled into the parking lot of the very busy diner.

"Is that line out the door?" Rae asked.

I groaned. "Well, fuck."

"Care to get a cone instead? We could walk home while eating them."

"Are you up for walking home after working this afternoon?"

She shrugged. "If we go slow, sure."

I grinned. "Slow and steady is my specialty."

She shoved me playfully and I laughed as I paid the driver. We hopped out and pushed our way inside, then placed our to-go order for ice cream cones. Rae ordered a banana-mocha swirled cone dipped in hardened caramel coating. And that damn thing sounded so good I ordered myself one, too. I paid for the ice cream and we pushed our way back out of the diner, heading in the direction of school.

Keeping a languid pace as we cracked into the hardened caramel shell.

"Mmm, my God, this damn thing is always so good."

I moaned. "I've never had the hardened shell before."

Rae gasped. "Oh, you wound me, Clint. That hurt. Physically hurt."

"I think you'll have to introduce me to more of your favorite treats around this area."

"You mean now that you're staying?"

I paused. "Was there ever a fear that I wouldn't?"

She shrugged. "I don't know. I guess there was always a fear that you'd use this opportunity to leave. And no one could have blamed you for it. Not even me."

I slipped my free arm around her shoulders. "I'm sorry I made you feel that way."

"It's okay. I'm just glad you've made the decision to hang around."

"I've got too many options on my plate not to."

She snuggled into me. "So, any idea what you might do after you graduate?"

I snickered. "No fucking clue. I mean, there are plenty of avenues. So I'm finding. But they all require a great deal of money. Money I might not have at my disposal if I move in with my stepmom."

"Why's that?"

"I mean, I'll be helping her with bills and such. Neither of us will have a ton of money. At least, until she gets through the official divorce with my father. Which you know he'll drag out in an attempt to get her to shut things down instead of raking him clean."

"I hope she drags his ass through the mud."

"Me, too. He fucking deserves it. But if my father's coming at us this hard, I can only imagine what she'll go through during the divorce."

"You think you might stick around and help her with that?"

I shrugged. "I honestly have no clue. I'm still just trying to not fail my classes. That'll be the key to getting a decent enough job to support me while I'm on my own."

"Did you ever think you'd say those words?"

"Actually, no. I didn't, to be honest."

She giggled. "They sound good. I know you can do this. We all know you can. And you won't fail your classes. Because you have me and Allison and Michael to help you get to graduation."

"I still don't know how I ended up with friends like them."

She scoffed. "Me, you asshole. I was your 'in' with them."

The two of us laughed as we rushed across the road. Cars honked at us as our laughter grew, and we continued running until we got into the shade. We stood there, panting and eating our ice cream cones as the autumn breeze kicked up. We began to shiver as we stood to catch our breath.

"Still a damn good cone," she said.

I smiled. "You're right about that one. But you haven't answered your own question."

"What?"

"What are your plans after graduation, smarty pants?"

She started walking again. "Well, it was to move with Allison into an apartment near her college campus. But I'm not so sure about that anymore. I mean, she and Michael are becoming a thing. And I'd hate to be a constant third wheel because I'm living with her. Plus, I'd really like to do something with my doodling and love for graphic design. And I can't afford a four-year institution."

"What about two-year? Or whatever?"

"That's an option, if I go part-time. But none of the community colleges around where Allison's headed have those programs. Which means I'd be on my own."

I held her close. "You're not alone, so long as you have me."

The two of us talked and laughed as we made our way to her house. I wanted to walk her home. I wanted to make sure she got there safely. Especially since the sun had fully set. I was still paranoid from that night. I wouldn't head toward my house until I knew she was safe within hers. But, as we slowly approached her home, we heard voices.

Her mother's voice, and a man's.

"Who is that?" I asked.

"Shh," she said harshly.

Rae tugged me into a neighboring yard before we crept closer. We stayed in the shadows, hanging out as Rae's mother stood on the porch. I narrowed my eyes. The man looked familiar, but I couldn't place him or his voice. But, my question was answered by the next thing that flew from Rae's mother's mouth.

"D.J., you're not coming inside. I've already told you no."

He snickered. "Come on, baby. It was just a stupid fight. We have them all the time."

D.J.? This was the fucker Rae always complained about?

Rae's mom sighed. "I know we do. But we've had our last fight. This isn't happening anymore. It can't. I can't do it anymore with you, D.J."

"You're being unreasonable. Why don't I take you out? You love that wine at that little Italian place—"

"I'm not going anywhere with you, either."

He took a step toward her. "You're not done with me. I'm not done with you, either. I'm not giving up on this. On us."

"Well, good thing you aren't the only one who can make decisions around here."

He paused. "Did your daughter get under your skin? You know she doesn't like me. But she won't be around for much longer. She's off to college soon. Or wherever. Then it'll just be us, baby. Like we always wanted."

"Like you always wanted. It's not my fault you were

a jerk to my daughter. You had your chance. And now, I want you to leave."

He took another step toward her. "You'll never be done with me, Lucy. We still love one another. There's still love here between us."

I went to step out of the shadows and confront this asshole. Because he was already pissing me off. But Rae slipped her arm in front of me, stopping me in my tracks.

"Hold on. I want to see how she handles this."

So I held my ground. Even though I wanted to jam my fist into that fucker's face.

"You know, Deej, I never thought I would be, either. You've been a big part of my life for a long time. And at one point in time, I thought maybe you were the one. That we just had some kinks to work out and struggles to work through."

He sighed. "See? I knew you still loved me. Just let me come in. We can talk rationally about this."

She shook her head. "No, Deej. You're not welcome any longer. It takes more than love to make something like this work. And we don't have it."

He pointed his finger. "You don't get to tell me that. You're not the only one who dictates what happens here."

"And neither are you. But this is my home. Not yours. And I don't want you here."

"I'm coming in."

She lifted her chin. "If you push past me, I'm calling the police. I won't repeat this cycle with you anymore. It's amazing to me that you haven't already replaced me with some young, dumb, perky little thing. I don't know why you keep coming back, either. Why I keep letting you treat me like shit. But I need to grow up. And so do you. I need to be the mother my daughter deserves, and you need help. Just like I do."

"I'm not fucking crazy like you and that spoiled bitch are. Where the hell are you gonna be without my money, huh? How are you gonna eat? Pay your bills? Remember what I do around here, Luciana. Remember it before I walk away. Because if I walk away, I'm not coming back."

She sighed. "Good. Now, get the hell off my lawn before I call the cops. And don't you dare step foot on my property again."

I felt Rae sigh with relief. I looked over at her and saw happiness fill her eyes. They sparkled in the darkness. The pride that washed over her made my heart soar. We watched D.J. walk away and get in his car. And as he peeled out of the driveway, I heard Rae's mom sniffle before heading back inside.

"Go see your mom. She needs you. And I'll see you soon, okay?"

I gave Rae a kiss on the cheek before I watched her head for the front door to go take care of the mother she deserved.

34

RAELYNN

M y eyes opened and I stared at the ceiling with a smile already falling across my face. Monday morning never felt this good, and my heart soared with joy. Last night with my mother was fantastic. I held her while she cried. I told her how proud I was of her. And after venting to me about how stupid she'd been for so many years, we sat down and took stock of her life. We cuddled up on the couch together and came up with a budget. We looked up the exact totals of all our bills and searched around for all sorts of services in the area. Mom was eligible for a great deal of help, from food stamps to free resume services to help her nail down jobs. We created a vague outline of what needed to happen. What bills were due when. How much money we needed a month in order to keep our heads afloat.

Then we figured out where we could cut back.

To an outsider, it sounded boring as fuck. But, to

me, it was the proof I needed to know Mom really was turning over a new leaf. We looked up jobs online she was already eligible for and jotted them down. Most part-time work. But part-time was better than no time at all. With the last of the money D.J. had offered Mom, we figured we had three more months of smooth sailing until we hit an issue. Because even though my paycheck from the grocery store could cover most things, it couldn't cover everything.

By the time we were done, we had a very confusing outline of what needed to happen. Ways we could cut back our bills. Things we could get rid of completely to save money. I promised her I'd research cheap meals for two and she promised me she'd put in two job applications every day from now until she snagged one.

And as I slipped out of bed, I felt the dawning of a new day upon us.

My feet planted into the ground and my body didn't feel so heavy. Getting dressed didn't feel like such a burden. I didn't bust a sweat taking a shower because I had to move around to get myself clean. I even took the steps downstairs two by two, jumping at the end before scooping up my backpack. I felt great. I felt alive. For the first time since Clint and I came together as one, I didn't feel burdened. Or stressed. The hopelessness that had plagued me no longer reared its head.

What a damn good feeling for a Monday morning.

Things were finally back on track. I made sure I had all my books in my bag, then double-checked my purse. I had my wallet, my keys, my phone. I had some snacks and some chewing gum. I even had some lip gloss in here, in case I wanted to spruce up a bit.

All I needed was something to snack on for breakfast.

"Rae?"

Mom's voice pulled me into the kitchen.

"Rae, you got a second?"

I plucked an apple from the fruit bowl. "Not much more than that. Gotta get to Clint and everyone."

"About that."

I paused. "Everything okay?"

Mom's face looked worried. That is, until a grin slowly slid across her face. I sighed as I bit into the apple, ready to chuck it at her for worrying me like that.

"Come on. Spit it out. What are you hiding, Mom?"

She sipped her coffee. "I called your school this morning."

"Oh? Why?"

"To tell them you aren't coming in today."

I paused. "Wait, why?"

She grinned. "Because we're going shopping for accessories to go with your graduation dress."

"We are?"

"Mm-hmm. I take it you probably didn't get any while you were out?"

"I mean, I have a pair of shoes that probably match."

"You know good and well 'probably' isn't good enough for an accomplishment like this. And plus, you have your ears pierced. I hardly see you wearing earrings. Is the dress low-cut?"

"No, but it's strapless."

"I'll need to see the colors of it so we can pick something out accordingly. But if it's strapless, a nice bracelet will accent things well."

"But… our budget?"

She sighed. "I can buy my daughter some accessories to go with her graduation dress."

I narrowed my eyes playfully. "You found some money in your purse, didn't you?"

"Yes. And I want to spoil my daughter with it."

I shook my head, but deep down I was screaming with delight. I hadn't spent a day with my mom in years. And I couldn't wait to go out with her. Plus, I had a bit of my own money to spend. My paycheck from the grocery store had a nice bump in it because of my raise. So, I silently decided to treat Mom to lunch while we were out.

But first, I had to tell the gang I wasn't coming.

Me: Hey, Clint. I won't be at school today. Mom and I are spending some time together. I'm sorry for missing school, but Allison can help you with things today for classes. Text me if you need anything.

I sent the message off and didn't have to wait long to get a response.

Clint: You two have a blast. Have fun, and I'll let you know how things go at the apartment after school.

I slipped my phone back into my purse and dropped my backpack to the floor. Mom came over and hugged me, holding me for the longest time. I sighed. I relished her touch. Her embrace. Her companionship. I closed my eyes and sank my cheek against her shoulder, feeling embraced by a mother I'd lost some time ago.

"I'm so sorry, Rae."

I shook my head. "Stop. It's in the past. We can only go forward, okay?"

Mom snickered. "I don't know when you grew up on me."

"And that's okay. Just keep getting better. For me, and for yourself."

She set her coffee down and swayed side to side, rocking me like she used to when I was a child. I felt myself falling back into those memories. Into the first memory I had of gazing up into my mother's face. I'd been sick with the flu. Coughing and unable to sleep. Hurting in places I didn't understand. And she had been there, with her own version of the flu. Making me sip water, giving me popsicles, and singing my favorite lullaby.

"Hush little Raelynn, don't say a word. Momma's gonna buy you a mockingbird."

My eyes welled with tears as she started singing it to me. Right there, in my ear, as we swayed in the kitchen. I didn't even try holding back my tears. I simply let them fall, dragging with them the pain and anguish I'd dealt with for all of my teenage years. I shook against my mom. I felt her wrap me up tight. My knees clicked together and my toes curled as I tried keeping up my strength.

With Mom singing in my ear.

"I've missed you so much, Mom."

She sighed. "I love you so much, Rae."

"Can we just—stay like this for a bit?"

"For however long you want, princess."

I don't know how much time we spent in that kitchen. But after a while, Mom started moving. Walking me down the hallway as I kept clinging to her. She walked us into the living room. We sat down on the couch we had occupied for hours last night. I crawled into her lap. Eighteen years old, five-foot-six, and one hundred and fifty-two pounds. All of me curled against her. And her arms somehow still wrapped around me. Her hands locked, her lips fell against my forehead, and she kissed me. Repeatedly. As the tears continued falling.

"Hush little Raelynn, don't you hurt. Momma's gonna promise to keep her word. And if this Momma does relapse, you have permission to kick her ass."

I sputtered with laughter as I sniffed back more tears. My head fell against her shoulder as she looked down at me. Still the giant of a woman I'd always known, despite the fact that we were the same height. My tears dried up as she smiled at me. I slowly raised my head as I slipped off to the side. With her arm around my back and my legs tossed into her lap, she settled into the couch. Smiling at me with a happiness I hadn't seen in her face since… well?

Since, ever.

"Independence looks good on you, Mom."

She snickered. "Let's just hope it stays that way. I'm getting old, you know."

"Oh, boo. You're hardly in your forties."

"That's almost mid-life crisis age."

"Don't tell me you're going to go out and get yourself a hot rod."

She giggled. "Don't be silly. Women go out and bring home a pool boy. Not a hot rod."

I threw my head back with laughter as my back fell to the couch.

"You're absolutely insane, you know that?"

Her hand wrapped around mine. "You had to get it from somewhere."

I smiled up at the ceiling. "So, any chance I can talk you into having lunch with me while we shop?"

"I take it you got paid?"

"And got a raise at work."

She gasped. "Rae! That's fantastic. When did that happen?"

"Not too long ago. I'm only, like, five days into my raise. But that five days gives me enough extra money for us to get lunch somewhere. Like that sub place you love so much."

"Oh, they have the best roast beef sandwich."

"I don't know how you eat that stuff. It stinks."

"Now you know how I feel when I watch you drink pickle juice."

I hummed. "Mmm, pickles. I need to pick some up the next time I'm working."

"You can keep your pickles and I'll keep my roast beef. How's that sound?"

"Fine by me. Just don't burp in my face. I'm not liable for my actions if you do."

She began tickling me and I started squealing my head off.

"Mom! No!"

"I don't burp. Take it back."

"Mom! I hate being tickled! Mommy!"

She giggled profusely. "Take it back."

"You don't burp! You don't burp! Uncle! Uncle!"

She stopped tickling me and I gasped for air, rolling off the couch. I hated being tickled. It was the worst sensation. But, as I slowly stood to my feet, a grin crossed my face.

"You fart like an old man, though."

She shot up. "You've got double tickles for that."

And as I took off up the stairs, I laughed my ass off, hearing her hot on my heels as I darted into my room.

35

CLINTON

A horn honking caught my ear as I walked out of the front of the school. Cecilia sat there in her bright red car, shining like the sun as she waved me down. She smiled brilliantly, and I couldn't recall ever seeing that kind of smile on her face. I jogged over and dropped down into the car, discarding my backpack between my legs.

"You look nice. What's the occasion?"

She rolled up my window. "Because today, if we play our cards right, we'll have a new home."

I chuckled. "I take it you're excited."

"I'm more than excited. I'm ready to get this party started."

The second I had my seatbelt buckled, she took off, zooming out of the cul-de-sac in front of the school and careening down the road. She had the music blasting with classic rock as she bobbed her head to the beat. Driving barefoot, of all things, as we raced down the road. I rolled my window down and let my arm rest out in the sun. I couldn't stop stealing looks over at her. How happy she looked. How carefree her hair was tossed on top of her head. It looked as if her own bonds had fallen away. Her face was barely covered in makeup. Her ears displayed simple stud earrings instead of the expensive, glistening diamonds I was used to seeing on her.

Simple suited her.

We drove in silence, but by no means was it empty. We jammed out to music and she played air guitar behind the wheel of the car at stoplights. I laughed at her as she yelled the words to her favorite songs. I'd never seen this side of her. Hell, I would have never guessed it existed. If she was nervous, the only thing that gave it away was how hard she gripped her steering wheel.

Her knuckles were practically white with tension.

We drove for maybe four miles before she turned on her blinker. Got into the left-hand lane. I looked over and saw the sprawling complex scattered with trees and greenery. It looked so different from the other places in Riverbend. The apartment buildings were brightly colored on the outside with stone work peppered in that felt pleasing to the eye. It looked like each apartment had its own private balcony. Beautiful white-washed wrought iron. This place screamed 'Cecilia'. It was definitely the kind of place I'd find someone like her in.

I hoped, for her sake, we qualified for something like this.

We pulled up to the parking lot in front of the lobby and got out. She slipped her heels on and stood up, smoothing her hands over her dress. She looked over at me and smiled. I held my hand out, ushering her toward the front door. And as we walked inside, a man dressed in a pale pink button-front shirt stood up, holding his arms out for her.

"Cecilia. You look amazing."

She hugged him softly. "Matthew, it's really nice to meet you in person. Finally."

I waved. "Hey there."

The man grinned. "And you must be Clinton. Cecilia called me and told me you were coming with her today. Nice to meet you."

He held his hand out to me and I shook it.

"Yeah, I wanted to come along with her and check out the place for myself."

He quirked an eyebrow. "Oh? Cecilia made it sound like you were moving with her."

I grinned. "If that's the best course of action for everyone, yes. But I'd like to see the apartment before either of us make a decision on anything."

He nodded. "Of course. I've got the golf cart cranked up and ready to go, if you guys would like a tour of the complex?"

Cecilia nodded. "We'd love one, thank you."

We followed Matthew out back and hopped onto the cart. Me in the back and Cecilia up front with him. We drove around the massive grounds, racing by the tennis courts, the beautiful blue pool that housed a deck, a small cobblestone pathway to the enclosed hot tub, as well as grills for the people living in the complex to use. It really was a nice place, tucked back away among lush trees and rich, green grass.

It felt more and more like home as we continued pressing onward.

"So, are we seeing a model room? Or the actual apartment you're wanting to rent to us?" I asked.

Matthew pulled into a parking space. "Oh, no. This is the actual apartment. And it's a good one, too. First floor, back right corner. Only one side of the apartment gets the harshness of the sun, so your energy bills won't skyrocket during the summer."

I nodded. "And all the appliances come with it?"

Cecilia snickered. "Why don't we get inside and see?"

Matthew smiled. "He's okay. It's good that he's asking questions. It means he cares about where you end up. Remember that."

I liked this guy.

We walked down the small hallway before he pulled out some keys. And the second the door to the apartment opened, Cecilia drew in a soft breath of air. Even I stood there, shocked. In all the best ways.

"Holy shit, this looks better than the pictures."

Matthew chuckled. "I told my boss those pictures we threw up there online were shitty. Excuse my language."

Cecilia slowly walked in. "The hardwood floors are beautiful."

I furrowed my brow. "Are those granite countertops in the kitchen?"

"And look! A built-in breakfast nook!"

I shook my head as Matthew ushered us in. He closed the door behind us and gave us the grand tour, with my jaw dropping to the floor. There was so much room in this fucking place. I mean, for an apartment? Hell, yeah. I went into the kitchen and checked all the appliances, which I found had been recently updated. I walked over to the balcony, shaded by the trees and the balcony above it. The white-washed wrought iron made the little nook cozy, and it overlooked a long stretch of grass that led softly down a hill.

Where I heard people splashing in the pool.

Rae and I could spend the summer by the pool after graduation.

I imagined her in a cute little bikini. Me, slathering tanning oil on her back. Driving me wild all summer while I wrote in my notebook and she rested between my legs. I hadn't even seen the bedrooms, and already this place felt like home.

Michael and Allison could even join us.

"Clint? Honey?"

I whipped around at the sound of my stepmom's voice.

"Yeah? Sorry. Just thinking."

Matthew grinned. "About that nice pool you saw?"

I snickered. "It was nice."

"We have the biggest apartment complex pool in Riverbend. And the hot tub comfortably seats fifteen people."

Cecilia's eyes widened. "Fifteen? That's a small pool in and of itself."

"We pride ourselves in providing the best for our apartment dwellers."

I sighed. "So, what's the catch?"

They both fell silent and all eyes were on me.

"There is no catch," Matthew said.

I snickered. "There's always a catch."

Cecilia cleared her throat. "We already talked about this."

I nodded. "I know. But you guys will be losing a profit on our lease at twelve hundred for a place like this. I want to know there isn't some catch. Something you expect us to do in exchange for paying such a low cost of rent here."

Matthew walked over to me and placed his hands on my shoulders. I didn't like him being so close. But it was better than my father being that close. I stood my ground, keeping my eyes connected with his. I wasn't backing down on this. I wouldn't let my stepmother get swindled by anyone else. Not again.

Not as long as she protected me.

"I'm not going to assume to know everything about your story. But let's say I get the gist."

I furrowed my brow. "Okay?"

Matthew licked his lips. "I watched my mother, for many years, get treated as less than by my stepfather. I watched her get taken advantage of for years. And she didn't live long enough for me to see her become the strong woman I knew she was, deep down."

I sighed. "Dude, I'm sorry."

"I got a soft spot for your stepmother's story. For

what I think she's gone through. And I'd like to think I'm pretty good at reading between the lines."

"I'm sure you probably are."

His hands fell from my shoulders. "There are some catches. But they're small. You'll provide your own bulbs. Batteries for the three smoke detectors. If any major plumbing issues pop up that our maintenance men can't resolve, you're responsible for the bill. But that's it. If you blow a bulb, the maintenance men will use your bulbs and replace them. Same with the batteries. It'll all be written out in your lease agreement. Along with the twelve hundred for rent."

"And that's it?"

He nodded. "That's it. Those three things. That will keep our cost down substantially on this apartment and give us the ability to offer this at a price that suits you and your stepmother's current situation."

"And your management knows about this?"

"They're the first people I convinced of it."

My eyes darted over his shoulder to Cecilia, who was standing anxiously waiting for my response. I didn't mean to make her so nervous. I just wanted to make sure she'd be okay here.

That we'd both be okay here.

I shrugged. "Well, can we apply today, then?"

My stepmom stepped forward. "Yes. I'm prepared to apply today, if we can."

Matthew smiled. "I'll do you one better. The place is yours if you can pay the deposit today. Equivalent to first month's rent."

I nodded. "Done."

Cecilia smiled brightly. "Will you accept a direct transfer? Or Paypal? Or anything like that?"

Matthew chuckled. "We can do Paypal. Let's get back to the office and get it set up. We'll get you confirmed before you leave here today."

The air smelled fresher as we rushed back to the front office. Cecilia transferred the money and I practically forced her to let me cover half of it. Going in together, so she knew I was coming with her. Moving in with her. Staying with her. We sat there in Matthew's office as everything percolated. As Paypal loaded and emails were sent off and confirmations sat there, pending.

Then, things started dinging on the screen.

My electronic transfer dumped into Cecilia's bank account. The apartment complex got our deposit. Our confirmation number popped up on screen and Cecilia laughed with joy. I wrapped my arm around her, pulled her close and kissed the top of her head. This was fantastic. Finally, things seemed to be looking up for the two of us.

"All right. So, when do you two want to move in?"

Matthew's question brought a still to the room as Cecilia sat up.

"Is it possible for us to move in soon?"

He shrugged. "That depends. How soon?"

I butted in. "Two weeks from yesterday sound okay?"

"So, not this coming Sunday, but the Sunday after?"

Cecilia nodded. "Yes. Do you guys do move-ins on Sunday?"

Matthew typed around on his keyboard before a smile crossed his face.

"We do now. Just put myself on the schedule to be here in two Sundays to welcome you guys to the property. Once you get here, I'll hand over the keys and we'll sign the lease agreement then."

Cecilia clapped her hands. "This is fantastic! Thank you so much, Matthew. Really."

I nodded. "But the apartment is ours even though the lease isn't signed?"

He nodded. "Yes, sir. That money secured your spot. It's yours, as of two Sundays from now."

And the sigh of relief that left my mouth relaxed me from head to toe.

36

RAELYNN

"Sweetie, can you pass me the—"

I tossed her the seasoning. "Catch!"

"Girl! Wai—shit!"

I giggled. "You owe me another cookie."

Mom glared at me. "You're doing this intentionally now."

"What? What did you think would happen when you promised cookies for whoever cleaned up their cursing first?"

"Look, all I'm saying is that it's not becoming for either of us to walk around dropping 'fuck' and 'damn it' all throughout the day."

I grinned. "Do those words count toward the deal?"

She slowly looked over at me. "No. They don't."

I snickered. "Fine. I'll let you off the hook this time."

As I stood at the stove, saucing up the enchiladas, I

giggled to myself. Things with Mom were going wonderfully. After shopping yesterday, though, Mom came to the conclusion that both of us cursed too much. Between getting poked with earrings, dropping jewelry on the floor, and looking at the prices of some accessories, she thought we needed to tone down our language a bit. So, we made a bet: whoever could go the next week and curse the least got to have their choice of cookies with ice cream next weekend. Complete with their own movie night that the other had to suffer through.

And since I had no intent on changing how I spoke, my goal was to make Mom curse more than me. You know, by pissing her off and shit.

"What other meals did you find that were under three bucks a pop to make?"

I scooped the enchiladas out. "All sorts of things. Buffalo chicken wings with mashed potatoes. Vegetable stir fry. Burgers and sweet potato fries. The list goes on really. It's all about cooking it in-house. I've found a cheap recipe for just about everything I know you like, with the exception of steak. Steak just isn't cheap."

Mom shrugged. "Eh, steak can be one of those things we go out and treat ourselves to."

"I'm fine with that. Because while it might look easy to cook, it's also easy to fuck up. And I don't think either of us want to sink twelve bucks a pop into steaks only to make them like hockey pucks."

I felt Mom grinning at me and I rolled my eyes. I tossed the rice into the enchilada pan and started cooking it up a bit. Letting it soak up all those juices.

We had some in the back of the fridge that had been sitting there for a couple of days. It needed to be eaten, otherwise it would spoil. And if there was one thing Mom had ingrained into me, it was the fact that food had to be eaten. Never spoiled. Never thrown away. And never, ever wasted.

"Pretty sure that makes us even now."

I snickered. "Not even close. I heard you upstairs trying to wrangle your clothes off."

"Wait, what?"

I tossed her a smile. "What? You think I wouldn't hear? I don't know what the hell you were wearing up there, but I'm pretty sure I've got the whole night to let my tongue fly before we're even again."

"You were spying on me? You little—!"

I held up my finger. "Uh, uh, uh. Do you want your cookies next weekend, or mine?"

"Your cookies suck. Who likes oatmeal raisin?"

"I suppose the same people who don't like cinnamon pecan cookies. You weirdo."

The two of us started giggling at the stove. Mom swatted me playfully with a rag before she took the black beans off the stove. She started setting the table, with the rice almost ready in this beautiful enchilada flavoring. The sauce created this rich red color that went perfectly with the black of the beans and the red and white of the enchilada. With the salad Mom quickly whipped up, we had all sorts of colors on that table. Complete with some orange soda we found at the back of the pantry.

Though we said a small prayer over it. Because we had no idea how long it had been back in that pantry.

Mom cracked the soda open. "Bless this soda, Lord, for I know not where it comes from."

I snickered. "So dramatic. The worst it can do is burn holes in our throats."

Mom started pouring the drinks just as a knock came at the door. I furrowed my brow and she looked at me, but I saw her tense. Which put me on alert. I knew we weren't completely out of the woods with D.J. yet. We knew there was a possibility he'd be back.

"Want me to get the door, Mom?"

Then a soothing voice fell down the hallway.

"Rae! It's me!"

I gasped. "Clint."

I rushed to the door and ripped it open. I smiled as I lunged myself into his arms. He held me tightly as he spun me around. And I peppered his cheek with kisses.

"What are you doing here?" I murmured.

"Your mom wanted to surprise you tonight with me coming over for dinner."

I paused. "Since when do you and my mom talk?"

"Since he came over late the other night to check on us."

Mom's voice caused my brow to furrow. "What?"

Clint settled me to my feet. "I was worried about you two after D.J. left. I tried going home, but Cecilia knew there was something on my mind. So we did a little drive-by just in case he came back or something."

"You—you did?"

Mom rubbed my back. "Yep. He did. Came up and knocked on the door and everything."

Clint grinned. "Your mom invited me to dinner tonight with you two after my worries settled a bit."

"Which I think is really cute, how he wanted to check in on us," she whispered.

I cupped his cheek. "You're amazing, you know that?"

Mom reached for his hand. "Plus, I want to get to know him more. I hope you like enchiladas, Clint. Because it's a family recipe, and it's what's for dinner."

"Sounds fantastic, Miss Cleaver."

"Nonsense. Call me Lucy."

Clint's eyes widened. "Oh! I brought these."

I watched him reach for the chair on the porch and him pick up two gorgeous bouquets of flowers. One of them, green and white with dusted gold, he handed to Mom. And the other one, filled with beautiful fall colors, reds and yellows and oranges, he handed to me. I slowly looked up at him before burying my nose in the flowers. Oh, they smelled heavenly. Mom reached out with her arm and hugged Clint's neck, patting him softly on the back.

They murmured to one another, but I didn't catch what they said.

I did see Mom smiling, though. Which was a very good sign.

"We should get these in some water," I said.

Mom released Clint. "Definitely. Come on. I've got some old vases somewhere in the cabinets."

Clint stepped inside. "It smells incredible in here."

I closed the front door. "Mom knows how to throw down in the kitchen."

She laughed. "I'm teaching Rae how to, though."

Clint laughed as my jaw dropped open.

"Hey!"

Mom put her hand up. "I'm not saying you can't cook. You've got your dishes you're good at. But none of them are those traditional recipes that come from your heritage."

I scoffed. "I think I did just fine with the enchiladas."

"Yes, you did. After I walked you through the first batch. That's how you learn, sweetheart."

Clint snickered. "First batch? Sign me up. I'm starving, and it all sounds delicious."

I put my hand on his arm. "Just know we aren't liable for the damage the orange soda does to your throat."

He paused. "Wait, what?"

Mom and I laughed our way into the kitchen before getting the flowers in some water. Then we all sat down to eat. For the first time in as long as I could remember, it felt like a family again in this house. Mom telling stories to Clint. Him returning the favor with his foot pressed against mine underneath the table. Mom and Clint got along wonderfully. And as the two of them talked, I couldn't stop staring at him.

He had come back to check in on us.

My heart fluttered in my chest at the idea of it.

Mom took a sip of her drink. "So do you have any plans for after school and all that?"

Clint and I paused, staring at her as her eyes danced between us.

"What?" she asked.

Clint narrowed his eyes. "How are you feeling?"

She shrugged. "I feel fine. Why?"

I licked my lips. "So, the soda's okay to drink?"

She scoffed. "You two are made for one another. Eat your damn food and hush."

I grinned. "One more point in my favor."

Clint furrowed his brow. "One point?"

"Let's get back to the question at hand. I want to know what Clint's plans for after high school are."

I looked over at him, trying to let him know that he didn't have to answer. But he looked confident. Much more confident than I would have been at that question had I been in his shoes.

"Well, Miss Lucy, I know college isn't for me. Not that I don't like a good education, but I'm terrible at it. I don't do well in classes with formal testing and things like that. I'm more of a hands-on kinda guy. I think I'd be better suited to start from the bottom somewhere, get certificates as I go along, and work my way up. Learn at the lower level and apply those types of things at upper levels."

Mom nodded. "That sounds like a plan. Are you staying around here? Or moving away?"

"For now, I'm staying around here. But there are plenty of job offers I can apply for. And I'll have a small support system in the area with my stepmom and everything like that."

"Are things going okay at your house, Clint?"

He sighed. "They're going. I don't know how much Rae's told you and all that, but Dad's selling the house and she doesn't want to go with him. We're getting an apartment together on the other side of the high school so I can finish out my senior year."

"That's wonderful news."

He smiled. "Thanks. It took a lot of weight off our shoulders, finding that place. I'm really just playing it by ear right now. But I'm in a good place with money. Dad hasn't been around to say anything else about it. Thanks to Rae and Allison, things are looking up for my grades."

Mom reached over and patted his hand. "Well, if you ever need somewhere to go, we don't have much here. But you're welcome to it."

I nodded as my eyes found Clint.

"Yeah. You're always welcome here. Okay?"

He smiled gratefully. "I really appreciate it. Thank you."

"You seem like a great boy, Clint. I'm glad my daughter found someone like you. It was very sweet of you to check in on us the other night."

He shook his head. "It's not a problem. I was worried, so I figured I'd stop by. That's it."

"Well, thank you for it."

I nodded quickly. "Yes, thank you for doing that. Even though I didn't know shit about it."

We all laughed softly before we went back to eating. Mom and Clint went back and forth with questions, warming my heart as to how well the two of them got along. I felt full of sunshine. Full of hope. Full of happiness instead of despair. We scarfed down dinner and he helped us clean up, washing dishes for me to dry while Mom put away the leftovers. We each poured ourselves some more orange soda before popping some popcorn. Then we settled ourselves in the living room for a movie.

Thankfully, I got Mom to put on a comedy instead another one of her romantic comedies. Which meant Clint and I wouldn't be bored out of our minds.

Mom stood up. "Oh, I forgot napkins. Does anyone want a napkin?"

I nodded. "Yes, please."

Clint murmured with his mouth full. "Mm-hmm. Please."

I snickered as Mom made her way out of the living room. I heard Clint swallow hard before he chugged back his soda. Then he gripped my chin.

"I've been waiting all night to do this."

He guided my lips to his and his tongue fell against the roof of my mouth. I shivered against him, moaning softly as his lips pressed against mine. I opened myself for him. I tasted him for the first time that night and I felt heat pooling in my gut. I lifted my hand to cup his cheek, stroking the stubble on his jawline. Blood rushed through my ears, drowning out the sound of the movie as the entire world faded away.

That is, until Mom cleared her throat.

"Shit," I hissed.

She tossed the napkins at me. "Save that for a time when I'm not here, got it?"

I giggled. "Got it, Mom."

"My apologies, Miss Lucy."

She pointed at Clint. "Protection, young man. Use it."

My eyes widened. "Mom."

"I don't care that she's on birth control. Use it."

My jaw dropped open. "Mom!"

Clint laughed. "Noted, Miss Lucy."

"Good."

And as Mom fell back down beside me on the couch, I wanted to curl up and die from embarrassment.

37

CLINTON

Clinton Two Weeks Later

I sighed as I stood in the empty, grand foyer of the house I grew up in. I'd call it a 'childhood home,' except that it held nothing positive. No memories of Thanksgiving dinners where families laughed around a table. No family breakfasts where we all talked about our upcoming day. No sitting around a television watching the news. No movie nights.

Just destruction. And darkness. And death.

"I won't miss you one bit," I murmured.

I looked over my shoulder, out through the open front door. There Cecilia sat in her new SUV. Even after trading in her cherry red luxury vehicle this past week, she was able to purchase a new car with money still going back into her pocket. An affordable, family SUV. With regular fabric seats, a basic Bluetooth interface, an extended overall warranty, and twenty grand more in her bank account. No payments. No hassle. No fuss.

And sadly enough, all of our things fit into the damn car.

"Take your time, Clint!"

Cecilia's voice ripped me from my trance and I waved at her. I turned my gaze back into the house and slowly started walking around. Down the hallway leading into the kitchen. Back around into the living room. I walked upstairs, making sure we hadn't left anything behind. No jewelry. No chargers. No random pairs of socks. Nothing like that.

And when I got to my bedroom, I sighed.

Everything looked so empty. What Cecilia and I didn't sell off, Dad had sold off himself. He didn't even seem to notice the lack of silverware. Or china. Or items in the attic. He emptied the house for the new owners, who were due to move in tomorrow morning. Empty.

That was the definition of this house.

I walked back downstairs and slid an envelope out of my pocket. I set it on the one piece of furniture that had stayed behind. A curio in the corner of the foyer Dad hadn't sold yet. I remember that curio distinctly. I remember the day Mom bought it. Right out of a thrift shop that angered Dad to no end.

We buy new, sweetheart. We don't have to rummage through people's garbage.

Does it have termites?

It looks diseased. Take it back.

I'll buy you a better one for your birthday. Just get it out of my house.

That curio symbolized everything. It was the one fight my mother won over my father. The one fight where my father actually gave in. Granted, he left us alone for three weeks after telling Mom she wasn't welcome on his latest business trip to China. But that didn't matter. To her, that curio symbolized her strength. Her ability to put her foot down.

It gave her enough strength to walk away from the marriage.

It gave her enough strength to leave me behind.

Place the note and get out of here.

I sighed as I walked over to the piece of furniture. I pulled the tape out of my pocket and taped the bright blue envelope to the front glass. I knew the color would stand out. When Dad came by, I knew he'd see it. Whether he read the note addressed to him or not, I didn't know. And honestly? I didn't care. Getting it down on paper helped. Handing it over to him helped even more. I did my part. I said what I had to say in that note.

And now, it was time to move on.

I sighed before I turned my back. The note was the last piece. It wasn't much either. Just a paragraph or two on what he could expect of me from this point on. I told him I no longer wanted him in my life. Nor did I want to be part of his. I told him I'd find my own way. That I wouldn't ever ask him for anything again. That I wouldn't reach out, either. And I didn't expect him to. I wanted him to know that we could go our separate ways and be done with all this shit. All this abuse. All this insanity.

Writing that note helped bring me peace.

And I hope it served to keep my father far away from me.

I walked out of the house and closed the front door behind me. I jiggled the knob, making sure it was locked. Then I headed for the SUV. Cecilia rolled up her window as I walked around to the passenger's side. Ready to drive off into our new future. I climbed into the car and buckled my seatbelt. And as Cecilia reached over for my hand, I shook my head.

"I'm fine. I promise."

She squeezed it. "You want to go get some food before we head to the apartment?"

I shook my head. "No. I'm ready for this. We can unload everything, get the furniture arranged, and order something in."

"Mmm, I haven't done that in ages. How do you feel about Thai?"

I grinned. "Sounds like a plan."

My stepmom drove away from the house, and with every piece of distance I felt the last of the weight lift off my shoulders. Peace overcame me so intensely it pushed tears to my eyes. I didn't try to mask them, either. As Cecilia held my hand, I let them fall down my cheek. I let the memories assault my mind. I let myself feel the pain I'd been experiencing my entire life.

And she sat there, silently. Driving us to our new home.

Without an ounce of judgment in her form.

I wanted this. As much as it hurt, I wanted this more than anything in my life. I wanted a new chapter in my world. I wanted to start the part of my life where I made things right. Where I made good choices. Where I surrounded myself with good people instead of toxic people. I wanted kindness in my life. People like Rae and Allison and Michael. And Cecilia. I wanted to surround myself with people who were healing, too. Healing from abuse and hurt they couldn't always control, like Luciana.

"You okay, Clinton?"

I sniffled. "I am."

"Are you sure?"

I nodded slowly. "I'm ready, Ma."

She paused. "What did you call me?"

I smiled as I looked over at her.

"Is that okay? If I call you that?"

She smiled brightly. "You can call me whatever you want, son."

"Thanks… Ma."

"Is there anything else you want to do before we get there? Any place you want to stop?"

I shook my head slowly as we came to a stoplight. Right by the school. Only five minutes away from our new home.

"I just want to get the hell away from that house."

And with a snicker, she nodded.

"Then, allow me to speed as quickly as I can to the apartment."

I smiled. "Sounds good to me."

38

RAELYNN

Michael pulled to a stop. "I think this is it."

I looked at the apartment building number. "Yep. 1824."

"You going to take pictures for me?"

I snickered. "I'm sure you and Allison will get the tour soon enough."

"So that's a yes?"

I giggled. "You know that's a yes."

"Good. Because you know Allison's going to be bugging me over dinner as to whether or not you've sent them."

I reached over and gave Michael a big hug as I laughed.

"Thanks for bringing me over."

He kissed my cheek. "Anytime. You know I don't mind giving you rides."

I pulled back. "Have you talked to Clint about the new school riding schedule?"

"I haven't yet. I plan on it tonight, though. You know, after the two of you are done doing your thing."

"There's no 'thing' happening tonight. His step-mom's home."

Michael gave me a knowing look. "Uh huh. Whatever. Have fun, Rae."

I rolled my eyes. "Screw you."

"That's Allison's job one of these days."

"I'm telling her you said that."

We laughed as I unbuckled my seatbelt. I slid out of his car and waved him off, watching him drive out of the neighborhood. He and Allison had a dinner date. *The* dinner date, really. The one where he picked her up at her house and officially met her parents.

I'd already told Allison to text me and let me know how it went.

With Michael's car out of sight, I turned around and looked up at the massive apartment building before walking onto the first floor. I came to the apartment number and knocked softly on the door. I checked my text message, making sure I had the right place.

And when Clint opened the door, I smiled broadly.

"Come here, beautiful."

He picked me up and swung me around. I giggled as he carried me into the apartment. He closed the door behind me and set me back down on my feet. Then he proceeded to give me the grand tour.

"This is my bedroom. It's back down the hallway. Cecilia's is right off the main room."

I nodded. "So her bathroom is the one guests use?"

He paused. "She said that, too. Why the fuck is that such a big deal?"

Cecilia called out from her room. "Because boys have nasty bathrooms, and guests aren't using nasty bathrooms!"

I snickered. "She's got a very big point."

Clint rolled his eyes. "I'm not nasty."

I giggled as he continued leading me around the apartment. He showed me his bedroom and bathroom, which were much larger than I expected them to be. Cecilia showed me her room and bathroom. And I was shocked at the amount of furniture they had. The decorations that had already gone up. It looked like they'd been slowly moving in all week. The place looked phenomenal.

"Want to see the balcony?"

I smiled. "Hell, yeah."

Clint's hand fell to the small of my back and he ushered me out a door. The white-washed wrought iron was gorgeous, and it overlooked a stretch of land shrouded in green grass and trees. The leaves were turning colors, casting yellows and oranges and reds against the sky. I smiled brightly as Clint closed the porch door, giving us some privacy out there all by ourselves.

"Come here. Sit with me."

I squealed as he pulled me into his lap. We sat down in an oversized chair on the small private balcony, and I leaned against him. My legs curled up as he held me. My forehead fell against his temple. I hadn't seen Clint smile like this in a long time. And the smile stayed prevalent on his face. He looked more relaxed, more at ease. I kissed the shell of his ear softly and he turned his head, nuzzling his nose against my own.

"What was that for, beautiful?"

I snickered softly. "You seem happy."

He held me tight. "I am happy."

"No, I mean... happy. Really, truly happy."

He nodded slowly. "I'm relieved, more than anything."

"Have you guys been moving in all week?"

He shrugged. "More or less. We still have a storage unit filled with things. But we pooled our money and bought new pieces of furniture. A new couch. A new television and a place to set it. Things like that."

"It really looks nice."

"Thanks for coming over."

The porch door opened and Cecilia stuck her head outside.

"Sorry to interrupt. But I'm about to order some Thai. Rae, are you hungry?"

I paused. "Thai food?"

She nodded. "Mm-hmm. Is that okay?"

"I don't know. I've never had Thai food."

Clint gasped. "You what?"

Cecilia shook her head. "That won't do. I know exactly what to start you with."

"How the hell are we dating? How did this happen?"

I laughed as Cecilia went back inside and closed the door.

"How have you never had Thai food?" he asked.

I shrugged. "Mom's not a fan of it, so we don't eat it."

He sighed. "I have to rethink my life choices now."

"No more sex for you, then, I guess."

"Hey, now. I didn't go that far."

I grinned. "It's cute that you think I could actually resist you."

"Oh, really now?"

His lips captured mine, silencing my laughter. I moaned as I sank against him. I felt my phone vibrating, but I ignored it. I could get back to Allison and Michael at a later time. I sat up as I straddled Clint's lap, letting my arms languidly drape around his neck. The kiss was slow. Deep. My head fell off to the side as his hands journeyed around my back. I rolled against him, wanting him more than ever before.

If only this balcony were more private for us.

"Mm, Rae. Rae."

I kept kissing his lips. "Mm-hmm?"

"Rae, Rae. Listen."

I paused. "Yeah?"

Clint cupped my cheek. "Some other things have happened this week."

"Oh? Like what?"

His hands settled on my hips. "Things are moving forward with the court date."

My eyebrows rose. "Wait, what court date?"

"The one against the boys. You know, that pro bono lawyer?"

My jaw dropped open. "The woman who called you? You took her up on her offer?"

He nodded. "I did. And she's confident we have it in the bag."

"Are you serious?"

He chuckled. "Very."

"Holy shit. Clint."

I threw my arms around him as tears rushed to my eyes. I clung to him, feeling him wrap his arms around me. He stood up and carried me with him, opening the balcony door and walking us back inside. I curled against him, tucking my face into the crook of his neck as I heard Cecilia still on the phone ordering food.

I drew in shuddering breaths as I tried keeping my tears at bay.

"I'm so happy you decided to go with it," I whispered.

Clint kissed my cheek. "I know you are. And I knew it needed to happen. I guess with everything going on with the house and my dad, I didn't want more on my plate. But she's made this process pretty painless."

"I'm so proud of you."

A door closed behind us and I lifted my head. I watched Clint's bed come into view before he walked me over. He settled me down on the edge, then patted my back. Trying to get me to let go.

"I've got one more thing I want to show you."

I sniffled. "What is it?"

He stood up. "Something Cecilia helped me pick out."

I watched him walk over to his closet. He slid the doors open and plucked something out from the back. He turned around and my hands flew to my mouth, taking in the beauty of the pristine black suit. Crisp. Clean cut. Tailored specifically to him. The button-front shirt had a glossy texture to it, juxtaposing the matte black jacket. The black collar was velveteen. But it was the dark green bowtie that caught my eye.

The color reminded me a lot of that dress Cecilia gifted me.

"Clint, it's—it's beautiful."

He nodded. "It is. But it's nothing unless you're on my arm."

I blinked. "What?"

"Rae, will you go to prom with me?"

And as I rushed off the bed, I lunged at him. I wrapped my arms around him as tears welled in my eyes. I hugged him tightly, peppering his cheek with kisses. He chuckled as he wrapped his arms around me, the suit dragging along the hardwood floors of their new apartment.

"I've been waiting forever for you to ask."

He snickered. "Then say yes."

I nodded quickly. "Yes, Clint. Holy fucking—hell yes. Hell yeah, I'll go to prom with you."

39

CLINTON

I smiled into her shoulder as I wrapped her up tight. I tossed my suit over into the corner, wanting to hold all of her in my arms. I breathed in the scent of the luxurious body spray she started wearing a few weeks back. I loved its smell. Like cotton on a cool fall day. I kissed her neck, hearing soft moans fall from her lips. And as I journeyed up her neck, I felt her head fall to the side.

"No. I want to taste you, Rae."

I fisted her hair and brought her lips back to mine. I needed her. I wanted her. And now, I had her. Fully, without my attention being divided. No father to worry about. No being scared of going home. No fretting over the situation Cecilia was in. I was free. Free of worry, and doubt, and chains my father locked me in. I was free to graduate. Free to live my life. Free to come home and never wonder about having to brace for impact.

Which meant I could devote myself to the girl I loved.

My hands slid down her back. I felt her slipping my shirt over my torso. Our clothes came off in a flurry, our hands sliding against one another's skin. I puckered for her. Goosebumps flooded my skin. My cock jumped at the sight of her. At the sight of her naked body standing in front of me.

I licked my lips as my eyes traveled down her toned curves.

I slowly walked over to the door. With my girth at full attention, it wept at the need to be inside her. I locked my bedroom door. And the sound of the lock flipping snapped something inside Rae. She rushed me, pushing me against the door. My back fell against it, and I tried my best to muffle the sounds. Her fingernails slid down my skin and rumbled over my abs as she fell to her knees. My eyes bulged as she wrapped her hand around my girth. Stroking it. Spreading my leaking arousal up and down its shaft.

"Rae, you don—holy fuck."

And the moan she let out around my dick made my body shiver.

I groaned as my hand found her hair, twirling up in her tendrils, commanding her every move. Her tongue slid down the underside of my cock, licking me and stroking me as her cheeks hollowed out. My toes curled into the hardwood floors. I felt my thighs already quaking as she swallowed down my cock. I heard her gag and felt the tightness around me. And as my eyes rolled back, I started moving my hips.

"Yes. Rae. Shit, just like that."

The whispered words filled the space around us. She bobbed her head quicker. Faster. Hollowed out her cheeks harder. The suction was too much. Feeling the back of her throat made my head spin. I felt my balls curl up and my eyes jumped open. I didn't want it to end like this. I wasn't ready for it to end yet.

"Oh, no you don't."

I growled as I tugged at her hair and pulled her up from the floor. She fell into me, my lips capturing hers. And the taste of my cum on her tongue unleashed the animal. I dipped down and gripped her ass cheeks, hoisting her against me. I walked her over to the bed and tossed her onto the mattress, watching her tits bounce for me.

She panted. "Clint. I need you."

And she didn't have to say anything else.

I gripped her ankles and pulled her to the edge of the bed. I tossed them over my shoulders as I stood there, my cock falling against her pussy lips. She unfurled for me. Her clit throbbed for my viewing pleasure. I grinned as I stroked my girth, feeling it pulsate in my hands. Her hands fisted my comforter. I stroked myself up and down her glistening slit.

Then I pressed into her, giving her no time to catch her breath.

"Cli—!"

I folded her in half and fell down against her. With my hands on either side of her head, I snapped my hips against hers. I felt her hands sliding along my back, her nails marking me as growls came out of the back of her throat. Our bodies became one as she rolled against me and I pinned her beneath me. I swallowed her sounds, the cries for more and the chants of my name. I pounded against her. Quicker. Faster. Harder. And it was only by the grace of whatever god existed that the bed didn't rake across the floor.

"Rae," I grunted.

I felt her closing around me and her body trembling beneath me. Her legs locked out. Her thighs quaked. And her hands cupped my cheeks. She kissed me over and over, gasping for air and whimpering as I sucked on her lower lip. I felt my balls pulling up as her juices dripped down my thighs. And as I sank myself deep into her, I ground my pelvis against her swollen clit.

"Clint. Clint. I'm coming. I'm so close. Yes. Right there. Like that. Oh! I love you. Clint. I love you. I love you. I love you. I love you."

I grunted at her words. I gnashed my teeth together and forced my eyes open. I saw her staring back at me, with pleasure and desperation in her stare. She arched her back. I watched her eyes close. And as my cock finally spilled into her, I choked out her name.

"Rae—lynn."

I collapsed against her, sliding her legs softly off my shoulders. As she quivered beneath me, my cock still sheathed within her, my face fell to her shoulder. I nuzzled her pulse point, feeling her heart beating wildly against mine. I kissed her skin. Her jaw. Her cheek. All the way over to her lips as my trembling arms held me up.

"I love you too, Rae."

And as her hands brushed away tears I didn't know I had been crying, I opened my eyes. I stared into hers. Into the loving eyes of the girl I'd come to love. The girl I had loved for weeks now.

"I love you with everything I am," I whispered.

EPILOGUE

Raelynn
Four Months Later

Allison cupped her hand over her mouth. "Oh, my gosh."

I smiled. "How do I look?"

"Rae! Are you insane right now?"

I laughed as she rushed over. She wrapped her arms around my neck and hugged me tight. The tulle of her purple and pale yellow gown rushed against my legs as she jumped up and down, taking me with her. Jumping in heels while I stood there in flats, trying to make sure she didn't knock me down.

"You. Look. Amazing. Oh, my gosh, Rae. Mom! Lucy! You guys! Get up here!"

Allison's voice rang my ears as she finally released me. I stuck my finger in my ear and wiggled it around. But not too soon after that, the clicking of cameras filled the space around me. Flashes went off and I shielded my eyes. Allison got beside me and tried to pose me as best as she could. With my hand on my hip. With our arms around one another. One with us smiling, and one with us being serious. As if we were models.

"Allison, you're killing me here."

She sighed. "Just one more. Okay? One with our parents."

I snickered as I went and stood beside my mother. She couldn't stop stealing glances. Shaking her head. Letting her eyes well with tears. I mean, I knew prom would be a big deal. But, all this crying? The squealing?

It was a bit much.

"You look amazing, sweetheart."

I grinned. "Thanks, Mom."

"I won't make a big deal out of it. I've only taken a few. And I'll only take one of us together."

"I know you'll steal some from Allison's parents later."

She snickered. "You're damn right, I will."

The two of us started laughing and I ignored the sounds of the cameras. Mom held her arms out for me and I hugged her tightly. I tried my best not to cry, too. Because Allison insisted I wear makeup for the night. She'd worked on my face for almost an hour, trying to get everything right. The last thing I needed to be doing was ruining it with tears.

"I love you so much," Mom whispered.

"I love you too, Mom."

Allison called out. "Hey! Rae!"

I released Mom. "What?"

"Did someone order a limo?"

I paused. "No, why?"

"Because a limo just pulled into the driveway."

All of us looked at one another before Mom and I started rushing down the steps. Allison and her parents weren't too far behind us. And just as we got to the front door, the doorbell rang. Allison squealed her head off. I heard Michael laughing behind the door. But when Clint's chuckle followed behind, I felt myself blush.

"You ready for this, honey?"

I looked over at Mom. "I'm very ready."

Allison's father opened the door and there the boys stood. Michael, in a white tuxedo suit with a black collar and a black pair of pants. His button-front shirt was purple. The same color purple as Allison's dress. And his boutonniere was pale yellow. Just like the corsage he had for her in his hand.

"You look—"

Michael was stunned speechless. I smiled as Allison wrapped her arms around him. Her parents snapped pictures as Michael slipped the corsage onto her wrist and the two of them posed for pictures. I stood off to the side with Mom, taking in how happy and wonderful my two best friends looked.

Then I felt someone appear at my side.

"She doesn't hold a candle to you, Rae."

I slowly looked up and saw Clint standing beside me. In his all-black suit, except for this bowtie. The dark green bow tie that matched my dress perfectly. I smiled up at him and he turned to me, his eyes locked with mine. He had a boutonniere on his collar, too. Dark green, with little sprigs of silver that were dotted with the smallest of pearls.

"This is for you," he said.

I looked down at the corsage, and all eyes turned to me. Pictures were snapped. Mom wiped at her eyes. I smiled brightly at the matching corsage as Clint popped the plastic container open. He took my hand softly and slid the band over my wrist. And as my eyes rose to meet his again, he winked.

"The limo is courtesy of Cecilia, if you're wondering."

I snickered. "Why doesn't that shock me at all?"

He shrugged. "She wants us to have a good time. And she's going to want some pictures."

We looked around at the adults and they nodded. Letting us know he'd get them, in due time.

"Wait, how did Cecilia afford the limo?" I asked.

Michael snickered. "Not going to lie, I'm wondering the same thing."

Clint shrugged. "Her lawyer has informed her that, until the divorce is final, my dad can't completely cut her off. Especially after proving that he sold the house right from underneath us."

My jaw dropped open. "Wait, so…?"

He grinned. "Let's just say Dad's mailed her a new credit card to appease her in the hopes she won't bleed him dry before they can get papers signed."

All of us had a good laugh before Clint offered me

his arm. Allison's parents and my mother continued taking pictures as we walked outside, all the way to the limo. The leather seats called to us. They were soft. Like butter. And out of the corner of my eye, I saw something chilling on ice.

"What's that?" I asked.

Michael picked it up. "The finest sparkling grape juice. Chilled to perfection."

Allison and I giggled as Michael screwed the top off.

Clint grabbed crystal champagne flutes and we each had a glass. The driver had music blaring, preparing us for a wonderful night out. I cuddled against Clint as we drank through the juice. We sang to the songs and waved our glasses in the air. Toasting, over and over, a night to remember.

A night that signaled putting all this bullshit behind us.

The limo drove us to the hotel. To the ballroom the high school had rented out and decorated. I slipped my arm into Clint's, then Allison took my hand. And together, the four of us journeyed into the hotel. We followed the red carpet all the way to the ballroom. All the way into the entrance. And as the beat pulsed and lights flashed, a smile crossed my face.

This was going to be awesome.

"Care to dance?"

Clint's lips pressed softly against the shell of my ear to be heard. And a shiver worked down my spine. I peeked over at him and nodded, then pulled Allison over to me. I wrapped her up in a one-armed hug,

344 | REBEL HART

kissed her cheek softly, and told her how beautiful she looked. Then, I told her I'd see her out on the dance floor.

Just before Clint started tugging me toward it.

He twirled me around. The bass of the beat wound down. And as his arm slipped around my lower back, the music slowed down. The song became sensuous. He pulled me close, holding my hand up with his, swaying us softly to the beat.

"I didn't know you could dance, handsome."

He grinned. "I'm full of surprises at times."

I paused. "Michael taught you, didn't he?"

"First—and last—time I ever dance with a dude."

My head fell back in laughter as he dropped my hand. He slid his arms around my lower back, holding me close to him. I slipped my hands up his chest. My arms draped around his neck. My head came back up and our eyes connected as the music filled the small spaces between us. Nothing else existed. Just me, him, and the song. Our song.

A song I started softly singing as my eyes danced between his.

"I know you haven't made your mind up yet. But I would never do you wrong."

Clint smiled as his cheeks tinted with a blush.

"I knew it from the moment that we met. No doubt in my mind where you belonged."

He pulled me close and took over the lyrics.

"I could make you happy; make your dreams come true. Nothing that I wouldn't do."

Tears rushed my eyes as I changed the lyrics.

"Drop down into a ravine for you."

And as his nose nuzzled against mine, we sang the last of the song together.

"To make you feel my love."

Thank you for reading STAY WITH ME. Don't miss ~~DON'T~~ FOLLOW ME, the final book in Rae and Clinton's epic love story.

Have you already read Clinton's exclusive novella? Check out CLAIMING ME, book 1.5.

Get an SMS alert when Rebel releases a new book:
Text REBEL to (844) 339 0303

REBEL HART

Rebel Hart is an author of Dark Romance novels. Check out all of her books at www.RebelHart.net/Stories. And don't forget to join her Readers' Group to chat with Rebel and other fans: facebook.com/groups/rebelhart

NEVER MISS A NEW RELEASE:
    Follow Rebel on Amazon
    Follow Rebel on Bookbub

Text **REBEL** to (844) 339 0303 to don't miss any of her books (US only) or sign up at www.RebelHart.net to get an email alert when her next book is out.

authorrebelhart@gmail.com

CONNECT WITH REBEL HART:

ALSO BY REBEL HART

For a full list of my books go to:
www.RebelHart.net/Stories

Made in United States
North Haven, CT
19 April 2023

35629307R00211